Joseph R. Lallo

Heart Ally Books, LLC
Camano Island, Washington

Cover by Nick Deligaris

Published by: Heart Ally Books, LLC
heartallybooks.com
26910 92nd Ave NW C5-406
Stanwood, WA 98292

Published on Camano Island, WA, USA

ISBN-13: 978-1-63107-080-8 (paperback)

ISBN-13: 978-1-63107-081-5 (epub)

10 9 8 7 6 5 4 3 2 1

Table of Contents

Table of Contents

Chapter 1

Non Sequitur prepared himself. Times like these were the true test of a hero. On one side of the door were him and his partner. On the other, a legion of creatures driven to the brink of madness by a cocktail of hormones that would kill an adult man. They'd been gathered together, feeding off each other's hyperenhanced emotions until they were in a frenzy. They had been perfectly trained to spot weakness and prey upon it, each one desperate to assert its dominance, to ensure its place within the power structure lest it be forever shunned.

He tightened the straps on his uniform. He'd been stripped of weapons before he'd entered this place. It was like they wanted him to be at the mercy of this horde. But he'd faced this threat a thousand times in the past few years. He was a pro. He was a hero. More than that, he was a superhero.

His partner's suit creaked as she stretched and limbered up. Unlike Non Sequitur's red-and-white canvas-and-nylon outfit, which looked like a flashier version of otherwise standard military fatigues, his partner Nonsensica's outfit evoked more "traditional" meta-human crime-fighter attire. Skintight latex with dazzling red-and-white patterning, the formfitting suit made the chunky combat boots and padded MMA gloves seem comically large, but to Nonsensica that was a plus. Superheroes belonged in the comics, after all. She turned to Non Sequitur and shot him a fiery gaze through her thick red-rimmed goggles.

"Let's do this thing," she said, punching her palm.

She kicked open the door in front of them. The low rumble of the crowd dropped to near silence as she and Non Sequitur marched out to the center of the auditorium. Bleachers encircled the combination basketball court and performance space, wild eyes watching and waiting to see what these so-called "heroes" could possibly do. For a moment the only sound was the squeak of their boots as they found their place in the center of the scuffed-up wooden floor.

"I hate these high school gigs…" Non Sequitur muttered.

"It's all part of the job," Nonsensica said out of the corner of her mouth. She clapped her hands and raised her voice. "All right! Are you ready to learn about safety!?" she projected.

As with everything she did, Nonsensica poured so much enthusiasm and raw energy into the admittedly extremely lame opener that it almost got the crowd on her side. Almost. The first sound out of the audience was a snicker, and that broke the seal. Within moments the auditorium dissolved into a burbling mass of snide comments and side conversations.

"Strong start," Non Sequitur said.

"Yeah, yeah. I didn't write the script. Just be ready for it," she said, adopting a combat-ready stance.

A few seconds of rising chaos passed. Like clockwork, someone in the crowd got the bright idea to throw something. Usually it was a balled-up piece of paper. This time it was the icy remnants of some sort of coffee drink. The plastic cup spun through the air, headed straight for Nonsensica. She spotted it and stood firm. When it was inches from her face, it stopped. It didn't bounce, it didn't shatter. It didn't poof out of existence. It just stopped, half-melted cubes sloshing about inside like someone had deftly caught the cup and held it in place.

"Like I said, are you ready to learn about safety?" she said, eyes fixed on the confused senior who'd pitched the piece of trash. "Lesson one: safety is all about preparation."

Non Sequitur reached up and grabbed the cup, holding it in place for a second or two before pitching it into the garbage can beside the door. "Now, we happen to be superheroes. We have options if things start to go wrong," he said. "But preparation is a superpower that everyone has."

"That's right. So let's start talking about how each and every one of you can—impostor shiver!" she snapped.

A second would-be troublemaker had been winding up to toss a second bit of trash, no doubt hoping for another demonstration of genuine superpowers. He received one, in the form of a precision strike on the comprehension center of his brain. The two words were perfectly selected to force his brain to overextend itself in its attempts to connect them. He flinched from the mental effort, and the wad of paper slipped from his hand.

"Tract perfume. Terminal plant!"

Two more improvised projectiles either dropped away or flew well off course.

"Look, I can scramble all your brains, or we can just get on with this," she barked.

The words carried a sharpness and authority that, combined with the clear ability to manipulate their minds in some way, was enough to convince even the most disorderly of students to settle down.

"Good," she said, squeakily crossing her arms. "So. Safety…"

A soft chiming noise filled the arena. At first, Nonsensica visibly rankled, ready to give an earful to whoever hadn't silenced their phone before the assembly began. Non Sequitur realized the chime was accompanied by a vibration in his pocket. He fetched his phone. The screen was flashing with an unassuming bit of text: GP Priority. Nonsensica pulled her own phone from her belt and found she had the same notification. She tapped the screen. A loading ring spun for three revolutions. It vanished, replaced with the emotionless and steady face of a military professional, labeled at the bottom in plain white text Sgt. Roberts.

"We have a situation. Get yourself to a private location and prepare for a briefing," he said.

"We're in the middle of the safety spiel," Non Sequitur said.

"This is a GP Priority-level event," Roberts said.

"On our way, Sarge!" Nonsensica tapped off the screen and turned to the crowd. "Sorry, citizens. We've got a world to save!"

* * *

Six Hours Earlier…

"Do we have all the data?" Dr. Aiken said, anxiously flipping through pages of information on the screen of his tablet.

"You're looking at it, Doctor," said Pvt. Summers as she kept pace beside him, marching down the corridor in the DARPA headquarters.

"Right, but all of it. Gen. Siegel is a master of the pop quiz. Remember last time when he asked about calorie intake in comparison to apparent power output?"

"We've got it all in there. Exercise routine, favorite music, everything," Summers said. "Here, have a coffee. It'll calm you down."

She held out a steaming to-go cup. He waved it off.

"Not yet. You're the only person I know who coffee calms down. We ought to screen you for the meta-human gene. Maybe you're The Caffeinator or Ms. Coffee in your free time."

"Already got the screening. Standard procedure for all DARPA staff. Negative. I'd go with The Caffeinator though. Ms. Coffee seems arch to me."

The pair reached the door to Gen. Siegel's office suite and stopped. Dr. Aiken glanced to Pvt. Summers. She held up her arm. They both focused on the seconds on her watch ticking by.

"Five… four… three… and… 0900," she said.

The very instant the hour-indicator rolled over on Pvt. Summers's watch, Sgt. Roberts opened the door. He gave them a stiff nod of acknowledgement for their punctuality.

"Gen. Siegel will see you now," he said.

Dr. Aiken hastily stepped past him and headed for the door to the general's actual office. "Every time I do that, I feel like a dog jumping through a hoop," he whispered.

"The man likes procedure. It's a military thing," she whispered back.

"At least dogs get treats for jumping through hoops."

They entered his office and took a seat. Gen. Siegel was the sort of man who probably should have been assigned his uniform and rank at birth. No one capable of a crewcut that ruthlessly straight and having a jawline that rugged and square could ever be anything but an angry CO. Today, though, the perpetually smoldering anger was uncharacteristically subdued. The unlit cigar in his mouth had barely been chewed.

"Doctor. Private," he said steadily.

"General," they each said in return.

"Let's have it," he said.

Aiken nodded and glanced at his notes. "We've seen very little noteworthy change in the team since our last briefing two weeks ago. As you know, Bomb Sniffer requested a transfer from active duty to the support team, specifically as a communications coordinator. This isn't, strictly speaking, a role that is enhanced by her powers, but she's shown a strong aptitude. We've seen a marked improvement in her mental state, particularly a decline in anxiety, and her rapport with the team has been an asset. I'm recommending her to replace Sgt. Roberts for all project-based communications going forward."

"I'll take it under advisement. What else?"

Aiken rolled the notes forward. "I've heard from the team of analysts in prison that Chester St. John's mind has only become more thoroughly set into the supervillain archetype. I'm worried that placing supervillain-type meta-humans in special custody only reinforces their villainous mindset."

"Are you suggesting we should move a master manipulator from special detention to general population? I'm not the psychologist here, but that sounds like a recipe for a prison break."

"I certainly agree that special accommodations need to be made to prevent St. John from using his powers to escape, but investigation into alternate means is probably called for. If we can address his psychological drive toward villainy, in the long run it will markedly improve matters."

Siegel drummed the desk. "I'll take it under advisement. Next?"

"Um… Johnny On the Spot scored us another PR win. He crossed the street without looking, which caused a school bus to slam on the brakes and narrowly avert a runaway semitruck that burst through the intersection at the same moment. It was caught on camera, of course, and people are eating it up as an act of heroism. As usual, there is also a low buzz on social media suggesting these things are staged. We'd like permission to return Johnny to military housing to try to keep him out of the spotlight for a few months. Just long enough to let those claims die down."

"I'll take it under advisement," the general said.

Dr. Aiken furrowed his brow. "With all due respect, sir, you're taking an unusually large number of things under advisement today."

"You're my advisor, aren't you? Next."

"The only other thing I've got is our continuing youth outreach program with Nonsensica and Non Sequitur. We've been getting generally positive responses from students and staff. They're really proving to be a positive face to the project. I would recommend expanding to colleges."

"I'll take it under advisement. That's all?"

"That's my briefing, yes," Aiken said, tapping his notes closed and preparing to stand.

"You aren't dismissed," Siegel said, sternness returning to his voice. "Do you know what today is, Doctor?"

He blinked and glanced at Summers. She shrugged.

"The morning of our semimonthly project briefing?" Aiken guessed.

"Today is the day of our quarterly budget assessment."

"Oh."

"So far what you've told me is one of our soldiers is simultaneously praised for preventing and accused of causing disasters. You've reminded me that the one unqualified success the team has achieved—which just so happens to be the defeat of a member of our own organization—remains a potential threat. And you've told me that the main skills we've built via our training program have been teaching adolescents how to avoid household accidents. Do you know what our budget is, Dr. Aiken?"

"I don't, sir."

"I do. And in three hours I suspect it'll be cut in half, or eliminated entirely, unless I can give the directors something more than what you've just given me. It is frankly astounding we haven't been shuttered already. This was supposed to be a secret recruitment initiative to form a military team of meta-humans. But that's now how it happened, is it Aiken?"

"No, sir."

"No. What happened was word got out, immediately, and the whole thing turned into an intensely public cattle-call of maladjusted 'superheroes.' It was a reality show by the end of it. That's not just a reason to defund the project, but dismiss all involved. If I were to guess, the only reason we're still on the budget is as a publicity tool, but publicity isn't a reason to keep a military squad together. We need to prove utility. We need to prove results. Give me something."

Aiken opened a different file. "I can give you some updates on my personal research, but it's a bit dry and so far inconclusive."

"What about the enhancement project?"

"Sir, I told you at the time that—"

The general thumped the desk and clenched his jaw. It was almost comforting to see him slide into the more familiar "barking commanding officer" role.

"Six months ago I instructed you to look into the possibility of improving the powers of our team. We need better utility. Something to justify the continuity of the project. Right now we have a guy who grows grass on the ass of people who thank him. And that's one of our top guys!"

"Uh… he grows grass on the ass of people whom he thanks, sir," Aiken corrected.

"Explain to me how that makes a difference. But if we're so interested in accuracy, let's run the list, shall we? Nonsensica: able to make people flinch by speaking random words. Non Sequitur: able to have the result of an action precede its cause by up to thirty seconds. Phosphor: able to pull endless fluorescent bulbs from his bag. Chloroplast: with the power of photosynthesis. Bomb Sniffer: able to detect explosives via their scent. The Number: able to compel people to dance if they hear the same music as him. And Gracias: able to make grass grow on the posterior of people whom he thanks. And that's it! That's the mighty team of heroes."

Aiken tipped his head and squinted his eyes. "That's seven. Aren't there eight?"

The general flipped through his notes and found a Post-it. "Ah, yes. The Afterthought: with the power to be forgotten. Frankly, if it wasn't for their discipline problems, I'd pull in some of the backup squad. Undo has the ability to undo a prior action. That has endless applications. But only your eight team members have shown any real aptitude as soldiers, and I can't keep claiming that the American taxpayers should be funneling money into this project when the best we can offer is Johnny-on-the-Spot, a dope who lucks his way into situations that benefit him."

"I suppose that's more of a politician thing than a military one," Summers said.

"Lord help us if that idiot ever runs for office..." Siegel said. "Can we get actual worthwhile powers out of these people?"

Aiken cleared his throat. "First, we need to reestablish some basic information about meta-humans and their nature. All superpowers share a common mechanism. They are psychic in nature, and are made possible by an evolutionary adaptation present in a small percentage of the populace called the Liefeld lobe of the brain. Superpowers manifest for two reasons, usually in conjunction: self-defense and wish fulfillment. The reason so many heroic origins involve near disaster or tragedy is because in a moment of psychological or physical stress, a mind with an active Liefeld lobe will concoct a means to defend itself from the source of that stress. Lightning strikes, chemical spills, animal bites. Most of them won't be life threatening, but they'll strike at just the right moment of physical or psychological vulnerability and the lobe will activate. That's the self-defense aspect. The wish fulfillment is less about offering a would-be hero any particularly potent power, but more about making that individual somehow distinctive. That covers natural-power occurrence and behavior."

Siegel looked at him impassively. For the moment, though he was keeping his patience in check, Aiken could see the smoldering in his leaden gaze.

"It isn't unheard of for the nature or potency of powers to change, though it is rare. We have done our best to measure the exact parameters of the powers displayed by our operatives, and we have observed sometimes substantial increases in those abilities when the heroes are stressed."

"Then we only need to stress them," the general said. "Work those powers like a muscle."

"I'm afraid not. There's never been any indication that the enhanced powers retained their elevated potency much longer than necessary to deal with the present threat. Or that repeated application allowed further enhancement. We've seen this most markedly in Nonsensica. The so-called 'mental short circuits' she produces in her targets can actually be measured quite precisely in an MRI, and to a lesser degree with a polygraph or an EKG. When she is instructed to try to 'set a record' or otherwise exceed her usual parameters, she's able to do it seventy-three percent of the time on average. She can only achieve it twenty percent of the time when she's not aware of her own performance, but she can do it ninety-eight percent of the time when she's given real-time feedback. A hero can, to oversimplify it, choose to be more powerful if it would fulfill the psychological need the powers manifested to serve."

"Then why don't these idiots just choose to be something worthwhile? We did that whole competition to get them a place on the team. They must have known that a little superstrength or some laser vision would have clinched it for them."

"Because it's not a conscious decision. And again, it's only to do with the need that the power manifested to serve. Nonsensica fully understands the nature of her powers. They are a part of her identity, and if they were to change their nature, she would be abandoning her identity. But she also has a foundational need to prove herself. So if it is within her abilities to achieve her goal with her powers, even if doing so would exceed their base levels, she will do so. ... Usually."

"I don't like when my researchers start adding qualifiers to their reports, Doctor."

"This is psychology, General. None of it is set in stone. She also has to believe she can achieve it. If she lacks the confidence to achieve her goal, even if her powers would be able to facilitate it, she could easily fall short. The same mechanisms that can enhance powers can weaken them. It's the theorized operating principle behind the frequent pairing of powers with weaknesses."

"Are you telling me I need to start handing out magic feathers and security blankets if I want my team to perform properly?"

"I'm saying that mental health is an important component to powers with a mental origin. Which is to say, all powers."

The general ground his teeth, causing the cigar to mash and droop. "You said self-defense is part of it. Can't we just place these people in danger? Put them in situations that they'd need better powers to get out of?"

"I would advise against it. First, the threat would have to be genuine, or at least appear to be so. If they even suspected the threat wasn't real, it would have no impact on their powers."

"So we really put a gun to their heads to make them bulletproof."

"General, even if we set aside the ethical ramifications of that—"

"We are a semisecret military research program. Setting aside the ethical ramifications is what we do best," Siegel said.

"It probably wouldn't work."

"Why the hell not?"

"Because this is a hero complex. And self-sacrifice would for many of these people be seen as a fulfillment of their role as a hero. There may be a more reliable means to cause temporary or permanent power enhancement if self-sacrifice isn't a possible means to succeed, but the number of variables is just too great. We're talking about juggling the safety of the individual or those around them, plus the confidence and dedication of the individual. And even if we succeed, we may not like the results."

"You give me someone with superspeed or weather control and I assure you, I'll like the results."

"As I've said, the powers are a part of the meta-human's identity. If the powers change, it could cause something of an identity crisis. When we're dealing with people whose minds can influence the world around them in physics-defying ways, any mental instability is not to be taken lightly, and certainly not to be caused purposely."

Siegel huffed a breath. "So to summarize your six months of research?"

"I believe our heroes will rise to the challenge, if they are challenged. But they are who they are, and it would be unwise to attempt to change them."

"General. Priority dispatch in the secure text channel," Sgt. Roberts interjected.

"Holy hell!" Aiken yelped, nearly sliding out of his chair.

As far as he knew, the door had been shut behind him and Roberts was at his desk until seven microseconds before he'd uttered the update. The man was a wizard when it came to arriving silently and unannounced. The doctor looked to Summers, who had handled the sudden appearance only slightly better, which was fortunate since a similar leap would have doused all involved with the contents of two steaming-hot coffees.

"Are you sure everybody gets checked for the meta-gene?" Aiken whispered to Summers.

"You have access to his file," Summers said. "You could double-check."

Aiken turned to the general. He'd tapped out something on his keyboard and was now staring at something on his screen. Though the doctor couldn't see what the general was reading, something about the military man's demeanor was unsettling. Until this moment, Dr. Aiken had only ever seen three emotional states from this man: open rage, barely restrained rage, and on one notable occasion, pride. Right now, there was a steadiness and clarity to his expression.

"Dr. Aiken, how many members of the team can you get here by 1600?" he said calmly.

"Bomb Sniffer is already in the complex. As are..." He glanced at Summers.

"Phosphor, Gracias, and Chloroplast. The rest are on leave or on assignment," she said.

"Get a core team together. As many of them as you think can handle a global priority assignment. A team, B team. Anyone with codeword clearance and enough stability to follow some very tough orders. Top priority. Roberts, book us a conference room, and tell logistics to crack open the emergency travel budget," he instructed.

Roberts slipped from the room.

"What's this all about?"

"We've been summoned by the chairman of the joint chiefs of staff. An egg we've been watching has just hatched. We'd hoped we had more time. Just have everyone here and ready for overseas deployment. This is the big one. Get moving. I've got calls to make."

* * *

Dr. Aiken marched back and forth at the head of a conference table easily large enough to seat forty people. The call had gone out, a few hours had passed, and soon they would be assembled. Pvt. Summers leaned against the wall behind him, notebook in hand, ready to take notes. A curious-looking group of people had assembled at the table. Phosphor, the eldest of the group, was sitting near the head of the table. A few months of steady income and a military training regimen had toned him up slightly, but he was otherwise the same middle-aged former janitor he'd always been, complete with the beat-up messenger bag full of fluorescent tubes that was, as far as he was concerned, the source of his power. Bomb Sniffer, now officially old enough to be part of the team, was seated beside him with a rather impressive-looking laptop set up before her. Gracias was, as always, joined by his reluctant partner Chloroplast. Most of the heroes were dressed in some variation of red-and-white-camo military gear. The one exception was Chloroplast, who wore a mesh shirt and shorts that were just shy of scandalous, the better to reveal every inch of green skin he could to soak up the sun's rays. Despite the fact all it would really allow him to do was skip lunch, like most of the team he was keen to put his powers to use whenever possible.

"I wish they'd let me weigh in on the uniforms," Gracias said. "Since when does a hero team have to wear matching costumes? Nobody does that."

12

"The X-Men wear matching uniforms in the comic books," Chloroplast said.

"Sure, sometimes," Gracias said. "But there's always the exception even then. They let Beast wear just his skivvies, right?"

"Not until after he got blue and hairy," Pvt. Summers pointed out.

"Okay, see? So if you're a weird color, you get to be basically naked. That explains my man Chloroplast here. But we're Team Green. I should be allowed to wear green. Team within a team, you know."

"They're uniforms," Phosphor said. "I think they're supposed to match. Wouldn't be very uniform otherwise."

"I got grass powers! You're telling me the guy with grass powers has to wear red and white? Whoever heard of red-and-white grass? And we're the official superhero team of the US Army. Where's the blue, huh?"

"Yeah. At least there's blue grass," Bomb Sniffer suggested.

"She gets it!" Gracias said, pointing in her direction.

The door burst open, and Nonsensica and Non Sequitur rushed in.

"We didn't miss the mission briefing, did we?" Nonsensica said, adjusting her slightly askew goggles. "I had a heck of a time talking my way out of a speeding ticket. The cops do not respect secret identities, even when you have a government pass."

"Hey, you two!" Gracias said, jumping to his feet and trotting around the table to give them each a fist bump. "Been forever since they got the whole team together."

"It'll be a while longer," Dr. Aiken said. "The Number couldn't get here until tomorrow. We'll have to catch him up when he arrives."

"But that's it, though, right? We're one man shy of the whole crew," Gracias said.

Bomb Sniffer counted. "With him, I count seven. We're The Other Eight. Who else are we missing?"

Nonsensica grabbed a coffee from the center of the table while the group attempted to fill the missing gap.

"It's not Primadonna, is it?" Phosphor suggested.

"No. She's still on the other team," Dr. Aiken said. "Best to separate similar powers when possible. The Number is our dance-based hero."

"If Undo wasn't such a jerk, I'd've figured he'd be on the team by now. Decent powers on that guy," Chloroplast said.

Pvt. Summers scratched her head. She flipped through her pad and quickly came upon a yellow sticky note. "It's Afterthought," she said.

"Afterthought," the team said in unified realization.

"I don't suppose we remembered to invite him," Aiken said under his breath.

"I'll get on that," Summers said quickly.

"Whatever it is, it can wait," announced Gen. Siegel, appearing in the doorway just before she could duck out.

Sgt. Roberts trailed two steps behind him, arms heaped with folders, each sealed with red tape. He placed them on the desk and popped a panel in the center of the conference table, revealing a series of ports. He plugged a thumb drive into one of them.

"Lock the door and drop the screen," Siegel instructed.

Roberts did as he was instructed. A tap at a keyboard beside the door sealed the room, and a toggle switch on the opposite side of the door brought down a retractable projection screen. When it was fully deployed, an image faded into view. It simply read Department of Defense Classified Data.

"Chances are the whole world will know about this before too much longer, but for now, this is top secret. None of this leaves this room. Understood?"

Gracias rubbed his hands together. "Oh, baby. We're into the good stuff."

Roberts clicked to the first slide of the data. It was a scan of a heavily redacted document written in Cyrillic characters. As he spoke, slides clicked by, illustrating some of his claims with spy photos and other stolen documents.

"In the early nineteen sixties, the Soviet Union launched what we believe to be the first modern attempt at incorporating meta-humans into an active military. They called it Red Polaris. It was a multipronged attempt to recruit, indoctrinate, or create heroes that suited their needs. It was not a pronounced success but served as the inspiration for, and in some cases the framework of, multiple other such programs. Germany had the Clear Gate Initiative. France and England had a joint project they called Iridium Shield. We had the Guardian Project. China had Operation Dǐngjiān. When the Cold War ended and the Soviet Union broke up, several of their researchers took their findings and methodology to the highest bidder. This gave rise to a handful of second-generation meta-human operations. Red Polaris 2 in Russia. The White Crescent Program in Iran. And something which came to be called The Icon Project. We have been able to confirm the collapse or dissolution of each of these programs except for the last. The Icon Project seemed to have vanished, but we couldn't confirm its failure."

Sgt. Roberts clicked a new slide, showing a map of East Asia. "In 1997, an unrelated conflict over a small piece of land straddling the Yalu River had been simmering for decades. Both North Korea and China laid claim to the land. It was home to approximately seven thousand people and, more importantly for the two nations involved, an aging nuclear power plant. Neither of the governments involved wanted to cede the land to the other, but they also didn't want the obligation of sunsetting the power plant or the lost face of handing over nuclear technology. Negotiations began in December, and by 1999 the decision had been made to slough off the region entirely. The city and a few kilometers of surrounding land were disincorporated from both North Korea and China. It is not officially recognized by any global governing body, serving instead as a functionally independent city-state, the Chinese-North Korean Disincorporated Zone or ChiNoKo."

Gracias snorted. "Like Texarkana."

"No comments from the peanut gallery," the general said. "ChiNoKo has been a thorn in the side of global politics since its creation. While it has been too small to draw much international press, the fact that it falls under no legal jurisdiction of any kind means that it has served as a safe haven for all manner of international criminal activity. It's been kept safe from retaliation both by its proximity to two nations the world would rather not antagonize and because the locals know all too well their continued existence depends upon them avoiding any sort of genuine wrath turned in their direction. Any operation that drew the concern of either China, North Korea, or any of its allies was swiftly snuffed by the locals for fear of retaliation. All, we have learned, except one."

"It was The Icon Project, wasn't it?" Phosphor said.

"Glad to see someone's paying attention," the general said.

"Oh, from me it's the peanut gallery, but from him it's a gold star and a pat on the head. I see how it is," Gracias said.

Siegel glared at him.

"… sir," Gracias added.

"A few months ago, a member of the Guardian Project was able to acquire intelligence from a protected North Korean database. It was spotty, but it suggested that The Icon Project had been operating at a level of such high secrecy that even the committee that negotiated the formation of ChiNoKo didn't know that it was the location of the ongoing meta-human project. The location of the territory has made detailed surveillance impossible, but we've done our best."

"This is a lot of information in a hurry," Non Sequitur said.

"We're just about at the end of it. Two weeks ago, there was a minor radiological incident. Radiation sensors in China detected a brief period of slightly elevated radiation. A spike of zero point zero three millirems for a period of two hours. It is believed this was part of a safety drill. Regardless of what caused it, within seven hours the entire region was in lockdown. A few hours ago, we received a message from our counterparts in the Chinese military that a meta-human event has occurred. They are requesting aid in the form of advisors and meta-human peacekeepers."

"That's us!" Gracias said.

"I prefer 'crime fighter,' but keeping the peace works for me," Nonsensica said.

"In a frankly unprecedented amount of cooperation, China has granted us supervised access to their side of the ChiNoKo border. Dr. Aiken and Dr. Liefeld, each with their own assistants, have been specifically requested."

"Liefeld is going to be there?" Aiken said, wincing a bit.

"He's the world's foremost expert in the meta-human condition," the general said. "We are making any and all meta-humans in the program available to the two of you. They will be permitted on the Chinese mainland pending clearance by their security bureau. The people in this room have already been cleared. You'll all be on a plane tomorrow morning. Any questions?"

"What do we know about the supervillain responsible for whatever happened?" Nonsensica asked.

"Nothing. We've only been in contact with the Chinese military, so we can assume whatever happened had to have been on the Chinese border. Everything else has been kept under strict secrecy. We don't know how many individuals were responsible. We don't know what their powers are, if any. We don't know what their demands are."

"I don't like it," Chloroplast said.

"You don't like anything," Gracias said.

"I don't think it's unreasonable to dislike the idea of getting on a plane and flying halfway around the globe to fight some number of supervillains we don't know anything about."

"That's what heroes do!" Nonsensica said.

"I'm not arguing that. I'm just saying I don't like it," Chloroplast said.

"Eh, you're just the brooding hero-type. Every team needs one. You're the Batman."

"I always sort of considered Phosphor to be the Batman. His powers are kind of gadget based, and he's old and wise," Bomb Sniffer said.

"Well thanks, folks," Phosphor said with the utmost of humility.

"None of you are Batman," Gen. Siegel snapped. He turned to Roberts. "He's the billionaire, right?"

Roberts nodded.

"Right. We don't need a Batman. There's plenty of billionaires giving us their two cents on how to run things, and I've yet to meet one who would be worth listening to even with his bank account. And I can't believe you've got me talking about comic book heroes. First plane leaves in six hours. Make whatever plans you need to make and be on it. We'll ship over any additional gear and personnel on a second flight once we have a proper assessment. Doctor, I want a psychological profile on the target by the time we arrive."

"But we don't know anything about—"

"No excuses! This is your first real assignment. I'm not asking you to make me proud. I just want you to get it done."

He stormed out of the room, Roberts in tow.

"He's pretty bad at pep talks," Bomb Sniffer said.

All eyes turned to Aiken. He raised his eyebrows and blew out a shaky breath of air. "I hate to break it to you, but I'm not exactly a pro at pep talks either. But over the last few months, the people in this room, plus The Number and…" He snapped his fingers. "Who's the other guy?"

"There's another guy?" Gracias said.

Summers flipped to the sticky note again. "Afterthought."

"Right, and him," Aiken said. "You're the best of the best. Some of the other team have powers that score as good or better than yours, but you've consistently outperformed them. You've all been building your skills. Daily exercise routines. Combat training. Power-specific drills. Non Sequitur, how many different types of locks have you learned to disassemble and reassemble?"

"Somewhere around two hundred," Non Sequitur said.

"And Bomb Sniffer, how's the resolution of your explosive tracking?"

"We've got it down to three yards in terms of distance and five degrees in terms of spread," she said.

"Exactly. You were the best we could find, and you've gotten better. The US Army and the Chinese Army both believe you'll be an asset. So let's get out there and prove them right." He tugged at his shirt. "Now if you'll excuse me. I have to figure out how to produce a psychological profile on a mysterious operative who was probably in North Korea and/or China at one point and who may or may not be a group of people."

"Right, so…" Gracias paused. "Oh, man. We never came up with a rallying cry for The Other Eight."

"I thought we agreed 'Eight is Great' was the winner," Phosphor said.

"That's a Sesame Street song," Bomb Sniffer said.

"So? Sesame Street is the bomb!" Gracias said. "Oh, hey. That should be your catch phrase. I'm the Bomb."

"But I'm not the bomb. I sniff out the bomb."

"Sure but—"

"We'll figure it out later! I don't know about you guys, but I've got some gear to pack. I'm gonna need my stealth suit. Two extra sets of my trademark non-chucks. Those night-vision goggles I bought. The Other Eight have arrived, baby!" Nonsensica crowed.

Chapter 2

"When the heck are we going to arrive…" Nonsensica moped.

In a rare occurrence, Nonsensica had opted not to wear her full superhero suit during the ride. She and Non Sequitur had been all over the US doing their public outreach events and they were perpetually stuck in coach. At the time, it seemed like just about the worst way to travel, but with each flight at least providing them with a cushioned seat and air-conditioning, she was willing to stew in her rubber bodysuit in order to keep up appearances. As it so happened, military transportation accommodations were considerably less luxurious. It would have been one thing if they'd been stuck on a standard international flight. At the moment the whole team would agree that the extra legroom a Boeing C-17 Globemaster III provided wasn't worth the fact that the aircraft provided precisely the same creature comforts to the passengers as it provided to the cargo heaped at their feet. Thus, most of the team wore standard military fatigues. Not even their special red-and-white ones. At the moment, they were soldiers and little else. No sense putting on the whole superhero show. Nonsensica had thrown in her trademark goggles to preserve her secret identity. Just about the only one who seemed to be handling the trip completely in stride was Chloroplast, though that was mainly because he'd been asleep since they'd reached the Pacific Ocean. Their only major stop had been in California to pick up The Number from his day job running an exercise/dance studio. For his part, The Number had spent most of the flight with headphones on, jotting down choreography notes.

"Hey, look at the bright side," Non Sequitur said. "Now we know what it's like to be in the luggage section of a normal plane."

"I think it's cool," Gracias said. "We're literally in the rear with the gear."

"Being in the rear with the gear isn't cool," Nonsensica said.

"Speak for yourself. That's exactly the assignment I requested," Bomb Sniffer said.

"Come on," Nonsensica said. "You're telling me you tried out for, and got onto, a superhero team and now all you want to do is be a glorified tech support agent?"

"First off, a glorified tech support agent is better than a not glorified tech support agent. And second, I sniff out bombs! That's my power! It's by definition a support power. You need me to help find a bomb, great! I'll be out there with my nose to the grindstone. Literally."

"Nice," Gracias said.

"When push comes to shove, I'm sure she'll be in there pushing and shoving with the rest of us, right, Sniffer?" Phosphor said.

"I'll do what I have to do. I'm a hero. I'm just not quite as super as the rest of you."

"I don't know about that," Gracias said.

He gave Chloroplast a shove. All it managed to do was produce a briefly more intense snore from his partner.

"At least you haven't been asleep for twenty hours because the windows in this plane are too small to get enough sunlight," he said. "I always kind of thought showing all that skin was a fashion choice."

"I think he's faking it. Building the brand, you know?" Nonsensica said.

Gracias clapped his hands and rubbed them together. "All right. So we're going to be butting heads with another supervillain, or supervillains. What sort of powers you figure they'll have?"

"I'm betting it's going to be one person, first off," Nonsensica said. "At least, one person in charge. Maybe some lackeys we'll have to boot our way through, but evil is all about consolidating power."

"I'm betting it's a superteam," Gracias said. "One of those deals where we'll all have to face our evil opposite. I'm gonna have to butt heads with someone called the Weed Whacker or something. Mark my words."

"I'm with Nonsensica on this one," Non Sequitur said. "A little city-state no one's ever heard of? This smells like a banana republic situation."

"… So, like… selling pants?" Gracias said.

"No, like a tin-pot dictator," Non Sequitur amended.

"Ooooh. So magnet powers," Gracias said with a nod. "That's a good guess."

"No, I…" Non Sequitur shook his head. "The point is, I think we're dealing with someone with delusions of grandeur who took control of his little city and wants to rule the world."

"Yeah, yeah. You get someone with delusions of grandeur and you're going to need the world's most powerful superhero team to defeat them, for sure," Gracias said.

"Still doesn't tell us what powers they'll have, though," Phosphor said. "This must be a real heavy hitter if the army needs us."

"Eh, it's probably just a hostage situation. Or maybe a doomsday device," Nonsensica said. "Can't just send in the troops. You'll need something a little more elegant and precise. A crack team of heroes."

The door to the forward section of the plane opened, and Dr. Aiken stepped through.

"Forty minutes to landing," he said. "We're actually going to be touching down on a temporary airfield they constructed twenty miles northeast of the border of ChiNoKo."

"They built a whole new airport for us?" Non Sequitur said.

"A landing strip, anyway. Evidently they foresee the need to get huge numbers of troops and huge amounts of equipment to the border quickly."

"This really is a big one," Phosphor said.

"The Chinese government has provided an interpreter fluent in regional dialects of Cantonese and Korean, but apparently most of the people we'll be dealing with directly will speak English," Aiken said.

"I sort of figured Nonsensica would be our language expert," Gracias said.

"I'm Chinese American. Accent on the American. You're Mexican American. Do you speak Spanish?" Nonsensica said.

"¡Por supuesto que sí! Mi papá se aseguró de que hablara con fluidez. Es muy útil."

She blinked at him. "Okay... Well, I only know enough Chinese to understand my grandmother when she yells at me for not knowing enough Chinese."

Aiken continued. "We'll be going right to the front from the airstrip to what they're calling the forward operating base for a quick briefing on any new developments and whatever intelligence they couldn't give us before we arrived, then it's straight to the front to see the state of things."

"The front?" Phosphor said. "As in, this is war?"

"I'm just telling you what they told me. I'm here to weigh in on the psychology, not the terminology," Aiken said.

"Have you made any progress with that?" Non Sequitur asked.

"What progress is there to make? We know next to nothing."

"You've been working on it for a solid twenty-four hours," Nonsensica said. "You must have come up with something."

"I can theorize, but this should be taken with a heap of salt," Aiken said. "If I were to be pressed right now to make predictions regarding the potential perpetrators, and I'm sure I will be as soon as we land, I'd say this. This person is the result of a government program, and if there's been no formal declaration of war, then something's gone wrong. Based upon the materials they've given me on how similar programs to The Icon Project have gone, this was a long-term project, so this person or group of people is likely to have a view of the world that's been manipulated by the project's organizers. They will have an incomplete worldview and will be taking orders from someone not out of duty but out of some sort of ingrained loyalty designed specifically as a means of control."

"That's it?" Phosphor said.

"Even that is a bit much. More speculation than I'd be willing to make solid decisions on." He flipped down one of the collapsible chairs along the side of the plane and took a seat to strap in. "Now as for Liefeld, I'm sure he'll have all sorts of definitive statements to make. That guy is nothing if not certain about stuff."

"Oh, yeah. Dr. Liefeld," Non Sequitur said. "He's sort of your big rival, right?"

"No. Saying he's my rival is overstating my role in history. He's the expert on the meta-human condition, and I'm the guy you get when you can't get him. I'm the 'is Pepsi okay?' to Liefeld's 'I'll have a Coke,'" Aiken said.

"Oof," Nonsensica said.

"How come you ended up with Earth's finest team of heroes, and he's just this shadowy figure in the shadows?" Gracias said.

"Because he comes at the meta-human condition from the biological point of view. Brain structure. Gene mapping. Power measurement. I came at it from the mental side of things. Theory versus application. His stuff is rock solid, incontrovertible. Data. He's never focused on actually putting theory into practice. My side actually includes human behavior. A lot harder to hit the kind of bulls-eye that military strategists want scientists to hit, but if you do, you end up with a team as opposed to a checklist of things a team could conceivably have."

The door to the forward part of the plane opened, and Pvt. Summers stepped out. She sat beside Aiken and strapped in as well. "We just got a message from our Chinese military liaison. They're doubling our armed escort for the trip to the ChiNoKo border," she said.

"Oof. Sounds like things are getting tense," Gracias said.

"How long until we land?" Nonsensica said.

"A few more minutes," Summers said.

Nonsensica stood. "I'm going to get properly suited up. Gotta have my game face on."

* * *

A surprisingly smooth landing and a very bumpy ride across a dirt road brought them to what was apparently called FOB

Alpha in the documents Aiken had been provided. In his limited time with the military, Aiken had come to learn that any given nation's corps of engineers were as near to wizards as the world was likely to see, unless one included Madam Witch-Wizard, Class O applicant for the Guardian Project who had the ability to "bewitch" frogs into doing her bidding so long as that bidding was hopping in the direction she pointed. It was quite evident that the base was entirely temporary. It probably had only been installed within the last few days, but it was nonetheless impressively robust. A satellite uplink kept it in touch with the intelligence and information systems of the rest of the military. Three heavy-duty antiaircraft guns had been installed, and there was a fully equipped barracks to house two hundred soldiers, in addition to separate accommodations for The Other Eight.

As they approached the main entrance, they were greeted by a stout, serious-looking officer flanked by two armed soldiers. Dr. Aiken stepped forward and extended his hand in greeting. The rest of the seven attending members of The Other Eight formed a line behind him.

"A pleasure to meet you, Dr. Aiken. News of your exploits and the achievements of those under your guidance and command precede you," he said. "I am Gen. Luo. I apologize if we are not able to provide a more formal greeting, but the situation has been escalating. If you are prepared, I would like to provide an update to you and your team and formulate an immediate plan of action."

"Of course," Aiken said.

After an impressively efficient security check—it turned out an unmistakable group of misfits like The Other Eight were very easy to positively identify—they were gathered in one of the sturdier temporary structures. Rows of folding chairs had been set up, and a desktop PC with a standard monitor had been placed at one end of the room. Gen. Luo dimmed the lightweight LED lighting dangling from the ceiling and pressed his thumb to a reader on the computer's keyboard.

"I assume you have been made aware of the minor issue detected with the Disincorporated Zone's power plant," Gen. Luo said. "It was well within safety levels but well above alert levels. As a matter of procedure, we dispatched a team of technicians to investigate and address the issue."

"You did? I assumed ChiNoKo would have their own crews," Aiken said.

"The Disincorporated Zone's local staff is, to be charitable, of limited skill. I am more inclined to define their skills as inadequate, but I am told such opinions are undiplomatic. It is in the best interest of the People's Republic of China that the reactor continue to operate safely and efficiently, so we have made an informal agreement with local authorities to provide supplemental technicians whenever regular maintenance and safety inspections are called for. Our inspection determined that there was no structural flaw responsible for the brief increase in emissions. It was probably operator error. However, a number of mechanical faults previously flagged for closer inspection had been determined to have risen to a caution state and plans were made for immediate replacement. Some preliminary maintenance, placing the reactor in what was effectively a maintenance mode, was initiated."

He tapped the keyboard. Shaky body-cam footage began to play.

"This footage was captured by the maintenance crew, three days later," he explained.

The language was unfamiliar, but a translation was hardly necessary. A skittish-looking man dressed in a military police-man's outfit was urgently warning maintenance crew away. He was continuously looking over his shoulder. Voices rose and the body cam shifted. A blurry figure streaked through the sky, then a deep thump caused the crew and the MP to stumble. The MP shakily stepped aside to reveal a young man, perhaps twenty years of age. He was quite thin and dressed in a silver bodysuit with a capital I on the chest. He stepped forward and proclaimed something. By the rather wooden delivery, the phrase was likely rehearsed, and followed by a second statement delivered in English.

"You will back away from our humble soil, outsider! The people of ChiNoKo have endured your tyranny for far too long. Off with you, or you shall face my wrath," he said, speaking with a confident grasp of the language.

A murmur of confusion and anxiety washed over the maintenance crew. The supervisor stepped forward and held some papers up. From the intensity of his words, he was making a very spirited case that the crew's work had to be done regardless of how he felt about it. The silver-dressed man grasped him by the shirt and, with a seemingly effortless thrust, heaved him off his feet. The audio from the recording was swallowed in shouts loud enough to become garbled by the limited capacity of the microphone. The video jostled and blurred as the maintenance workers ran. A few seconds later, the footage settled to reveal the supervisor, badly injured and moaning. He was lying at the end of a bloody smear on the side of the road, like he'd been hurled twenty yards and come down hard.

The footage blurred with a snap-turn and settled into the first properly centered view of the man responsible. The maintenance worker must have grabbed the camera and manually aimed it to capture a proper shot. The silver-suited man held his hands out to either side, palms up and fingers curled. Slowly, he rose into the air until he was drifting ominously over the heads of two more MPs who had rushed to the border.

He delivered another rehearsed line, then stated in English, "Such is the fate of any who would threaten ChiNoKo. So says... The Icon."

The footage ended. The eyes of the assembled team of heroes were wide.

"That was real? What we just saw was real?" Nonsensica said.

"Holy cow," Non Sequitur muttered.

"Dude, he could fly. He had super strength and he could fly," Gracias said. "That's not fair! Why does he win the power lottery?"

"If you will permit me to finish the briefing," Luo said.

"There's more?" Chloroplast said.

"This unidentified subject, still known only as The Icon, assaulted official representatives of the Chinese government. The supervisor of the maintenance crew is still in the hospital. This attack could not be allowed to stand, and the person responsible could not be allowed to remain free and active. He was a threat to national security."

He tapped the keyboard. A somewhat higher-quality piece of footage played. This one was recorded by a dedicated hand-held camera, either by a journalist or by a surveillance expert judging by the skill at keeping the relevant action properly framed and sharply focused. It showed a team of fifteen soldiers moving at a low run, weapons held at the ready. They wore body armor, complete with protective air-filtration masks of the sort normally worn by riot police. They approached the very same border crossing. When the lead soldier was a few paces from the well-marked border, a silver streak shot down from above. The Icon struck the ground with enough force to send a rush of debris scattering against the soldiers. As before, he spoke first in Chinese, then in English.

"Do not cross this border. I do not want to hurt you, but I will defend my home."

The lead soldier shouted orders. The Icon weathered them with arms crossed.

"Our soldiers are informing him of his crimes," Gen. Luo explained. "They are instructing him that he is to surrender to their custody and that further hostilities will not be tolerated."

The lead soldier held his ground. The others spread out behind, weapons at the ready. More orders were barked. Canisters of tear gas launched across the border, billowing up in a toxic cloud. In time, the wind cleared the gas, leaving The Icon unblinking and unhurt. The ominous figure remained still. Finally, the lead soldier approached.

The moment he crossed the border, The Icon moved in a blur and caught the soldier by the throat. The others raised their voices and raised their guns. The Icon raised the stricken soldier and slammed him to the ground, leaving him broken and twitching. The soldiers opened fire. Chattering fully automatic weapon fire caused The Icon to stumble back and drop to one knee. The rifles didn't stop firing until the place where The Icon once stood was lost in a cloud of debris. The soldiers held their ground and skillfully reloaded. They stalked forward. One by one, they crossed the border.

The Icon stood up from the smoke. He was unhurt. Aside from some minor burns on his bodysuit, there was no sign he'd just absorbed enough ordnance to wipe out a full squad. He burst toward the soldiers. Rough, graceless blows struck each soldier. There was no sign of training, no sign of martial prowess. It didn't matter. Strength alone was sufficient. The scene was grotesque. Fifteen heavy blows. Fifteen broken men. When they were past the point of combat, Icon dragged each of them to the border and heaved them over. He lingered for a moment, eyes wide and chest heaving with exhausted breaths. He looked shakily to hands splattered with the blood of other men, then shut his eyes tight and dashed into the distance with startling speed.

Gen. Luo stopped the video. "Four of those soldiers succumbed to their wounds. The rest remain in critical condition."

The room was silent for a few seconds. Chloroplast was the first to speak.

"We're going to die," he said.

No one felt compelled to contradict him.

"There have been no further direct contacts with The Icon, but following that hostility, we have kept the Disincorporated Zone under constant satellite surveillance. Furthermore, we have been broadcasting warnings that until The Icon is delivered to us, the Disincorporated Zone will be considered a hostile territory."

"Does he have any demands?" Aiken asked.

"You have observed the only two instances of direct contact. The only demand appears to be that the borders of the Disincorporated Zone be respected."

"I think you should do it," Gracias said. "That guy's hard-core."

"We cannot, for two reasons. First, he initiated hostilities against the People's Republic of China. That cannot stand. Second, you'll recall the mission of the maintenance workers was to replace and repair some components of the reactor that were in danger of entering a fault state. Specifically, the reactor was placed in a maintenance mode. The local reactor crew does not have the expertise to remove it from that state, and it was not designed to remain in that state for long periods of time."

"Oh jeez," Non Sequitur said.

"What is going to happen?" Aiken said seriously.

"Impossible to be certain. If the workers leave the reactor untouched and the mechanisms slated for repair do not fail, then the reactor will stall and require a lengthy procedure to safely return to full output. If they attempt to return it to full capacity, or if any of the flawed components fail, there are scenarios that could result in a prompt criticality event and subsequent meltdown into groundwater. The resulting steam explosion could spread radioactive particles across much of East Asia. We have attempted to contact and coach the crews, but all two-way communication channels have been systematically shut down. We must assume this was done by The Icon himself."

"Son of a..." Nonsensica muttered.

"How long do we have?" Aiken said.

"If the reactor is left alone, no less than three weeks will pass before it fully stalls. At that time, the local crews are likely to begin attempting to restore functionality and thus risk pro-ducing the undesirable outcome," Luo explained. "Before then, hardware faults or user error could potentially cause similar un-desirable outcomes."

"Undesirable outcome is a heck of a way to describe Chernobyl: Take Two," Chloroplast said.

"The only other relevant information I can give you is, of the local population of seven thousand, six thousand two hundred fifteen have fled the zone. Five thousand refugees have been processed here. The remaining refugees are estimated and were observed entering North Korea. The Icon made no attempts to prevent them from leaving."

"You know things are bad when refugees are fleeing into North Korea," Phosphor said.

"What about the rest of the population?" Aiken asked.

"We must assume they are either unwilling or unable to leave."

Gen. Luo pulled a small metal case from beneath the table and clicked it open. Inside was a thick envelope. He held it out to Aiken.

"This contains all the information we have about the Disincorporated Zone that we believe may be of use. I would prefer it not leave this room without supervision."

There was a knock at the door. Luo paused. After a moment, the door opened to reveal a frail old man dressed in a crisp white dress shirt and gray slacks and supporting himself with a silver-handled cane. Dr. Liefeld. He nodded to the others and hobbled to take a seat.

"Please," he said. "Don't let me interrupt."

Aiken scrabbled to regain his train of thought. "Does this include anything about The Icon himself?"

"What little there is," Luo said. "We've yet to process all interviews with former residents of the Disincorporated Zone. We would appreciate you study the materials. I am in contact with your Gen. Siegel to discuss tactical options. Any meta-human-specific insight and operations are welcome, as are any areas of investigation you feel we may have missed."

"One question leaps to mind immediately," Aiken said. "Why has The Icon allowed service crews to enter until now? Why did he choose after this maintenance process had already begun to bar further entry?"

"Because The Icon did not exist before now," Dr. Liefeld said. "I should think that would be obvious. The origin occurred at some point shortly before the second maintenance crew arrived. I suspect the reactor itself may be responsible for the origin."

"Yeah. Yeah, that's classic," Gracias said. "He was probably bitten by a radioactive... icon."

Liefeld gave Gracias a doubtful look, then scanned the room. "So. Here we have it, then. The fruit borne by the Guardian Project. The Other Eight, I believe you call yourselves?" He squinted his eyes and adjusted his glasses. "Despite the fact that there are seven of you."

"It's sort of an informal name. And there's one member who by their nature tends to straggle... I think..." Aiken said.

"Not to undermine the decisions made by the US military, and not to cast any undue criticism in your direction, but I question the value of bringing your people here to face this threat."

"We're superheroes. He's a supervillain. We're exactly who is supposed to fight him," Nonsensica said.

Liefeld fiddled with his cane. "The Icon is most certainly a supervillain. His appearance, I would say, redefines the very meaning of meta-human. The bar has been raised. And it is delusion to suggest otherwise."

"Hey!" Gracias said. "I'm good at delusion."

"With all due respect, Doctor," Aiken said. "I think you're overlooking the psychological aspects of the situation. Nonsensica is right. Superheroes are supposed to fight supervillains. The Icon will be expecting to fight superheroes. Or, rather, he believes himself to be a hero and expects to be facing supervillains."

"Do you really believe that The Icon's mental state matters in light of the amount of raw power we've seen on display? When a man has a rifle, do you believe his intention matters when he pulls the trigger?"

"So why did they bring you in, exactly?" Non Sequitur asked. "To just sit there and talk about how the bad guy is really strong?"

"I'm presently revising my calculations on the maximum potential energy output of the Liefeld lobe. My current theory is that The Icon may have a stamina issue. He seemed winded after his clash with the soldiers. I needed a break from my calculations, so I thought I should come to congratulate you on how far you've come since your troubles with your doctoral thesis."

"You mean when you repeatedly rejected me for being too correct about something that was top secret?" Aiken said. "I'd say I've come along quite well. But I do have a tremendous amount of material to get through, so I appreciate the visit and insight, but I need to get to work and collaborate with my team."

"Of course, of course. I look forward to your assessment." Dr. Liefeld stiffly stood and paced for the door.

"Oh, and Doc," Nonsensica said. "Stress tournament."

He flinched, then sneered. "Ah. Yes. No doubt an indispensable skill in the face of a flying, invulnerable powerhouse. Fine team you've assembled, Aiken."

"Doctor Aiken," he snapped as Liefeld left.

"I'm calling it right now," Gracias said. "That guy's going to start a rival team of heroes and they'll turn evil."

"So what do we do now, Doc?" Nonsensica said.

Dr. Aiken ran his fingers through his hair and pulled a chair up to the table with the computer on it. "You should get to the barracks and get yourselves ready. Maybe catch some sleep if you can manage. I've got to go through this information and come up with some idea of who and what The Icon is."

"I'll go see what the coffee situation is," Pvt. Summers said.

"Good thinking. We're going to need it."

Chapter 3

The team had assembled in a temporary barracks. Two rows of six bunk beds suggested it was intended for two dozen troops. With just the seven of them, there was at least plenty of room. Like the cargo plane that had brought them here, the amenities were a little slim. It was drafty, lacked any sort of air-conditioning, and if they wanted to use the bathroom, they'd be hoofing it across the base. At the moment, none of that mattered. There were far more pressing things on their minds.

The entire crew had taken advantage of the showers. Those who still had an appetite after what they'd seen and heard paid a visit to the mess hall. For the last ten minutes, they'd milled about or tested various beds, each trying to ignore the elephant in the room. It was Gracias who finally gave voice to what was crowding everything else out of the minds of the team.

"A flying brick. The world gets one flying brick and he's a villain," Gracias said.

"Yeah… What are we supposed to do about this?" Chloroplast said.

"We're supposed to fight," Nonsensica said. "We're supposed to defend the innocent and punish the wicked."

Of the group, she'd been the most busy. She'd taken the opportunity, and the near-certainty of a clash with the enemy before too much longer, to change back into her full supersuit after her shower, complete with gear. And while the others moped about, she'd interspersed some twirling non-chuck practice.

"He slaughtered a crack team of soldiers," Bomb Sniffer said.

34

"They weren't superheroes."

"They had guns, though," Chloroplast said. "Don't get me wrong. I know I'm super. I know we're all super. But in this particular situation, 'has gun' is a more useful superpower than most of us have, and it didn't do any good."

"Well then it wasn't a more useful superpower, was it?" Nonsensica said. "And having a gun isn't a superpower, anyway."

"It's the Punisher's superpower," Gracias said.

"The Punisher isn't a superhero, he's an antihero. And his power isn't 'has gun,' it's the raw, seething dedication to vengeance that drives him to superhuman acts," Nonsensica said.

"He's also fictional," Non Sequitur said. "I'm not sure we should be trying to make points and counterpoints with people who don't have to worry about reality."

Nonsensica waved a hand dismissively. "Reality is what we make it. Phosphor can pull an endless series of fluorescent bulbs from his bag and light them up. Gracias can conjure grass and dirt from little more than the concept of gratitude. The rules are different for us. And that's how we'll win this. All of those soldiers? They had to do their thinking, and fighting, inside a box. We're gonna stand on that box and do a jump kick off it."

"Is this the same box that's got the dead cat in it, or a different one?" Gracias asked.

"No. That's Schrödinger's box. I'm talking about the 'think outside the box' box," Nonsensica said quickly, hoping to maintain the rhetorical momentum.

"To be fair," Chloroplast said, "the presence of a dead cat in a box is a pretty good reason to think outside of it."

"But sometimes there's a live cat in it, right?" Bomb Sniffer said. "That's a pretty good box."

"Is this the cat everyone's trying to figure out how to skin in different ways?" Phosphor asked.

"Hey, yeah," Gracias said. "That'd explain why there needs to be more than one way. Sometimes the cat's already dead, and sometimes you have to kill it, then skin it. Oh, hey. And there's a thing called a Skinner box. Does that fit in somewhere?"

"Why do all of these sayings and experiments involve cats and boxes?" Chloroplast asked.

"Cats like boxes, everyone knows that," Gracias said.

Everyone took a moment to nod appreciatively at the sage wisdom.

"Enough about cat boxes!" Nonsensica snapped once she realized how thoroughly they'd lost the thread. "In a couple of minutes, the doc is going to walk through that door. He's going to have a plan, and we're going to have to execute. Now let's talk strategy. What can we do?"

"Well, we can't shoot him," Phosphor observed.

"Which is good, because none of us has the 'has gun' super-power," Bomb Sniffer said.

"I think all we've got is distraction," Non Sequitur said.

"Right! That's one thing. Phosphor can dazzle him with hurled fluorescent tubes. I can zip-zap his neurons with my words. The Number can get him dancing, right?" She craned her neck. "Where is The Number anyway? He's being awfully quiet over there."

She marched over to the bunk in the corner, where The Number was limbering up with headphones on. She pulled the headphones from his ears.

"Care to join in the conversation here, dance man? We're talking about how we can save the world."

"Hmm? Oh. Sorry. It's just... look, these dance moves don't write themselves. It takes a lot of preparation to put together a full routine, and I figure we're going to need one. It's the only thing I have to offer," he said.

Nonsensica looked to the others, then shrugged. "That's fair. What's your playlist, by the way?"

He held up his phone. She thumbed through the songs and whistled. "If nothing else, this clash is going to have a killer soundtrack," she said.

***

Dr. Aiken marched back and forth in front of the computer table in the same room the initial briefing had been held in. It had only been two hours since then, but he looked like he'd had three sleepless nights. Pvt. Summers and Gen. Luo were seated, waiting for his presentation. Gen. Siegel and assorted high-ranking military advisors were on a secure video call on the screen. Dr. Liefeld and the heroes were notably absent. A technician was just finishing the AV setup that would allow Aiken to share his data with those on the call.

"Are we ready?" he asked.

The tech nodded, then excused himself from the room. Aiken took a sip of coffee and cleared his throat.

"To get the key point out of the way, the main thrust of this presentation is that we need more information. This problem can't be solved without learning more about The Icon, the precise methodology employed by The Icon Project that sought to create him, and the specific nature of his origin. I can, however, provide some basic assertions that I am confident can be applied. First, and foremost, he is not a villain."

"He's killed my men," Luo said. "And he's holding eight hundred people hostage, with the potential for hundreds of thousands more if the reactor fails."

"Please, I fully understand, but this is a matter of behavior and terminology. There exists a supervillain behavioral archetype in meta-humans. It is far rarer than people would believe. To be a supervillain, one must not be driven by the same morality that drives the rest of society. It is very simple to see the earmarks of supervillainy. These individuals are driven by greed, control, and notoriety. They so monomaniacally pursue these ends that they inevitably overextend themselves or self-sabotage. If The Icon was a proper supervillain, this situation wouldn't have been nearly as easy to contain for as long as it has been. He does not seek notoriety. No message has been delivered in any grand fashion. Not to the greater world, anyway. No demands have been made to spread that message. He is not driven by greed. There is nothing of value in ChiNoKo. Not that we know of, at least. And, again, he hasn't made any demands. Control? There is evidence of that. Clearly he wishes his homeland to be kept from the control of others. But as evidenced by his willingness to allow refugees to leave, he doesn't seek to control their lives. He is not a leader. He sees himself as a protector. And that is, at its core, a heroic trait. From this point forward, we must view him as a misguided hero. To do otherwise would improperly model his potential behavior."

"Heroes don't kill soldiers," Luo stated.

"No. They don't. And that was the point that stumped me the longest. Again, I can't stress this enough, I can't be sure until I have some solid understanding of The Icon Project. But if the goal was to create a superhero that could be used as a tool, then it would stand to reason that one would want to render morality as black and white as possible. In short, the creators of The Icon Project would attempt to sculpt the worldview of their creation into something as comic-book-like as possible, with themselves or their creators in a position of unassailable virtue. They would want to remove as many barriers to action as they could and remove as much doubt as they could. In a comic book, and particularly in the mind of a meta-human with a hero complex, superheroes and supervillains are the focus. A hero fights villains. A superhero fights supervillains. And there is only one type of foe that a proper superhero is free to destroy. Stormtroopers, or mooks."

He brought up a still image of the soldiers immediately before the attack. "Gen. Luo, your men initiated the assault with gas. They were wearing masks, and they were wearing uniforms. This is what cost them their lives. The defining characteristics of a mook are conventional weaponry, interchangeability, and anonymity. You unwittingly supplied him with precisely the type of foe he has been taught is disposable. And so he disposed of them."

He changed the view to a still of The Icon shortly after the battle. "Here you can see that he has blood on his hands, and the realization is clearly disturbing to him. He didn't see the soldiers as human, and the evidence that they are has visibly shaken him. This supports the theory that he is acting not out of a desire to do harm but out of a desire to defend his own principles, whatever they may be. I believe our best bet at defeating The Icon is to illustrate that our principles align with his own."

"But we don't know what those principles are," Luo said.

"Not yet. But if we accept the premise that he has been molded as closely to the hero archetype as possible, then when he is confronted with other meta-humans, people he considers to be his equals, he will not only engage them in nonlethal combat, he will likely voice his principles as a means of reinforcing his nobility to himself and to them. He will want to prove to those he considers to be villains that he is a hero. This will be doubly necessary for him, as he has taken lives and must now justify to himself and to the others that he was right to do so."

"You propose we send your people, then. We send The Other Eight."

"Not all of them. It is frequently in the nature of a hero to assume he will be outnumbered. The ones with the biggest army are almost always the bad guys in their mind. I propose a small sampling. No more than three members of The Other Eight. We bring them to the border, but do not cross it, and we tease as much information out of the confrontation as we can before we withdraw. With any luck, there will be no violence, and we will conclude the confrontation with a far greater understanding of The Icon's mindset."

"And then what?" Luo asked.

"And then we can pursue a diplomatic solution. We can reason with him."

"And if he proves unreasonable?"

"More data are always better," Aiken said. "What we learn will make us better capable of dealing with whatever comes next."

"Presently, I prefer the course of action proposed by Dr. Liefeld," Luo said.

"I concur," said Siegel.

"Forgive me, but was there a briefing I wasn't invited to?" Aiken asked.

"Dr. Liefeld has been running his calculations based upon the proposed maximum capacities of the Liefeld lobe, the observed capabilities of The Icon, and the visible fatigue after his first battle. He believes a prolonged, high-intensity assault can overwhelm The Icon. Because his durability is merely a manifestation of the influence of the Liefeld lobe, that influence must be maintained for his defense to remain intact. If he becomes exhausted, both his strength and his durability will diminish, and he will eventually become vulnerable."

Dr. Aiken shook his head. "I would vigorously advise against that course of action, Generals. A major assault, particularly with overwhelming numbers, will reinforce his belief that he must protect his land and/or his people. He will match the level of force and feel justified in doing so. He won't hold back."

"But there is an upper bound on the capacity of the Liefeld lobe," Siegel said. "That's just science."

"I read Dr. Liefeld's reports on the lobe once I was recruited into the Guardian Project, and everything we've seen is outside the upper bound of what he proposed was possible. He was wrong then, who is to say his new numbers are correct? For this plan of overwhelming The Icon to work, you need to hit him with excess force. Falling short by even a single bullet will cost all of your soldiers their lives and harden his resolve. The cost of your plan's failure is dozens of lives. The cost of my plan's failure is some time."

"And, in the worst case, as many as three members of our team of meta-humans," Siegel said.

"It won't come to that. I assure you."

"Your assurance notwithstanding, you've made the argument that your plan has the better worst-case scenario. What is the best-case scenario? The Icon must be neutralized. How do you propose we achieve it?" Luo said.

Dr. Aiken rubbed his face. "There is an aspect to the meta-human condition that, until now, we haven't been able to study in any quantifiable terms. That is the subject of limitation. Dr. Liefeld obviously believes limits exist. Hard limits based on biological capacity. And he is probably correct, but we can't know how high they are, particularly considering The Icon so drastically exceeds prior estimates. I am of the belief that the limitations, like the powers, are self-imposed. Every meta-human I've discovered has their powers limited in some way."

"Most of the meta-humans you've studied have pointless powers to start with," Siegel said bluntly.

"Value judgments aside," Aiken said, "some of these can be explained as potential measurable limits. Non Sequitur's ability to precede cause with effect is limited to thirty seconds. Not precisely thirty seconds, by the way, but by what he perceives to be thirty seconds. In the absence of a timing device, we've observed his powers failing in as little as twenty-two seconds or persisting for as long as forty-eight seconds. And Gracias. He is able to manifest biomatter from no apparent source, but only if circumstances can reasonably justify him speaking a key word. That is an utterly arbitrary limitation that can only have been self-applied.

"I believe that psychologically, meta-humans justify their own powers by forcing them to adhere to rules. Those powers can exist, even if they violate the laws of nature, because they are balanced by their own laws. And we have observed that the more potent the power, the more tangible the limitation. To use the relevant parlance, someone like The Icon is bound to have their kryptonite. Literally bound, in that the power cannot exist without the weakness. If we can find that weakness and apply it, then they will, as you put it, be neutralized."

"And you are certain this weakness exists," Luo said.

"All evidence I have supports it. That's as certain as I can reasonably be."

The two dour military men glared at each other across the video link.

"What is your timeline, Gen. Luo?" Siegel asked.

"Eighteen hours to equip, brief, and deploy what I would consider to be an adequate response team."

"Are you comfortable permitting Dr. Aiken to pursue his research in the intervening time?"

"If he is capable of doing so without endangering the potential success of my mission or the safety of my troops, that is permissible."

"Just so I'm clear, you intend to attack regardless of what I do?"

"With a threat of this size, multiple avenues of engagement are advisable. Your information-gathering mission is authorized. Logistics will provide you with transportation and an operational window. Expect to be ready to deploy in two hours."

"Yes, sir. Thank you. I'll make the appropriate preparations."

He gathered his things. Pvt. Summers opened the door and held it for him.

"That went better than it could have," Summers said. "You're a psychologist talking to two career soldiers. Usually the only sort of psychology they like to hear about is intimidation."

"They're going to attack someone who very likely will become more hostile and dangerous when under attack. That they don't understand that means I didn't do my job," Aiken said.

"You could be wrong. Their way could work," she suggested.

"I'd really rather not find out. If we're lucky, we'll get everything we need from my plan and I'll be able to form a more compelling argument. But to do it, The Other Eight are going to have to really prove themselves to be the professionals I believe them to be."

They reached the barracks and he opened the door. An argument seemed to be raging.

"No, the cat wouldn't land, because if you buttered its back, it would want to land on both its back and its feet," Gracias insisted.

"A cat isn't a piece of toast!" Chloroplast said. "And toast lands butter side up all the time!"

Aiken shut his eyes tight and furrowed his brow.

"Professionals can have spirited discussions," Summers said.

"Oh, hey, Doc!" Nonsensica said. "What's up?"

"Things are moving quickly. I need three volunteers for an information-gathering mission," Aiken said.

"Not it," said Chloroplast.

"Not it," said Bomb Sniffer.

"Dibs!" Nonsensica said. "What's it gonna be, Doc? Stealth? Is it a stealth mission? Should I put on my stealth suit?"

"No. This will be a face-to-face encounter with The Icon himself. We will see if he has any demands and generally try to learn more about him. His history, his motivations, anything we can. Our goal is to root out some indication of a weakness."

"You want us to just go toe to toe with a guy who wiped out a squad?" Chloroplast said. "Double not it."

"Again, it's not combat. All evidence suggests he won't assault anyone who stays on the Chinese side of the border. We just want to keep him talking. I want three of you, in cost—er, uniform. The Other Eight uniform, not military."

"I'm in. I've got the best uniform," Nonsensica said.

"She's my partner," Non Sequitur said. "If she's going, I'm going."

"One more," Aiken said.

The rest of the team cast glanced back and forth. Eventually, it was Phosphor who stood.

"Seems like if the job's about shedding light on things, I ought to be on the crew. I'm an old pro at it," he said.

"Great. Get ready. No weapons. Nothing offensive, at least. Defensive is fine. We don't want this to escalate. I'll go see about transportation. Meet me in the briefing room across the way. I'll coach you on what to say."

"You aren't coming?" Non Sequitur said.

"I'm coming, but I don't think I'll be doing much talking. If I'm right, you three will be the only ones he'll respect enough to address directly."

Nonsensica grinned and nudged Non Sequitur with her elbow. "You hear that? The most powerful villain who ever lived and we're the ones he'll respect. Meanwhile, we have to do a bunch of stunts to get high schoolers to respect us."

"High schoolers have a lot in common with power-mad supervillains. Spend enough time as a janitor and you'll work that out," Phosphor said.

Dr. Aiken headed for the door.

"Oh! Doc!" Gracias said. "Settle an argument. If you buttered a cat's back and dropped it into a box, would the cat be on its feet, butter-side down, or both until you opened the box up and looked at it?"

Aiken stared wearily at Gracias.

"You're under a lot of pressure right now. We'll circle back," Gracias said.

* * *

Nonsensica sat beside Non Sequitur in the back seat of an open-top jeep. Phosphor and Aiken were in the front row, with Aiken at the wheel. Two other jeeps trailed them to fill out the convoy, each with six soldiers. As they'd left the base, any semblance of light faded away. There were streetlights, but they weren't illuminated. Possibly damaged by The Icon, possibly cut off on purpose. Either way, the pools of light cast by the jeep on the badly maintained road ahead only worsened the atmosphere of raw, undiluted anxiety in the vehicle. Aiken in particular looked like his teeth would shatter if he clenched them any harder. Nonsensica probably felt about as wound up as he did, but the fear was crackling and popping amid a cocktail of other emotions. She was terrified of what might happen, but at the same time, she felt like this was the job she was born to do. She held on to that thought and let it steel her against all the doubts and concerns.

"I wish they'd given us something with a roof," Non Sequitur said, trying to shield his eyes from the wind while still watching the road ahead.

"This is why you ought to wear goggles. It's not just about identity, it's about utility," she said.

"They shouldn't have given us an escort," Aiken said. "This is too many soldiers. I told them I didn't want any soldiers."

Phosphor slapped Aiken in the back. "Tell you what, Doc. We'll make sure we steal the show, right? Keep his eyes on us."

"If there's one thing I'm good at, it's being the center of attention," Nonsensica said.

"One more turn." Aiken turned and signaled the trailing jeeps. They pulled aside and slowed down. "Remember what I told you. Don't antagonize. Everyone got their recorders on?"

The heroes reached up and tapped the compact body recorders the Chinese army had provided. Phosphor and Non Sequitur wore theirs tucked into the chest pocket of their red-and-white fatigues. Nonsensica wore a head-mounted one affixed to her goggles. The jeep rumbled past the furrow in the ground where the hurled maintenance supervisor had landed.

"How are we supposed to get his attention?" Phosphor asked.

"They say he keeps a very close watch over this border crossing," Aiken said.

"You think maybe he's got super-hearing and super-vision, too?" Phosphor asked.

"If he had any supervision, he wouldn't be running amok, would he?" Non Sequitur said.

Nonsensica glared at him. He shrugged.

"I figured since Gracias wasn't here, someone had to be the jokester. Lighten the mood, right?"

"Now's not the time for lightening the mood. Now's the time for game faces," Nonsensica said.

The first lights became visible ahead: their destination. The border crossing was an unassuming one. The briefing said that ChiNoKo straddled the Yalu River, but it was more accurate to say it was entangled by the river. The little city-state was composed of two peninsulas of land with the river curling in an extremely tight S shape. This border crossing was a pinch of land between two bends in the river. It was wide enough for the two-lane road and a bit more before tapering off to muddy shoreline and then rushing water. Nonsensica stood on the seat of the jeep to get a better view of the city beyond. Not much of it was visible from this vantage. The streetlights within ChiNoKo were lit, unlike those leading up to the crossing, but the illumination was dim and flickering. A few scattered houses that seemed more like the kind of thing you'd find in a suburb than a piece of contested land between a superpower and a dictatorship were all they could make out of the city nearby. A few taller buildings could be seen in the center of the peninsula, mostly visible thanks to the blinking lights affixed to the top to ward off aircraft. The only truly well-lit part of the city was the bridge that connected the two peninsulas. If Nonsensica squinted, she could see the characteristic shape of the cooling towers of their reactor in the distance, silhouetted against the power plant's lights.

"We've been spotted," Non Sequitur said.

Nonsensica, out of habit, looked to the road. Their target, of course, didn't much care about roads. She didn't think to look to the sky until a few moments before he struck the ground. The impact felt like the sort of shock wave that rolled through the ground after a controlled collapse of an office building. It kicked up dust and gravel that plinked against Nonsensica's goggles and caused the others to shield their eyes. When the dust cleared, they got their first look at The Icon in person.

In the flesh, he seemed smaller than in the harrowing videos that had been taken. Though around the face it was clear he was in his early twenties, there was a strange lankiness to him, like an adolescent that had just been through a growth spurt and hadn't quite filled out. Though he didn't wear a mask, something about his expression seemed to be hiding something. If Nonsensica didn't know better, she'd think he was scared of them.

"You're up, big guy," she said quietly, slapping Phosphor on the back.

The burly elder statesman of the group cleared his throat and stepped out of the jeep, followed by the others. The Icon pointed and shouted, first with crisp forcefulness in his native tongue. Then in somewhat flawed but well-practiced English.

"Stay back. I've warned you," he said.

"Hey now. No one's looking to start a fight," Phosphor said. "We're just here to talk."

"You arrived in a Chinese Army vehicle. You have two more vehicles filled with troops waiting down the road. You will not fool me."

"Look, Icon? You stirred up a real hornet's nest. Friend or foe, no one's coming down this road without the army keeping an eye on it. But do I sound like I'm a member of the Chinese Army?" Phosphor asked.

"No. You sound like an American," he said.

"That I am."

"Americans are no less warlike. You are all outsiders."

"I can't help that I'm an outsider, but I don't need to be a stranger, right? Let's start this off on the right foot. My name's Phosphor. This here's Nonsensica. That's Non Sequitur."

Icon squinted his eyes and raised his chin. "The Other Eight."

"Ha! Our reputation precedes us!" Nonsensica said.

"Tools of your government. Weapons of the oppressor," Icon said. "It saddens me to know you use your powers to such shameful ends."

"We want to do what's right. What about you?" Phosphor said.

"All I want is for my land and my people to be left alone."

"That's going to be a little difficult, Icon. See, maybe you felt like you didn't have a choice, but you killed some soldiers."

"I was defending my home."

"The Chinese Army doesn't see it that way."

"I warned them. All they had to do was back away. All they had to do was leave us alone," he said.

"You attacked a crew that was trying to come in and help, Icon."

"We do not need help. The world beyond our borders is a cesspool of deceit and corruption. We will not have that poison here."

"You speak for your people?"

"I speak for my homeland."

"The land maybe, but I'm asking about people. Because it seems like you're running pretty low on population," he said.

"If they wish to abandon ChiNoKo, so be it. The weak flee. It is in their nature. The strong remain. The good remain."

"But you care about the ones that are left, right?" ·

"I am their protector. I am the shield that keeps the wrath of a twisted world from destroying them."

"Oof," Nonsensica said under her breath.

"See, I'm glad to hear that. Because that reactor's going to be a real threat if you don't let someone in to help."

"Those were the same lies the first outsiders told."

"Is there anyone left to take care of the power plant?"

"Of course!" he snapped. "The power plant is the heart of ChiNoKo. The strength of ChiNoKo. The workers remain because they know that it requires sacrifice to keep ChiNoKo strong."

"You don't need to take my word for it. Go talk to them. See if they need help. See if the power plant needs maintenance."

The Icon flared his nostrils. He curled his fingers. Slowly, his feet left the ground.

It was truly unnerving to see a human simply will himself into the air. It was one thing to be aware it might happen. It was one thing to see it occur on a screen. Decades of cartoons and movies had depicted the impossible so frequently that one came to accept and dismiss such wonders, even when they were real. But before one's own eyes, a person shrugging off the pull of gravity and rising up sent a chill down the spine. It was wrong. Awesome in the oldest meaning of the word. The Icon must have seen the look in their eyes. A grin curled his lips. Then, in a motion so swift it produced a thunderclap, he darted into the city.

"That boy is not right," Phosphor said shakily.

Nonsensica slapped him on the back. "You're doing good, big guy. Real 'kindly assistant principal' vibe."

"We're all still in one piece, so there's that," he said.

Aiken heard a chirp from a handheld radio in the jeep. He picked it up and held it to his ear. "Spotters say he's entered the power plant," he said.

"He's actually checking," Non Sequitur said. "That's good, right?"

"I suppose we'll find out," Aiken said.

"You getting a read on this guy?" Nonsensica asked.

"I am, and it isn't encouraging." He held the radio to his ear again. "He's on his way back. Try to get him to talk about something personal. His family, his origin."

A distant clap signaled The Icon's departure from the power plant. In seconds, he was once again at the border. His expression was stern. He remained drifting over the ground, arms crossed.

"What's the word, pal?" Phosphor asked.

"We are the people of ChiNoKo. The power plant has been at the center of our world since we gained independence. It is within our power and expertise to repair."

"Is that the power plant crew talking, or is that you?" Phosphor asked.

"That is none of your concern," The Icon said.

"It is our concern," Nonsensica said, stepping forward. "Because if that thing blows its top, it'll kill your friends and family, and a whole lot of other people who are just minding their business. You do care about your friends and family, don't you? This is your homeland, isn't it? You want to keep them safe."

His gaze became more intense. "Do not question my devotion to my people."

"If you're devoted to your people, you'll do what it takes to protect them. From threats outside and in. That power plant is dangerous," Nonsensica said.

"No one understands the dangers of the power plant more than me. But I also understand that outsiders are the greater threat."

"Have you at least seen to it that your family has been evacuated? If something goes wrong, you wouldn't want to lose them."

"ChiNoKo is my family. The people. The very soil," The Icon said.

"Tell you what," Phosphor said, signaling to Aiken. "We trust you when you say your people can fix up that plant just fine. But everybody could use some backup. Tech support, that sort of thing."

Aiken trotted over and handed Phosphor the satellite radio the army had provided.

"This is just a way to talk to the experts. We noticed you took down every other way for the folks out here to talk to the folks in there, so this should give your crew a way to double-check they're crossing their Ts and dotting their Is when they get the plant back on its feet."

Phosphor stepped forward, radio extended. The Icon watched, eyes trained on the ground. Non Sequitur grabbed Phosphor by the belt and held him back as he came dangerously close to the clearly marked border line on the crossing.

"I'm just going to set this here. You can pick it up and see for yourself it's just a radio. Can't do anything but give your crew a little advice and instruction if they need it."

He placed the radio on the line and stepped back. The Icon regarded it with disgust and turned his back on them. He rose up, clearly about to abandon the little confrontation. Before he could dart away, the twin spotlights casting their glow upon the border crossing flickered briefly. A similar, sickly waver rippled through the already-dim cityscape behind him.

"Seems like maybe you should get that radio to them pretty quick," Nonsensica said.

The Icon drifted down until his feet touched the ground. He crouched and plucked up the radio. The lights wavered again. The Icon's lips curled back. He raised the radio, clearly meaning to throw it.

"Uranium plow!" Nonsensica barked.

The Icon twitched, rather more than most who feel the wrath of Nonsensica's verbal attack. He looked as though he'd been slapped in the face and shook so much that the radio slipped from his grip. It dropped and seemed like it would strike the ground well past the border line. But it bounced in midair, easily six inches away from the ground, and flipped awkwardly to the Chinese side of the border. Nonsensica caught it. Non Sequitur reached over and slapped the bottom of the radio, roughly in the way it would have had to be batted to take the inexplicable trajectory it had taken.

"If you're not going to help your people save the day, you can at least respect other people's property," Nonsensica said.

For a moment, a look of shock and confusion flickered across The Icon's face. It slipped quickly to smoldering fury. He surged up from the ground. In two lightning motions, he smashed both spotlights with his fists. The border was suddenly nearly pitch-black. The only light came from the weak glow of the city, painting The Icon as a subtle silhouette hanging in the air above them.

"Go," he ordered, his voice trembling. "Flee in the darkness like the villains you are."

Nonsensica held her ground and quietly cursed herself for not bringing the night-vision goggles after all. The short slide of reverberating glass rang out beside her, then a soft yellow glow swelled to illuminate the border. Phosphor was holding a fluorescent bulb over his head, hands gripping either end. The bar of light grew brighter and clearer.

"Heroes prefer to create their own light rather than spread darkness," Phosphor said.

In the glow of the bulb, they saw another flicker of confusion on The Icon's face. He dropped heavy to the ground, not with the thump of a piledriver but with the simple crunch of boots on stone.

"Leave us alone. Just… leave us alone," The Icon demanded.

He lurched almost drunkenly back into the air and rushed into the distance. When he was gone from sight, Phosphor huffed a breath and slouched, his own light dimming. Aiken started the jeep and turned it to shine the headlights on the border crossing.

"Are we calling that a success or a failure, Doc?" Nonsensica asked.

Dr. Aiken hopped out of the jeep again and approached the border, eyes focused on the ground. "Phosphor is a fairly able diplomat. Nonsensica, you could use a bit more practice," Aiken said.

"He's a supervillain. I'm a superhero. Things are going to get tense."

Aiken waggled a finger. "Not a supervillain, a misguided hero. Remember that. Everything he says screams indoctrination. He's regurgitating a script, but he's doing it too naturally to be repeating something he's just been told. This is deep in him. This is his education. Distrust for outsiders was a core principle of his upbringing. That's going to be hard to overcome."

He crouched at the base of the spotlight's tower and scooped up some of the dirt, shards of broken glass atop it. He carried it over and held it to the headlight. "Non Sequitur, get a bag from under the seat. Nonsensica, get the shovel from the tool kit. Phosphor, get the light over by the border. The people at the base are going to want to see this."

Non Sequitur returned with a large zipper-top plastic bag. Aiken dumped the dirt and glass inside, then held it to the light again. Along the edges of two of the larger shards of glass were glistening beads of blood.

"I'm prepared to call this a success," he said.

Chapter 4

The base had been buzzing with activity from the moment Aiken had given an update on their findings. He and the bags of glass were swept into the research tent for debriefing and analysis respectively. The heroes had been stripped of their cameras, though evidently the overall feeling was that the content of the footage would tell the tale better than they could, so no official debriefing was requested. Instead, they were sent to rejoin the others, who were all-too-willing to have their own far less formal briefing.

"So, what? Did he give you an alien vibe? That's my bet. He's an alien. Probably they get better powers on other planets," Gracias said.

"He didn't seem like an alien to me," Phosphor said. "Though, I guess I don't have much to compare it to."

"This guy was pure human. I guarantee it. And he might be able to take a bullet, but he is defenseless against me. Seriously, high school students take a mental zap better than he does. He's sturdy, but he's not invulnerable," Nonsensica said.

"It seems like anytime things get off script he gets a little shaky," Non Sequitur said. "Like, if things are going the way he expects them to go, he's rock solid. But use some powers in front of him or keep him from doing what he wants to do and he loses his temper or sort of fumbles his powers a bit."

"And he cut his hands on glass, right? That means his weakness is glass?" Chloroplast said.

"Glass is sort of everyone's weakness, isn't it? It's not like we can just start swinging glass around," Bomb Sniffer said.

"I can," Phosphor said.

"Oh, right! Bulbs! Oh, man. This is going to be epic. We're going to go down there and Phosphor can just bash him with light bulbs," Gracias said. "We should start working on one-liners. How about 'Here's a bright idea!'," he suggested.

"Yeah. And 'Nice tube meet you!' That one needs a good follow-up, though. Sort of a 'Have a nice trip, see you next fall!' kind of thing," Nonsensica said.

"I feel like we could probably get a pain/pane of glass thing going on," Phosphor said.

"Oh man. Too good. I'm gonna get a pen," Nonsensica said.

"Not to rain on everyone's parade," Non Sequitur began.

"No one who has ever said that has ever done anything but rain on everyone's parade," Gracias said.

"Shouldn't we be planning more than just the banter? If this does come down to a fight, it seems like we should have some tactics prepared."

"Non Sequitur, we're surrounded by military people. Strategic geniuses. Probably the reason they're taking so long is because they're making maps and drawing circles and Xes and stuff," Nonsensica said.

"That's football," Phosphor said. "Army maps have the little men you push around with a stick."

"Oh man! You think they got a little-man table? I always wanted to mess with one of them," Gracias said.

"The point is, division of labor. We work on the hero stuff, they work on the strategy stuff. Because if one thing's for sure, it's that no one in that big debriefing is working on the banter."

* * *

"Of course, it could be light bulbs specifically and not glass in general," Pvt. Summers said. "I could envision Phosphor doing some 'shed some light on the situation' lines."

"That is a fairly fertile avenue for wordplay," Dr. Aiken said.

Despite the considerable amount of activity going on behind the curtain separating the two halves of the research tent, Dr. Aiken had been left largely to his own devices during the investigation, hence the divergence to less professional areas of discussion.

Gen. Luo pulled the curtain aside and exited the analysis section of the research tent. "Ah, Doctor. I'm glad you're still here. We have some results," he said.

"Excellent. I've also organized my assessment on his behavior."

"All in good time," Luo said. "We've done a chemical analysis of the glass. It is standard industrial high-impact glass. About a decade out of date for similar applications but easily available. I have a team knapping some blades out of it. We are also working on glass-load shotgun shells. A few of our technicians believe standard ceramic blades have a similar enough chemical structure to potentially produce the same effect, so we have requisitioned a full complement of them, and they are en route."

"A strict focus on the glass may not be the best course of action," Dr. Aiken said.

"I assure you, it is just one prong of our research. We have also finished the DNA analysis of the blood. There was no record of this individual in any of our official databases. We've determined he is of Sino Russian heritage. It should come as no surprise that he has the meta-human gene. The absence from our databases suggests he has been in Project Icon since birth."

"Why?"

"Our records of meta-humans within our nation are comprehensive, Doctor."

"Comprehensive as in all meta-humans are expected to come forward, or comprehensive as in compulsory blood testing?"

"Comprehensive," Luo repeated without further clarification. "We've compiled an improved visual profile drawn from the footage from the body cams. Like the DNA, we have no visual records of this individual. We can thus state with relative certainty that he has never left the Disincorporated Zone on the Chinese border. We are attempting to collaborate with our North Korean counterparts, but cooperation has been limited. The visual profile is being circulated in the Disincorporated Zone refugee camps in hopes of determining The Icon's identity. At your suggestion, images enhanced with an assortment of eyewear and facial hair have been included in the profile to help identify potential secret identities. We'll update you if we have any useful information in that regard. Now, I believe you had some assessments?"

"I do. Should we head to the debriefing room?" he asked.

"There are significant tactics and strategies that need to be dealt with. A formal debriefing would take more time than I can spare at the moment. A verbal summary now and a written submission with my staff will have to do."

"So you're still going forward with the assault."

"We believe your discoveries have only increased the likelihood of its success."

"I wish you'd reconsider. There are likely to be casualties even if it's successful. If we can just take the time to learn a bit more—"

"Every military mission risks casualties, Doctor. Now please. I will handle the military aspects. What is your assessment?"

Aiken considered making a more vigorous plea to postpone hostilities, but he could sense Luo's patience wouldn't last much longer. It was better to deliver his findings while he was still willing to hear them.

"The first thing I can say with confidence is that The Icon is the product of lifelong indoctrination centered very specifically on distrust and xenophobia. He has an immaturity and uncertainty that shows in particular when those views are challenged in a meaningful way. I believe his entire upbringing was centered on ensuring those views were depicted as inviolable. His distrust is fundamental."

"Evidence that negotiation and diplomacy will fail," Luo said.

"Not necessarily. I've read through the proposed tactics in the unsealed records for precursor projects, and in nearly all cases direct control is intended to be achieved through a mentor figure. Either a parent or a teacher. If we can find and communicate with this person, The Icon can be controlled."

"Noted, Dr. Aiken, though that The Icon is responsible for multiple deaths and has not been reined in suggests if the mentor is still in contact with the Icon, said mentor approves of the present behavior at the very least or directed it at the very most. And in any case, we have no intention to open negotiations with a terrorist leader. Anything else?"

"There is significant evidence to support the theory that the power plant is central to his motivations. He has particular objection to foreign interference with it and seems to regard it with both reverence and fear. I believe his origin may involve the power plant in some way."

Luo nodded. "Anything else?"

"I have some additional theories on the specific nature of his weakness."

"We have determined it is glass, have we not? It was able to pierce his skin when nothing else could."

"You need to remember that this weakness has its roots in psychology. Understanding why glass is his weakness will help us perhaps amplify and extend its effects. The glass was a part of a light, and the light draws power from the nuclear power plant, so perhaps—"

A technician stuck his head through the curtain and said something Aiken did not understand. Luo replied, then turned to Aiken.

"I thank you for sharing your expertise, and I invite you to continue your research and analysis, but my available time has run out. You are free to use the briefing room to contact Gen. Siegel. I will keep in touch with all relevant discoveries and developments."

He paced back to the analysis section of the tent, granting Aiken a brief glimpse of Dr. Liefeld dictating some sort of instructions to what appeared to be an entire team of researchers. The curtain swung shut, and Pvt. Summers and Aiken were once more alone.

"Why do I get the idea he'd have had a lot more time for me if I was telling him which machine guns to use?" Aiken asked.

"I doubt that, sir. I'm pretty sure he already knows which machine guns he's going to use. So, what now?" Summers said.

He checked his watch. "Fourteen hours until the military of one of the world's last superpowers declares open war on the world's first person with the superpowers they wish all their soldiers had. I'm going to see if we can get access to the refugee camp. Maybe get the team involved. One of the only things we're absolutely certain of is that The Icon is entirely a product of ChiNoKo, born and bred. If we can't get access to him, we can at least learn a little more about the other people who share his homeland."

* * *

It took nearly four hours to negotiate their way into the nearest of three ChiNoKo refugee camps, and despite their best efforts, they were not able to arrange to forego the armed escort. The camp, considering the hastiness with which it was assembled and the general attitudes of the two nations involved, could certainly have been worse. In fact, it was nearly identical to the barracks in the forward operating base, albeit with far lower quality and far more numerous bunks in each of the tents.

"I'll be honest," Chloroplast said, keeping his voice at a diplomatically low volume. "I kind of expected things to be a lot more unpleasant in here. The phrase 'refugee camp' paints some unpleasant images in the mind."

"I think they may have upped the quality a bit in the camp they thought we might end up visiting," Aiken said. "With any luck, we'll be able to defeat The Icon and get these people back home before they have to deal with anything horrible."

"I kind of get the feeling they've already had to deal with some horrible stuff," Nonsensica said.

They moved through passages between the tents as a group, armed soldiers leading and trailing. As they moved, the refugees watched them. There was a distant look in their eyes, like they weren't so much looking at the heroes as simply pointing their heads in their direction. It was a combination of hypervigilance and bone-weariness. Every man and woman had the look of a night watchman at the end of their shift. They were aware they should be keeping their eyes peeled but were so desperately ready to stop. The same could not be said, however, for the children. In what might be the most stirring example they'd seen for the triumph of the human spirit, despite losing their homes and despite being heaped on top of each other in a hastily assembled shelter, the handful of children in each group was laughing and playing. And when the heroes came near, rather than the dead-eyed stares, there were looks of wonder and awe.

"I think they like our costumes," Non Sequitur said.

"Oh man. It's more than that! Check this out!" Gracias said.

They gathered around a little girl who was playing with an action figure and seemed particularly excited to see them. The figure was of a man with a goatee and slicked-back hair, wearing a green shirt with a white G.

"That's me! That's a Gracias action figure!" he said.

Nonsensica crouched down and held out her hand. The little girl let her inspect the doll as she stared, jaw agape, at the heroes.

"I think this is Robert Downy Jr.'s head on a Green Bay Packer quarterback's body," she said.

"That's basically a description of me!" Gracias said. "Quick, somebody do me a favor so I can show her the thing."

"Not it," Nonsensica said.

"Not it," Non Sequitur said.

Chloroplast was notably silent. The sun had yet to rise, so he was a little out of it for lack of photosynthesis, and jet lag had hit him harder than the rest.

"Hey, buddy!" Gracias said. "Could you come over here for a minute?"

He shivered as if shaken from a doze and trudged over and raised his eyebrows, waiting to learn why he'd been summoned. Gracias shot him with finger guns. Chloroplast's eyes widened in realization.

"Don't you dare!" Chloroplast said.

"Grassy ass," Gracias remarked.

The green-skinned hero winced, and his shorts bulged with thick tufts of grass.

"Son of a..." he muttered, hobbling away. "That's friendly fire, man. That's low."

Despite his dismay as he tottered off to find someplace private to deal with the predicament, the stunt did not go unappreciated as all of the children squealed and clapped. A few of the downtrodden parents couldn't suppress a chortle.

"You speak English?" Gracias asked.

The little girl nodded.

"Where'd you get this?"

"Internet," she said simply.

"You people get the internet in ChiNoKo? I kind of figured you'd have the whole firewall problem," he said.

Nonsensica nodded. "That's a fair point. North Korea and China are both pretty notorious for information control. You'd think something that was cut off from both of them would have double the problem."

"We can't do much. But superhero things, we can do plenty," said the young woman who was presumably the little girl's mother.

"That's a weird limitation. Or lack thereof," Non Sequitur said.

"Comic books. Toys. The movies. Thank heaven for the MCU, we've had plenty to watch, at least."

"And the DCEU," Gracias said.

"Eh," the woman said.

"Hey! Wonder Woman was good! The first one anyway."

"But the only thing they give us that isn't censored is comics. If not for Captain America, I wouldn't know about World War II."

"That strikes me as quite on purpose. Are you aware of the reason?" Aiken said.

The young woman gave him a wary look and didn't answer.

"You can trust him. He's the guy who put the team together!" Nonsensica said.

"Yeah. He's like Professor X. Only no powers. And no wheelchair. So I guess not much like Professor X." Gracias scratched his head. "What's another person who put a team together? One without powers?"

"Nick Fury," the little girl said.

"Boom. Nick Fury. The girl gets it," Gracias said.

"I don't know why they let us see the comic stuff," she said, not quite convinced.

"What do you think about The Icon?" Phosphor asked.

The woman glanced with uncertainty at Aiken again, then with outright distrust at the armed guards. Nonsensica looked to Non Sequitur and motioned with her head. He caught eyes with Aiken and the pair nodded. Each of them walked to one of the guards and engaged him, rather noisily, in conversation. Nonsensica huddled a little closer.

"Not the sort of thing you want 'outsiders' to know about, huh?" Nonsensica said. "Look, the Chinese Army's been really going over the doc's head and ignoring his advice, so all things considered, we're not too fond of them right now either."

"I don't want to speak ill of The Icon," she said. "But…"

"Hey, I met him, you don't have to convince me he's not all he's cracked up to be," Nonsensica said.

"I'd expected him to be a little more… wise. It's what we were taught to expect."

"You expect more from superheroes."

"We expected more from The Icon."

She twisted her head. "You were expecting him?"

"You don't know The Icon?" the young woman said. "Surely if you know anything about superheroes, you know about The Icon."

"Nope," Gracias said. "First we heard about him was when that guy started throwing nuclear technicians around."

"It's the most popular radio show in ChiNoKo. I never got to collect any comics or toys, but twice a week they'd play the adventures of The Icon, hero of ChiNoKo and scourge of the foreign devils. Except the one from the show is wise. Clever. This one is just strong and fast like him. But I suppose we shouldn't have expected too much from someone like…"

She stopped herself and cast her eyes to the ground. Nonsensica huddled closer.

"You know who he is? His real name?"

"You don't reveal a secret identity. Not even to other superheroes," the woman said solemnly.

"That's a good policy. An excellent policy," Nonsensica said. "But here's the thing. You watched all the comic book movies, right? With all the heavy hitters like The Icon?"

"Over and over."

"How do those movies turn out for the city?"

61

The woman shut her eyes tight.

"If we don't find some way to get through to The Icon, to get him to take it easy, eventually this is going to be a knockdown, drag-out fight, and there won't be a ChiNoKo."

"Why do you think we left? We know what's coming."

"It doesn't have to be that way. Think of..." She snapped her fingers. "What's one where someone wins by talking sense and being reasonable?"

The group stood in silent contemplation.

"Spider Man 2," said the little girl. "The old one."

"Boom! Turns out the coolest little girl in the world has been right here the whole time," Gracias said.

"I can't tell you his identity. I don't know it. But I've seen him before. He worked at the corner store. Across from the bridge monument."

Voices rose at the edge of the group. The soldier dealing with Non Sequitur had apparently decided he'd been distracted from his duty for entirely too long.

"You've made a difference today. I promise you," Nonsensica said quietly.

Chloroplast wandered back over, still visibly uncomfortable but no longer sporting the bulging shorts.

"Hey, partner! Come take a picture of us with this little girl, so we can send it to her once this all blows over."

"I'm not doing you any favors," Chloroplast said. "Besides, I want to be in the picture."

"Fine. Hey, Doc! Take a picture!"

The heroes huddled together. Aiken produced the secured phone they'd given him. He snapped the picture and showed it to the girl. As they were leaning close to review it, Nonsensica whispered in his ear.

"We've got a location for The Icon."

He nodded. "Now we just need to figure out how to use it."

***

In total, Aiken and the others spent three full hours in the refugee camp before word came from the base that their time was up and it was time to return. By then it was less than seven hours before Gen. Luo's planned assault. He should have gotten some rest, but the lingering effects of jet lag combined with the heady mix of concerns and mysteries meant there'd never been any hope of him getting any sleep as the hours ticked by. He was too caught up in trying to solve the riddles laid out before him.

A handful of things had become quite clear. First, distrust was the number one product of ChiNoKo. He and the team were profoundly lucky to have found someone willing to cooperate. To these people, outsiders were a menace, as likely to steal your child as to tell you the time of day. The outside world was constantly after them, or so they were convinced. It didn't matter that they didn't grow any of their own food, that they didn't have any proper industry. That there was nothing truly valuable in ChiNoKo for outsiders to seek. Irrelevant. The outsiders hated and envied the angelic and pure city-state out of simple malice. Out of cartoonish evil. Out of raw villainy. And that was reinforced by the second lesson about ChiNoKo. Superheroes were the number one import. Every man, woman, and child had a depth of knowledge and a reverence for superheroics of all kinds. Heroes, antiheroes, villains. Never had a place been more primed to revere a hero should it arise. And combined with their certainty that the whole world was composed of beings capable of nothing less than demonic cruelty, never had a place been more certain that only a superhero could save them, and that one day a superhero would come.

By the time Pvt. Summers had joined Aiken in his quarters after her much more successful attempt at catching some sleep, it had all pointed to an unmistakable fact. She handed him a coffee and simply switched his internal monologue to an external one, as though Summers had somehow been privy to the sleepless musing.

"It wasn't just The Icon himself that was a part of Project Icon. It was the whole city," Aiken said quietly to Summers as he processed the data. "I can understand why it wasn't in the briefings we got about ChiNoKo. Any non-native has been trained since birth to hide it from anyone on the outside. But there's no doubt in my mind that ChiNoKo's entire purpose, at least for the last few decades, has been to generate a populace suitable for a 'proper' superhero. These people were some sort of a component in the program, even if they didn't know it."

"It didn't take, though," Summers said, gracefully boarding his train of thought despite the fact that it didn't make a stop for her. "When the time finally came, they didn't stick around to adore him or to be protected by him or whatever. They ran, and with good reason."

"Such is the nature of human psychology," Aiken said. "You can never truly sculpt a human mind into precisely the shape you want. It's possible that the most costly example of all is The Icon himself. Because this can't be the intended outcome of the program. An invincible guardian who won't leave his city? One who will antagonize a joint mission by two of the most powerful militaries in the world? One who won't even allow a crew to come and repair the power plant before a disaster? What's to be gained? Something went wrong. Someone lost control. But even so, there must have been control. Or at least the plan for control. If we could find that, that would be something…"

He trailed off and turned toward the north wall of his quarters. Somewhere out there, the odd rhythmic swish of a military helicopter sliced the air.

"I guess it's time," Aiken said. "How does this work? Is there a war room?"

"Beats me, Doctor. I haven't been involved in a sortie before," Summers said. "But I can tell you that the military doesn't arrange things and then hope people know their part. If you haven't been summoned, you're not invited."

He rubbed his face. "Just as well. I don't have a stomach for this sort of thing." He leaned heavily on the table and stared at the scattering of notes. "I don't even know what to hope for here. That the most significant individual in my field of study is killed swiftly? The alternative is that he kills the soldiers. I can't stand that it's come to this."

"The army doesn't do clean business, Doctor."

"No. No it doesn't. And this is going to be very messy. I can feel it." He cradled his forehead for a moment. "I was hired as a researcher and an adviser, not a strategist. But it's clear if I'm going to be taken seriously, I'm going to need to start framing my advice as strategy. You're the one with military experience. I'm going to need your help."

"I'm a private, and I've only ever served as security and as an assistant."

"You know how to use a gun, and you know what the word 'sortie' means. That makes you the expert in strategy in the room."

She glanced off to the side. "That's a little unnerving. But what little expertise I have is at your disposal."

* * *

Across the base, in one of the better fortified and more secure structures, Gen. Luo sat with the next two levels of the chain of command. Two technicians coordinated six different radios and three different screens. The only person in the room who was not a member of the Chinese military was Dr. Liefeld. The elderly professor sat in a folding chair beside the general, shaky hands gripping notes scrawled in large, precise lettering. Live video feeds from the helicopter and from two troop carriers cycled across the screen.

"One more time, Doctor," Luo said.

"Based upon my calculations, revised from recent evidence, The Icon will not be able to endure a concentrated assault for more than three minutes and forty-five seconds. Keep the pressure on for that amount of time and he will become increasingly vulnerable."

Luo nodded. He slipped a headset on and switched to his native language to address his troops.

"Gunship 1, you are confirmed for direct assault. Remain outside the border. Fire in controlled bursts. Sniper positions 2 and 3. Call out the target's location. Alternate fire, focusing on the gaps in the gunship assault. We are targeting full ammunition expenditure in no less than four minutes. Moderate output unless threat warrants otherwise. Strike teams 4 and 5, wait for my go-ahead. Advance only when target enters a weakened state. Once you engage, do not relent until we have a confirmed kill."

One by one, acknowledgements chirped through the radio.

"Target spotted," reported Sniper one.

"Visual," Gen. Luo ordered.

One of the monitors snapped to the indicated feed. The Icon had emerged from the streets of the fringe of the city. He was marching through a narrow strip of pavement between the city and the river. His eyes were fixed on the helicopter. He was speaking.

"Surveillance, get a parabolic on him," Luo instructed.

The audio feed, mostly garbled by the sound of wind and the distant thrum of the helicopter, picked up his voice.

"... the last time. You have no claim to ChiNoKo. Your evil has no place here. Leave or I shall be forced to teach you a lesson," The Icon said.

"Gunship 1, engage."

A Vulcan cannon burst to life, dumping rounds of ammunition into The Icon by the dozen. Fist-sized bites of concrete blasted out of the ground around him. He raised his arm to shield his face as bullets peppered his body. The raw force was enough to push him back, his toes carving shallow furrows in the pavement. The barrage of bullets relented and were instantly replaced by the heavy thump of sniper shots. They struck him on his side, stumbling him. He'd barely adjusted to compensate when a fresh burst rained down from the helicopter.

Gen. Luo watched with detached fascination as an assault that could have riddled a tank with holes did about as much damage to The Icon as a barrage of tennis balls. But they were taking their toll. He tried to take off, perhaps to assault the gunship directly, but the bullets drove him back to the ground, forcing him to one knee. He couldn't climb to his feet again, the bombardment was too intense.

"We have positive sign of injury. Repeat, positive sign of injury," squawked a voice over the radio.

"Give me a still and enhance," Luo instructed.

A technician scrubbed footage, isolated a frame, and pushed it to the big screen. One of The Icon's arms, raised to block the bullets, had no sleeve left, and multiple splashes of red were visible on charred and stained skin.

"Strike teams, weapons ready. Go ahead in seventy-five seconds," Luo said.

"Precisely as I predicted," Liefeld said.

They watched in grim silence as the assault continued. As the mission timer ticked past the four-minute mark, the communications started to light up.

"Primary ammunition hopper nearly depleted."

"Debris is fouling targeting from my position."

"Fire until empty and prep secondary ammo stock. Strike teams, you are go on ammo depletion. Hit him hard and finish the job."

Two armored personnel carriers squealed across the border and roared toward the rising cloud of dust that hid the injured Icon. The helicopter pulled forward, across the border, to use its rotor wash to clear the clouds of debris. The troop carriers came to a stop. Soldiers poured out and formed a semicircle around the collapsed Icon. They wore no masks, the one nod to Aiken's advice. Semiautomatic shotguns pumped special shells loaded with the superhuman's weakness unloaded into him. The assault continued until all soldiers had fired their first volley. Then, for a moment, silence.

"Target appears neutralized," one of the soldiers stated.

There was a subdued wave of celebration. Luo silenced it.

"Confirm," he instructed. "Strike teams, keep weapons trained."

The lead soldier stepped forward. There was a blur of motion. The Icon was suddenly on his feet, and his hand was around the soldier's throat. He heaved back and hurled the stricken fighter, sending him tumbling end over end into the river.

"Engage, engage, engage!" Luo demanded.

The soldiers opened fire again. The Icon darted from one to the next, shattering drawn knives, mangling firearms. Bone-breaking thumps knocked the men to the ground. Vicious throws dumped them into the river as well. In seconds, the whole of the strike teams was neutralized. The helicopter shifted position and opened fire. In another blur, The Icon was at the open door of the aircraft. Bloodied fingers closed around the rotating barrels, seizing the weapon. Maddened eyes stared into those of the gunner. The Icon grabbed him, tore him free of the harness, and dropped him to the river below. Finally, he shifted to the front of the helicopter and stared down the pilot. There was a moment of hesitation, then fingers clutched the nose of the helicopter, buckling the metal. He fought the helicopter's motion as it tried to maneuver, then entirely overpowered it, heaving the aircraft in a drunken twirl until it struck the ground and was swallowed in a fireball.

"Get eyes on the survivors. Get an extraction team in there, now. Sniper 2, get me a visual on The Icon."

The video feed from the sniper's nest popped up. The Icon was stationary in the air, heaving breath and dripping blood from a dozen gashes and slices. The arms and legs of his suit were a tatters, frayed ends smoldering. He spat some blood and darted into the distance, vanishing into the city.

Luo turned to Dr. Liefeld. "I don't understand it. You saw it, just as I did. The weapons were working. He was beaten. I don't know how he could have rallied."

Luo turned to the others with an impassive face. "I want an update from the extraction team as soon as the troops are recovered. And get Aiken into the briefing room."

Chapter 5

Forty minutes later, Aiken found himself in the briefing room. Unlike most of the other times he'd been summoned here, there wasn't a small crowd of assistants, experts, and advisors sitting in like some sort of lecture. Aiken, Luo, and Liefeld were the only ones in attendance.

"Do you know why I've summoned you?" Luo asked.

"I hope it's because The Icon has been dealt with. I worry it's because he hasn't," Aiken said.

"The Icon is alive. We are fortunate that there was only a single fatality, though several of my soldiers are badly injured. I'm told they will recover. The details of the mission are available for review, but the key points are that it failed—"

"After promising initial results," Liefeld interjected. "And that the one soldier killed was the only one wearing a mask. Your theorized behavior held true. He seeks direct lethal force only upon masked soldiers. The one piece of your advice I fully embraced likely saved a dozen lives. And so, I believe the time has come to employ your expertise more directly. First, and foremost, what reasoning can you provide for the initial promise but ultimate failure of our methodologies?"

"Without reviewing the combat information directly, am I correct in assuming he shrugged off the damage only once he was directly assaulted on his home soil?"

"That is correct," Luo said.

"It was the narrative," he said.

"The narrative?" Luo asked.

"You've read all of the same materials on precursor programs that serve as the inspiration and basis for The Icon Project. Even if we don't know the specifics of the project that created The Icon, we know that the goal had been to create him. As such, there is a structure that has been installed into his mind. Expectations. Beliefs. He believes the world is trying to destroy him and his people. And he believes he is the sworn defender of ChiNoKo. You played the precise role he was taught to expect of you. You were the villains to his hero. You reinforced his role, and his powers were thus reinforced."

"Are you saying we make him stronger by attacking him?"

"I'm saying he will endeavor to become powerful enough to ward off an attack, and he will ward off that attack in the way that he has been taught is appropriate. Faceless enemies are destroyed. Humanized enemies are repelled. And superheroes are met on their own terms."

"Are you suggesting your team could defeat him?"

"I am suggesting if my team were to come into combat with him, it is possible the clash would end in a stalemate by design."

"Why?"

"I've spoken to the people in the refugee camps. They have an almost biblical reverence for comic books. It is my theory that The Icon will treat an opposing hero the way a fictional hero would treat a villain. Defeat but ultimately spare them, with the full expectation of future clashes."

"That is lunacy."

"It's narrative structure. It's what he's been taught to expect. We already have some evidence of it. The longest conversation any of us have managed was with Phosphor at the border."

"How do we use this to our benefit? It seems that all we'd achieve is a series of nonfatal clashes."

"I don't think adhering to the intended narrative, at least as constructed in his mind, can ever lead to a meaningful end. It is in the nature of comic books, and thus comic book heroes, to continue in much the same vein for as long as they exist. But I think it means, at the very least, that the safest way forward is to ensure that only superheroes are used as operatives. Threat to life and limb will be reduced, and his behavior will be more stable, because he will be given what he expects."

"Dr. Aiken, I have thoroughly reviewed the reports on your team. They are not terribly effective soldiers."

"They're cut from the same cloth as The Icon. It is in their nature to rise to the occasion."

"And what occasion shall they rise to? You still haven't proposed a method to neutralize The Icon."

"He was created with control in mind. Either that control is still in place and we need to find the one who wields it, or it was flawed and we need to find a way to properly assert it. In short, we need to investigate his origins. Both the one he ascribes his power to, and the actual Project Icon. We send teams in to learn about his personal history, and we send them to locate what information is available for the project."

"Fine. An intelligence mission. But we still need to know how it will be done. And the timeline has been shortened considerably."

"What do you mean the timeline has been shortened? This is the first I'm hearing of this."

"According to our technicians, the helicopter crash damaged some underground power lines. The Disincorporated Zone's only source of power is now the power plant. Increased reliance on the plant, combined with the low expertise of the local crew in running it under these conditions, means we may be less than two weeks from a potential fault scenario. We need to act quickly. The increased danger of plant failure means that excess force is less of an option. I need you to present alternatives."

"What we need is for the mission, whatever it is, to proceed in a way that will feel natural and unchallenging to The Icon. That will cut down on volatility." Dr. Aiken rubbed his head. "I'm not sure you'll like what I'm going to suggest."

* * *

"You want us to plan the mission!?" Bomb Sniffer said.

Dr. Aiken and Pvt. Summers fought to get control of the members of The Other Eight as the realization set in. Some, most notably Chloroplast and Bomb Sniffer, were aghast at the idea. Others were spoiling for the chance to prove themselves.

71

"Oh baby. Finally," Nonsensica said. "This is where The Other Eight shines. This is how we won the spot in the first place! This is how we got to be the big team."

"A lot of people have already died, Doc," Non Sequitur said.

"We're going to give you all the support we can manage, but this is a job for superheroes," Aiken said.

"Do we have an objective?" Phosphor asked.

"Three objectives. First, you need to find out more about The Icon. The best source will be his home, as identified by the refugee. The next objective is a little less certain." He turned. "Bomb Sniffer. In the event future military action is necessary, it will need to be precise. There is concern that weapon or explosive caches could cause collateral damage that will endanger lives and, more crucially, the power plant. Have you detected—"

"Yes, there's loads of explosives in ChiNoKo," she said quickly. "Did you not know that?"

"It was assumed. But precisely where?"

She pointed. "That way. Toward the center of the city. I can tell you about how far away, but that's it. You want more accuracy, I'll need to get a whiff from more angles. They were training me on triangulating positions."

"I'll have them put you on a jeep and run a semicircle at minimum safe distance. Will that work?"

"I think?"

"Good. Let's get you moving. The faster the better. Because in order to give us the best chance of saving lives, we're probably going to have to find a way to disable those explosives. And then there's the third objective. They've looked at infrared signatures and estimated power usage. There is far more power being used than the city's current state could explain. They can't narrow down the power consumption beyond the certainty that it isn't near the border."

"Secret base…" Gracias said. "We're gonna find and invade a secret base! I bet there's lasers! Dibs on sliding under lasers!"

"Start planning, tell me what you need, what you need to know. Come up with a plan and I'll take it to the military. But don't take too long. We're on a time limit."

"Heroes work best under pressure," Nonsensica said.

* * *

Gen. Luo sat in his quarters and looked over the endless stream of updates coming from his equally endless stream of assistants and technicians. Lives hung in the balance. Such was the nature of any military campaign. But he'd not been prepared for anything of this sort. He supposed no one had.

No. That wasn't accurate. One person had, or such was the US Army's intent.

He checked the time. There was a thirteen-hour time difference between his present location and that of Gen. Siegel. Regardless, he fired off a request to his communications team to put him in contact. Within a minute, his secure line was ringing. He picked it up.

"General. I hope I did not disturb rest or more pressing business. Our extreme separation presents some scheduling issues, I realize."

"Nonsense," Siegel said. "In situations like these, there is only one time zone: Mission Time."

"I am very much in agreement. I trust my team has kept you briefed."

"I'm in the loop, General."

"Are you satisfied with the contingencies that are in place?"

"I don't think we can ever be fully satisfied with contingency plans. By definition, they exist to be called upon only when something has gone wrong. But from the information you've given me, I think you have all reasonable outcomes planned for. But then, this isn't a mission where reasonable outcomes are likely, is it?"

"No. That is the reason for this discussion, I am afraid. Forgive my frankness, but the team you have sent me is extremely irregular, and the reasoning behind their activities clashes with what I would consider sound tactical planning."

"General, I know precisely the thoughts going through your mind, though granted, in my case I was working through hypotheticals and you're working through realities. But I've seen these people work. I've seen them doing what they believe they were born to do, and I can tell you that once you've seen it, it'll make you a believer too. They are unorthodox, certainly. But Aiken has done his work. He understands these people like no one else. And I am convinced we've put together the very best of the best. Put them in a position to get the job done and they'll get it done. Maybe not neatly. Maybe not the way you'd like. But they meet objectives. And in the end, that's all we ask from our soldiers."

"I hope, then, that I leave this operation as a believer. Because as it stands now, I fear for the consequences of failure."

* * *

A few hours later, the time had come to assemble in the briefing room. Phosphor, after his success in dealing with The Icon, was selected as their spokesperson. Nonsensica was the only other member of The Other Eight in attendance. So far, Aiken was the only one they'd shared their ideas with, and his reaction had been, if not enthusiastic, at least encouraging. Now to see if the Chinese Army and Gen. Siegel would feel the same way.

One by one, representatives of the military filed in and took a seat. A secure line was set up for the US Army side. Phosphor fidgeted with the strap of his bag, glancing anxiously at the index cards he'd prepared.

"I haven't done something like this since I was in high school. I'd rather not talk about how long ago that was," he said.

Nonsensica slapped him on the back. "You're going to do great, big guy. And if you start to lose the thread, I'll pipe up to give it a little sizzle."

The audience settled in and looked expectantly to the heroes. Phosphor took a breath and began.

"This is a big task. Superheroes fighting supervillains. We've all got real respect for you and yours, what you folks do. Good training. And The Icon took some of your best, so we mean to take this seriously and do right by your—"

"What are your goals and how do you intend to achieve them?" Luo said sternly.

Phosphor shifted to the next card. "We talked to Aiken, and he says we need to know about the origin. The way we all figure it, we need to find out where he came from. How he got his powers. That'll let us get inside his head and maybe work out a better weakness. So we're going to find out about the man, and that's just going through the city and finding his history. It's a small place, relatively speaking. And if the whole city is more or less about making The Icon happen, it shouldn't take long to find where the signs are pointing. He doesn't wear a mask as The Icon."

"Fine. So will it be a grid search? Do you have a system in place?" Luo said.

"We'll get to that, General," Nonsensica said sharply.

"The other thing we need is to find out about The Icon Project. Bomb Sniffer sniffed out what might be a clue. There are all sorts of explosives and stuff, and she worked out that most of them are in the neighborhood of the bridge."

"Yes, we are familiar with that development. Our soldiers on the jeep relayed the information to us."

Phosphor flipped to the next index card. Then the next. He shut his eyes for a moment, then handed them to Nonsensica and crossed his arms.

"Here's what we're going to do. Me and the crew are going to get in there. Four teams. One team gets The Icon's attention and keeps it for four minutes and thirty seconds. Teams 2, 3, and 4 use that time to slip over the border at different locations. So far, The Icon has only ever had to keep an eye on the border crossing. If we cross somewhere else at the same time, we're thinking we can get into town and keep a low profile."

"You don't strike me as a group with a particular aptitude for keeping a low profile," Luo said.

"We're not going in with an attack helicopter and shotguns," Nonsensica said. "No wave of troops. You gave him something to expect, we're giving him something besides that.

"One team focuses on the bridge, tries to get in and get information. The other finds his home. We keep in touch with satellite phones and stuff. We'll need those, by the way. And we stay in there until we get the job done. Once Teams 2 and 3 have what they're after or decide it's not there to be found, we deploy Team 4 as a second diversion so they can get out."

"And that will result in the full extraction of the teams?" Luo said.

"No. That'll get us to phase 2 of the plan. Phase 2 doesn't need much. It'll sort of happen on its own. It'll give us direct contact with The Icon. Maybe we can reason with him. Maybe we can deploy a better weakness if we find it. But if nothing else, it will keep The Icon busy for a while to let more ideas roll out. Here's the full list of equipment we'll need. We also need to get some of our reserve members over here, specifically Primadonna. I figure we can be ready to go in twenty-eight hours, if you can get her here by then."

Luo took the index card containing the equipment list and looked it over. "Motorcycles with drivers, communications equipment," he muttered, scanning the card. "You have here 'High Quality Public Address System,' a request for smoke machines, and a lighting array? But no weapons. These are not the requests for a serious military mission."

"Hey. We don't need weapons, General," Phosphor said.

"We are the weapons," Nonsensica said.

"Our time is limited. We cannot be squandering it on foolishness. Request is denied."

"With all due respect, General, you haven't heard the full plan," Phosphor said. "Phase 2..."

"Nothing I have heard suggests to me that you are giving me or the current situation the respect that is due. We're through here." He stood.

"General, if you care about getting this job done, I don't think you can afford to ignore what we have to say. You're fighting a supervillain. We are superheroes. You run an army, and armies are used to fighting each other. You've never had to fight something like this before, and we haven't either, but the simple fact is, we're the ones who are supposed to. You train up your troops with all the finest tactics. You give them the best equipment. But this is a different thing entirely. Even if they managed to crank The Icon out of a program specifically designed to pull that off, everyone in this room knows this wasn't the first program to try, but it is the first program to succeed. That's capturing lightning in a bottle. Maybe you'd call it luck? Maybe you'd call it fate. Me? Call me silly, but I'm on the side that says it's fate. I'm of the mind that we don't have nearly the control we think we do. We're just strapped in and along for the ride. And the difference between a hero and a victim is, a hero recognizes those brief moments when the steering wheel is in our hand and takes control.

"Again, you churn out some good soldiers. But me? Nonsensica? Our whole crew? We were born for this. We were born with something special in us, and life wove its path just right to help us find it, and to find our way here. I don't think something like that happens for no reason. I think we were put here in this room, put on this Earth, for this moment. Us to make a plan and carry it out, and you to help us see it through. Are we outclassed? Sure. Is it a sure thing? No. Nothing is. But we're putting our lives on the line to make sure this turns out the best way it can. All you need to do is get us the gear to make it happen and turn us loose."

"It is not as simple as turning you loose," Luo said. "There are consequences for failure beyond risking your own lives. Every clash with The Icon gives him another opportunity to decide he will leave the borders of the Disincorporated Zone, or through error or direct action further accelerate the failure timeline of the reactor."

"You're listening to us because you don't have better ideas," Nonsensica said. "So far you've tried force and more force. That's cost you lives and time. We're giving you an actual alternative. Listen to the rest of the plan and then make your decision."

Luo gave Nonsensica a look with the sort of intensity only a general could give. It was no match for the kind of glare a superhero can return. He sat.

"Continue."

* * *

It had taken time, and it had raised the blood pressure of all involved, but they'd done it. Astoundingly, impossibly, The Other Eight were given the okay for their mission.

Chloroplast, Gracias, and Bomb Sniffer sat on the edges of their beds. Officially, they were supposed to be memorizing and drilling upon their roles in the mission, which would be launching the following evening. Presently, only Gracias seemed motivated to do so, though his progress had stalled a bit.

"And then it says 'Mode 2' and there's a weird little symbol," Gracias said. "This radio thing is complicated, and I get the feeling they didn't put as much effort into the English instructions, what with this being China and all. I don't understand why we can't just use our phones."

"I think it's probably about reliability," Chloroplast said. "And durability. And battery life."

"Yeah…" Gracias said. "Plus, probably they're worried we'll get a call about our automobile warrantee and spoil the whole mission. How's your thing coming along?"

The manual for Bomb Sniffer's equipment was on the bed beside her. It was all she had to work with because the device itself was too high risk to be kept anywhere but the armory.

"It's a bomb," she said. "A little sticky one. You stick it on the thing you want to blow up, hit the button to arm it, then go somewhere far away and hit the button on the detonator. It's not that hard. We're supposed to use it to bust open any doors."

"Cool! Hey, I'll bet it feels good to be getting to use some bombs instead of just sniffing them out," Gracias said.

"I thought I'd like the idea a lot better than I do," Bomb Sniffer said.

"Having second thoughts about superheroics?" Chloroplast asked.

"Yes. No. I don't know. I mean, I still feel the need. I want to be a hero," she said.

"You're already a hero. A superhero," Gracias said.

"You know what I mean. But I'm not sure what part of being a hero I can actually do. Nonsensica seems to get a jolt out of the danger. She's all about clashes and stuff. I think about a fight, and I just don't know."

"So you're a support hero. Or like a super spy, right?" Gracias said. "You get in and get out and never even have to fight because they'll never know you were there."

"See, the problem with that is, what if I screw up? Then I'm someone who can't fight, but has to."

"That's why you're on a team. Other people bring the muscle," Gracias said.

Chloroplast turned to him. "Are you seriously suggesting that either you or I is the muscle?"

"Uh… I mean, we could be. You saw that action figure of me. People view me as a beefcake, and rightly so."

"It was a bootleg. They used leftover parts, and they couldn't match your body type because people don't build action figures of regular people."

"Lucky for them, I'm not a regular person, I'm a superhero. And besides, it's not a bootleg. Bootlegs are rip-offs of things that are already available, right? And there aren't any other Team Green action figures that I'm aware of. So that was official. Legit."

Chloroplast put his hand to his face. "Failing to have a real action figure isn't an achievement."

"If there's no real version of something, then the fake version becomes the real version. That's the rules. So, let's go over it. We're Team 2. That means we're infiltrating Icon's lair."

"Well, at least we'll be infiltrating the place the little girl's mother indicated," Chloroplast said.

"So what do we do?" Gracias said.

"Kick in the door, look for useful information, steal it, run like hell," Chloroplast said.

"And if The Icon shows up?" Gracias asked.

"Get pummeled to within an inch of our lives, probably," Chloroplast replied.

"Hopefully an inch before the end rather than after," Bomb Sniffer said.

Gracias gave each of them a hard look. "There are only eight official members of The Other Eight," he said. "Me, you two, Nonsensica, Non Sequitur, Phosphor, The Number, and… the other one. Point is, you two make up a quarter of the team, and you're both kind of iffy about being superheroes. Me? I'm all about it. And I'm proud to be on a team with you two. I think we're better off with you than without. But if you're not one hundred percent on being heroes, there's a line around the block of people who would jump at the chance to take your place. Why stick around?"

"What's the alternative?" Chloroplast said. "I'm green. I realize most of us don't wear masks, but you take off your uniform and you fit in with regular society. Hero or not, I'm green. I'm a weirdo by default. At least if I'm a legitimate hero, I can offset some of the 'weirdo' with something positive. My options are being ostracized and failing to find a proper place in society, or do some good and maybe get some respect. But it doesn't mean I'm comfortable with the risks."

Gracias turned to Bomb Sniffer. "And you?"

"I uh… again, I want to be a hero. And I know I go by Bomb Sniffer. But up until a few weeks before I tried out for this team, it would have been better to call me the Bomb Collector. That's what I was mostly using my powers for: finding and keeping anything even remotely explosive. It got my parents worried. Rightfully so, I guess. There isn't much good that can come from having a fascination with explosives. But I always sort of thought 'oh, you don't understand me.' Typical teenager stuff."

"Aren't you still a teenager?" Chloroplast said.

"I'm gonna be nineteen. That's basically twenty," she said defensively. "But the point is, after a while I couldn't even convince myself I wasn't heading down a bad path. I don't know if I wanted to be on the team just to prove to myself I wasn't a burgeoning villain, or maybe I was hoping some training or some good influence would help me straighten out. Now I'm in China getting ready to trespass on the territory of a guy who throws helicopters around."

"Exactly. Right where a superhero would end up. So that proves it. You're a hero, not a villain," Gracias said. "And Chloroplast, seriously. You're totally green. That's just cool! And you know who else is totally green? A little hero called the Hulk."

"Setting aside that he's fictional, he also is super strong. I'm just able to photosynthesize."

"Exactly. That makes you the better hero."

Chloroplast crossed his arms. "Okay, I can't wait to see how you spin this."

"Anyone can go toe to toe with a supervillain if he's ultra strong and durable. That's not impressive. But we're going in there with powers that require cleverness and guile to be used properly. That takes fortitude. We're like if Bruce Banner lost his powers and still decided to duke it out with Ultron," Gracias said, without an ounce of irony. "Team Green is, therefore, more heroic than the Avengers."

"When you put it that way, we do seem pretty good. Not any less likely to get killed, but pretty good," Chloroplast said.

"Hey, we need to pick a new name! For this mission, we're a trio," Gracias said. "How about Team Green-sniffer?"

Bomb Sniffer winced. "Needs work."

* * *

Nonsensica stood between bunks and was running through a sequence of complex maneuvers with her non-chucks while Non Sequitur looked through a stack of surveillance photos. She was dressed in the casual version of her outfit, forgoing the rubber suit for now. A normal person might have made such a decision for the sake of comfort, but Nonsensica, as usual, had a more heroic reason. Both suits were laid out on her bed, and she was engaged in a bit of a one-sided debate.

"So, pros and cons," she said. "The traditional suit. Pro: it's a lot more broken in. I don't know if you've ever worn a latex suit—"

"You, in fact, know that I haven't," Non Sequitur said.

"But if they're new, they have a weird resistance to them. At least from the place I get them. So I've got more freedom of movement in the traditional suit. Con: highly visible. Bright colors are good for keeping spirits high and dazzling the enemy, but this is a stealth mission. I call it the stealth suit for a reason. Black suit, perfect for blending into the night."

"We're starting the mission during the day, and it might last more than one day," Non Sequitur said.

"Yeah… and the black suit doesn't blend in any better than the red-and-white one during the day. And it gets even hotter than the red-and-white one. Two cons," she said.

Non Sequitur rubbed his eyes and leaned back.

"Something wrong?" Nonsensica asked.

"I don't know why I'm looking at these. The spies have already been over them. It's not like I'm going to spot something they didn't."

"You never know."

"I now know that I will not. I don't see any doors, any hatches. I mean, their angles are all either really high up or from the west. So I guess that means it narrows down any entry points to the east side near to the water. But that's still a lot of bridge to cover while keeping our eyes peeled for The Icon."

"We'll get it done," she said. "We have to."

"Necessity isn't a guarantee of anything. We could just fail."

"Pfff. Maybe you. I'm planning to save the day, and if anyone thinks they can stop me, they're getting a frizzle-frazzled brain and a boot to the chin."

Non Sequitur made a noncommittal grumble.

"Out with it," she said, twirling the weapon with a little more flourish. "I don't need my partner out there mumbling to himself. Particularly not when you're the one who'll be opening any doors, so you'll need your head in the game."

"This is a real superhero mission," he said.

"Are you just now figuring this out?"

"No. But I'm just now failing to ignore the implications."

"What implications, that we've finally arrived on the world stage and proving to all of those turds on social media who said we didn't deserve to win the competition that they are as dumb as they look?"

"I'm thinking about my dad," he said.

"You've got Daddy issues, buddy boy," she said.

"That'll happen when your dad is a superhero who got killed in a mission against a supervillain, and then everyone you know, including your own mother, pushes you into following in his footsteps."

"You've got the best powers on the team," she said.

"My powers aren't as good as Dad's. Ambition could literally do anything he believed he could do, provided he had enough 'ambunition.' All I can do is put the cart before the horse."

"If this was all about powers, then none of us would be heading out there. There's more to the hero than the super."

"I'm not saying I'm not going to go and do my best. Too many people are counting on us to not. But I'm less of a superhero than my dad, and I'm going up against more of a supervillain than the man who got him killed."

"Great! Then we've got two reasons to look forward to this mission tomorrow. Not only is it going to prove to the world we're the pros we already knew we were, but it'll get you out from under the shadow of your dad. Now if you're done looking at the pictures, help me out with my suit dilemma."

He turned and looked to the suits. "Wear the red-and-white one."

"That just preference, or do you have a tactical reason?"

"Because he thinks we're villains, and villains wear black."

She stopped twirling the non-chucks and considered his statement. "Batman wears black. But point taken. A heroic outfit gives us a psychological advantage."

The door to the barracks swung open. Pvt. Summers walked in and shut it behind her.

"What's up?" Nonsensica said. "The doc got a message for us?"

"Dr. Aiken is with the Chinese brass making sure everything that you folks needed us to requisition is on hand. He's also discussing why he needs face-to-face time with The Icon. They're not so happy with how he's planned to get that face-to-face time, but it seems like we're going to be good to go, come the morning. The reserve team members are arriving as we speak. Plane touched down a few minutes ago. They'll be here in time for the final run through before lights out. I would have preferred to wait until the full team was assembled before I came and said my piece, but as it is, Dr. Aiken could only spare me for a few minutes and we'll both be tied up until basically mission time, so it's now or never. Gather around."

The heroes collected in a semicircle around the assistant to their mentor. She cleared her throat.

"I've been a part of the Guardian Project for slightly longer than even Dr. Aiken. Basically the only person who has been a part of this project in its current form for longer than me is Gen. Siegel. So I think I'm speaking from a position of experience when I say that you have all exceeded every reasonable expectation of the project. Versions of this project have been in operation, on and off, for decades. The team was assembled precisely for situations such as this, but no one involved at any stage of the process believed we had one chance in a million to find the kind of person we really needed. As far as I'm concerned, this team, when it is fully assembled, is the result of winning that lottery eight times over. I've worked with better soldiers than you. But for this task, for this moment, I don't think there is another group in the world with the skills and the spirit to succeed. The Icon is a terrible, terrible threat. He needs to be stopped. And tomorrow, you're going to give us all the insight we need to achieve it. I'm proud of you. And when you all come back, alive and well, I'm going to buy each and every one of you a coffee."

"Well thanks, Pvt. Summers," Phosphor said. "That means a lot."

"You know, not everyone is as motivated by caffeine as you are," Nonsensica said.

Summers shrugged and smirked. "Well, no one's perfect."

Chapter 6

The command structure gathered inside the portable war room. This time, Pvt. Summers joined the general and Dr. Liefeld in the room with the technicians. All were silent, watching high-quality video feeds cycle. The morning was disarmingly calm. The primary feed displayed a small contingent of troops that had been assembled three hundred yards from the border crossing. They were lightly armed, their faces were unobscured, and for the moment they were doing little more than standing in formation. The Icon was watching and had been since they'd arrived. He stood at the border, arms crossed and eyes locked on them. All around, the scars of prior battles were glaringly evident. Broken lights. Gouged ground. Bullet holes in every surface.

"We've got better light now," Luo said, speaking English for the sake of the others in the room. "Get us in close on the target."

The feed switched to a higher-quality camera as it zoomed in. The superhuman had not fully recovered from his previous clash, but to look at him, one would hardly imagine he'd been the focus of fire from a gunship. He wore a fresh costume. Faint pink lines and barely visible welts scattered across his face and hands were the only evidence of the assault. In another few days, one would never know he'd been attacked at all.

"Status on Operation Two-step," Luo said.

"Team 1 is in position. Teams 2 and 3 are on standby. Awaiting signal from Team 4," said a technician.

"What's taking them so long?" Liefeld griped.

"They are entering from the North Korean side. We are fortunate they were granted permission to do so."

"The North Koreans know what's at stake," Pvt. Summers said.

Minutes ticked on. The soldiers on the feed didn't budge, and neither did The Icon. Finally, the secondary monitor switched to a view on the northeast section of ChiNoKo. Unlike the primary border crossing, this one was bottlenecked not by the pinch of the river but by a tall, sturdy fence. In the past, this had been the primary border crossing to China, but it had become more securely locked down and largely ignored once ChiNoKo was formally severed from the larger nation. There were three reasons the southern border crossing between the curves of the river had taken over as the primary Chinese crossing. The first was its closer proximity to a major road. The second was its proximity to the main population focus of ChiNoKo. The third reason, and almost certainly the primary one, was that the circumstances of the Disincorporation redrew the border at the northern crossing to be fifty meters farther into China than the actual fortifications. If it was used for day-to-day comings and goings, the walls and fences would have been rebuilt and the additional land would have been reclaimed. By ignoring it, the shift in the border was reduced to a painted white line, and the Chinese could contentedly observe that while the land was not theirs on paper, the people of ChiNoKo were not benefitting from it either. Spite was a disturbingly powerful force in matters of diplomacy.

A technician pressed the cup of his headset more firmly to his ear. "We have word that all teams are in position," he said.

"Give the command. We are go for Operation Two-Step," Luo said.

The order was delivered. Subtly, the soldiers raised their hands to their ears, slipping them up beneath the edges of their helmets to depress a button on similar headsets of their own.

"Cutting audio from the feeds," the technician said.

The main video display shifted to the secondary border crossing. Large, rectangular forms were slowly wheeled out from the trees nearby. Then, a figure stepped out. He was lithe and dressed flamboyantly in an outfit bedazzled with red-and-white sequins arranged into camouflage blobs. He moved with a dancer's grace.

That stood to reason. He was The Number. Dancing wasn't just his career, it was his power.

"Get the audio visualizer on screen," Luo said.

A green waveform was superimposed over the bottom of the footage. It jumped now and again with a digital crackle but was otherwise flat. Then it began to thump with bassy vocal hits and rhythmic claps. The Number started to strut to the music. If they could have heard the lyrics, the command crew would have heard the song being dedicated to the hood girls, the good girls, straight masterpieces. Of course, if they'd been able to hear the music directly, they wouldn't have been of much use, as they too would have been stylin', wildin', and livin' it up in the city. When The Number danced, so did everyone else who could hear the music.

"Increase volume," Gen. Luo said. "Let's get footage of the city."

An aerial shot cycled into the rotation of views. The camera moved with robotic jerks and zooms until it got a clear view of the streets of ChiNoKo closest to the northern crossing. The city was all but deserted, but a scattering of people was gradually filtering from their homes and places of business, moving with precise rhythm, matching the moves of The Number despite lacking even the ability to see him just yet. On the main video feed, The Icon turned, fixing his gaze on the city and the curious sounds in the distance.

"He's not dancing. Deploy the supplemental distraction."

"I think you should give him time, sir. The Icon isn't close to the source of the music," Pvt. Summers advised. "The effect increases the closer you get."

"We cannot afford to learn that The Icon is resistant. Deploy the supplemental distraction," he repeated.

As the lyrics described a heat fit to coax a dragon into retirement, a second figure emerged from behind the camouflaged speakers. It was a woman, moving with every bit as much grace and style as The Number. Her uniform was markedly different, pink-and-white camo instead of red and white, and sporting a slightly ridiculous camouflage tutu. It was Primadonna, a reserve hero brought in for the operation whose powers precisely matched the Number. The moment her motions joined The Number's, the streets flooded with the remaining locals within earshot. It was quite clear that the two heroes, each with the same powers, were amplifying their influence by working in unison.

Their routine brought them forward, strutting toward the painted line that marked the border of ChiNoKo. The moment they crossed the line, The Icon took to the air and swept toward them. A low, rising tone within the music seemed to mirror the ominous path The Icon was taking, streaking with superhuman speed and single-minded purpose toward the dancers. The Number and Primadonna continued their dance, casting nervous glances at one another as the mighty Icon approached with no suggestion of rhythm. The two heroes watched tensely as he drew closer. The command crew waited for some sign that the plan was working. The lyrics and music reached a crescendo, entreating the listener. Don't believe me? Just watch.

The Icon came to a sudden stop in time with a clap in the music, then dropped to the ground with pavement-shattering force. Primadonna and The Number were knocked into the air by the impact but came down in time and continued their dance, now with The Icon matching their moves.

"The Icon is engaged. Repeat. The Icon is engaged. Move out. ETA to potential release, three minutes and twenty-three seconds," Luo ordered.

The camera views shifted. A group of red-and-white-suited heroes rushed from cover near the edge of the river, suited up for diving. Each carried a bag of gear and a powered turbine to help propel them through the water. Another view, this time from the body cams on the operatives themselves, accelerated as they moved on motorcycles across the border. By the time the song was calling upon the listener to flaunt their sexiness, the motorcycle team had reached a deserted parking structure and taken cover.

"Incredible," Luo said. "The target is almost completely immobilized. I had my doubts it was possible. This presents additional tactical possibilities. We could bring larger, less nimble weapons to bear and have no fear that he would dodge."

"Not without endangering The Number and Primadonna. It is taking the two of them combined to keep The Icon in check, and only at extremely close range. Anything powerful enough to take out The Icon would kill the heroes as well," Summers said.

"Given the severity of the worst-case scenario, that could be an acceptable loss," Luo said.

With thirty seconds left in the song, the river crossing was complete. The team scrambled to find similar cover within the city. With fifteen seconds remaining, two motorcycles arrived, their drivers notably without hearing protection. Their arrival was a part of the choreography, as was the elegant and fluid way that both The Number and Primadonna mounted the back of each motorcycle. As The Icon continued to engage in compulsory dance moves, the motorcycles streaked off, circling him in a flourish before burning rubber, heading for the border and the cover beyond. They were mere yards from the border when their distance was too great for their influence to overcome whatever superhuman will The Icon had at his disposal.

He turned, fury in his eyes. The motorcycles crossed the border. He raised his fists and brought them down with unimaginable force. The blow caused the ground before him to lurch up. The shock wave traveled toward the border, turning the pavement to gravel and rolling forward. The devastation raced past the border and overtook the motorcycles. They both lost control, spilling their riders at high speed. The waveform became discordant and then flattened as the PA system was rattled into silence.

"Medical teams, on standby. Strike team, be ready to defend," Luo said.

The Icon rose up, eyes fixed on the fallen heroes. He wavered above the ground, his toes scraping the dirt as he floated to the very edge of ChiNoKo land. His chest was heaving, and there was something more than anger in his eyes. There was a dash of confusion, and something more complex simmering beneath it. But he toed the line and finally turned his back on the heroes and soldiers struggling to pull themselves from the

fallen motorcycles. He dashed back to the heart of ChiNoKo at a superhuman sprint.

The command team swept their eyes across the footage. The teams of heroes were huddled into cover. Distant views of The Icon showed him dashing through the city. Medical teams emerged from cover and assessed the injured heroes at the northern crossing.

"Minor injuries to Primadonna, The Number, and both riders. Nothing critical. All teams are within ChiNoKo borders," a technician said. "One moment... The Icon is arriving at the primary border crossing."

They looked to the main screen. The Icon slid to a stop and scanned the crossing with vicious anger. As before, he did not cross the border. After a few seconds of trembling fury, he seemed satisfied that they had not made a move and their distance was sufficient. He resumed his vigil, arms crossed.

"No indication he is aware of the multiple incursions," Luo said.

"That is surprising. He seems so immediately aware of when someone crosses the border, I would have expected a component of his power set was an innate awareness of invaders," Liefeld said. "Simple hypervigilance rather than something meta-human, I suppose."

"Let's get the injured soldiers to medical. Starting now I want all transmissions from the Disincorporated Zone recorded, and dedicated comm teams on each of the teams of operatives. Evacuation and extraction teams need to be ready to move should the need arise to pull them out ahead of schedule. And I want real-time tracking of The Icon, with updates given to both me and the field teams. I know he moves fast, but I don't want anyone to be surprised by his whereabouts until all teams are clear of the border."

He stood and turned to Summers. "It's in their hands now."

* * *

Bomb Sniffer, Gracias, Chloroplast, Non Sequitur, and Nonsensica huddled in the basement of a school not far from the riverbank. The near-complete evacuation of the city, combined with the fact that what few people remained had been drawn into the streets by the dance routine, meant it was fairly simple to find a safe place to hide. Knowing they probably hadn't been seen didn't do much to reduce the tension, particularly not as they finished receiving their update on Primadonna and The Number on their communicators.

"Primadonna has a sprained ankle," Nonsensica said. "They may as well have snipped off a butterfly's wings."

"She'll recover," Non Sequitur said.

"Not before we need to get out of here," Chloroplast said. "Thank goodness we have a backup escape plan."

"The Number only hurt his wrist and elbow. You can dance without your arms, can't you?" Bomb Sniffer said.

"What's he going to do, get out there and Riverdance?" Gracias said.

"... What's Riverdance?" Bomb Sniffer said.

"Quit being so young!" Gracias snapped. "It's that dancing thing where you only show joy below the waist."

"That's a thing?" she said.

"It was in Ireland. And on PBS," Chloroplast said.

"Let's try to stay focused, okay," Non Sequitur said. "No one got killed, we're all in position inside ChiNoKo. We have jobs to do. Bomb Sniffer, any new insight?"

"Okay... okay, give me a second." She shut her eyes and took a slow whiff. "There's a storeroom in this school with some explosives. Firecrackers. I can smell the powder from the ammunition for the local law enforcement and military. It's sort of scattered and pretty sparse. Probably not much left in the way of defense besides The Icon. But the bridge explosives... Yeah... Yeah, they're more muted than they should be at this range. I think they're probably underwater. Or inside something with bad ventilation."

"But definitely the bridge?" Non Sequitur said.

"Definitely."

"So either the bridge is rigged to explode, which makes no sense considering it just connects the two halves of ChiNoKo, or there's some sort of... thing hidden under the bridge," Nonsensica said. "So far so good. Now all we have to do is find it and get in. How far is it?"

Chloroplast held up his arm and tapped at the still-dripping PDA he and the others had been provided. It was the military equivalent of a smartphone. And like all military equivalents, it was larger, more rugged, and a little rougher around the edges than its consumer counterparts. The device was capable of secure communication through their headsets, plus high-precision GPS navigation, cross-linked with the systems at the forward operating base for the purposes of laying down waypoints and providing updated aerial imagery.

"It's about… stupid thing's in metric…" Chloroplast crunched some numbers in his head. "It's about a mile and a half along the river. We can't afford to go there directly, though. We'd be out in the open, and it seems like The Icon can get to anywhere in town within fifteen seconds. Too risky."

"Right," Nonsensica said. "We'll make our way through the neighborhood until we get close. What about that bridge monument? Where are we in relation to that?"

He pinched and zoomed. "For something that's named 'the Bridge Monument,' it's not as close to the bridge as you'd expect. About a quarter mile from the bridge, at the entrance to a small park."

"Should have called it the Park Monument," Gracias said.

"All right. Let's get moving. We stay together as long as we can. Then we split up at the park," Nonsensica said.

"What's the fallback point? They said we should pick a fallback point to meet up at when we're done," Gracias said.

"I'm surprised you were actually listening to the mission briefing," Chloroplast said.

"Hey, I'm a pro," Gracias said.

"I don't think we can pick one until we know which decent pieces of cover are confirmed free of locals," Non Sequitur said.

"I say we pick a deserted restaurant. No offense to the Chinese military, but their food leaves something to be desired," Gracias said.

92

"ChiNoKo is a disputed territory. I don't think they're going to have resort-style food," Nonsensica said.

"Well, sure. But hard times and necessity always produces the best food. Nachos were a way to use up leftovers. Barbecue is just really cheap cuts of meat plus a lot of time and care. I bet the ChiNoKo... ChiNoKoan? ChiNoKoese? I bet these folks have some really great stuff," Gracias said.

"Okay, so the primary mission, find out The Icon's personal and secret history. Secondary mission, find a cute local cafe to post on Instagram," Non Sequitur said.

"What's Instagram?" Bomb Sniffer said.

"Now you're screwing with me!" Gracias said.

She snickered. "Yep."

"Let's get moving before you two start an intergenerational feud about MTV or something," Chloroplast said.

"I never really liked reality shows anyway," Bomb Sniffer said.

"What does that have to do—" Gracias began.

"She's baiting you," Non Sequitur said, securing his gear for travel. "She knows the M stands for music."

"It does?" she said.

"What did you think it stood for!?" Gracias raved.

* * *

The trip through ChiNoKo had taken nearly three hours. "Nearly empty" was a far cry from "entirely empty." Though nine out of ten of the buildings they passed through were empty, every fragment of the lingering population had to be carefully located and circumnavigated. The team had to assume that the remaining locals were either loyal to The Icon or too afraid of him to leave. Either way, they were a liability. Fortunately, The Icon's devotion to protecting the border meant he spent the bulk of his time standing watch at the main border crossing, where Gen. Luo kept troops constantly stationed to keep his attention. At irregular intervals, The Icon did leave the crossing to give the rest of the border a quick patrol, but each such trip was quickly called out over the communicators. Thus, they'd made it this far without anyone but the command crew knowing they'd penetrated the city. But they all knew that, barring extraordinary luck or astounding incompetence, that was likely to change within the next half hour.

The team had already split up. Nonsensica and Non Sequitur had taken the more overtly dangerous job of finding and infiltrating the bridge. Bomb Sniffer, Chloroplast, and Gracias were weaving into the residential neighborhood across from the park.

"This place is, uh… grim," Gracias whispered as they slipped into an alleyway.

The crew had known what to expect going in. They'd been briefed. They weren't going to be marching through the manicured lawns of a suburb or the bustling metropolis of a thriving city. They'd seen pictures of the brutalist cement housing complexes that made up most of the residential district. Even then, it hadn't seemed so bad. A little flavorless, a little claustrophobic. But the images they'd seen were from shortly after the development of the area. Decades of dispute and neglect had rendered them barely livable. Faults ran down many of the walls. Actual glass in the windows was a rarity, with the more common materials leaning in the direction of textiles or paper products pinned or wedged in place. An unpleasant black film formed ruddy streaks down the sides of buildings, staining the cement beneath every crack and corner as though the building itself had been bleeding. The smell was more industrial than residential, with a strange, heavy odor in the air that put one in the mind of a poorly cleaned dishwasher. It didn't feel like people lived here. It barely felt like people survived here.

"We're going to have to search this entire building," Bomb Sniffer said, "without alerting anyone inside that we're doing it?"

"They gave us the weird, rattly door-unlocker things and the explosive charges," Gracias said. "Though I guess the charges will probably give us away, huh?"

"We probably need to go door-to-door, listen for people within. Find evidence of comings and goings. If this is where The Icon lives, he'll be coming and going pretty frequently. I'd say we need to keep a lookout, but I guess drones, spy satellites, and a whole team of observers have got that handled. Not that it'll give us more than a few seconds of warning in the worst case."

Chloroplast peered up at the buildings on either side, then out to the street, across which the monument could be found. "We don't even know which building is the right one. I'd say any of these three qualify as 'across from the monument.' And that assumes we got the right tip." He rubbed his head. "This is going to take forever."

"Hold on..." Gracias said. "I'm having an idea."

Chloroplast squinted at him. "Are you sure it's an idea and not a dumb joke or weird hypothetical?"

"Hear me out. This whole town is sort of here to create The Icon, right?" Gracias said.

"So we're told," Bomb Sniffer said.

"And basically all we know about him for sure is that he loves his country and thinks he needs to protect it, right?"

"Yeah."

"Well, if I was trying to convince someone their country was great, I'd give them someplace comfortable to live and give them a great view of all the stuff that makes it great." He pointed. "Over there, we've got the park, then the bridge, then way over there, the power plant. And we know the power plant is impor- tant to him. And from this building, they're all in a nice, straight line. I'm betting his place is in this building, on this side of the building, and probably nice and high."

Chloroplast scratched his head and glanced at Bomb Sniffer. She nodded appreciatively.

"That's some solid thinking, Gracias. I only hope you're not the brains of Team Green, because if you're the smart one, then what's that make me?" Chloroplast said.

"Not the pretty one, because I got that covered too," Gracias said as they made their way to the back door of the indicated building.

"You're the PR friendly one. People love green, right?" Bomb Sniffer suggested.

"I am the world's only carbon-neutral superhero, what with me making my own oxygen..." he mused.

* * *

Nonsensica and Non Sequitur did their best to move quickly and invisibly as they approached the bridge. It wasn't easy. The best cover available was the guardrail along the side of the roadway. If they stayed low, it probably would have hidden them from people at ground level on the west side of the city. Alas, their main concern was someone passing overhead, and there was nothing but the bridge itself to offer cover from that. They'd have to keep moving and hope for the best.

"There's how many people in ChiNoKo?" Nonsensica asked, hustling as best she could.

"I think seven thousand, before they fled, anyway," Non Sequitur said, scanning the sky before rushing forward.

"Then what do they need a six-lane bridge for?" she said.

The bridge was, to put it lightly, excessive. A towering, steel-arch behemoth with three lanes of traffic in each direction and paths for bikes and pedestrians running through the middle.

"The whole city could drive across this thing twice a day," Nonsensica said. "Heck, the whole city could probably fit on this bridge at the same time. We've barely even seen any cars!"

"I think it's the same deal as the nuclear power plant," he said. "A big, impressive thing to prove they're big and impressive people. Like that statue of The Icon we passed. A lot of this place is all about seeming to be something. I think they just like a big spectacle."

"Yeah... or a big, expensive construction project to cover for a bigger, more expensive construction project," she said, peering over the edge of the fortified riverbank into the water.

She didn't need to say what she was thinking. Non Sequitur was thinking it too. A roadway that big needed some fairly massive supports to keep it up, such as the huge cement structures that vanished beneath the surface of the slowly flowing river. There was nothing curious about them in and of themselves. But if you were to remove the bridge and just look at the supports by themselves, the words "bunker" or "fortress" came to mind.

"Here," Non Sequitur said. "Check this out."

Nonsensica trotted over to the section of river wall that Non Sequitur was peering over and matched his gaze. A narrow path with a meager padlocked chain led under the roadway. It was labeled Maintenance.

He tapped the communicator on his forearm. "Can someone push the maintenance info for the bridge onto this thing?"

Almost instantly, a sequence of schematics and maintenance procedures popped up on the device.

"Man," he said, poking through the info. "I could get used to having a data team…"

Nonsensica hopped the chain and trotted along the narrow path.

"Wait. We don't know if that's where we're headed yet," he said.

"It's going to be the way in. How else would we get in? And besides, it's the only place for a quarter mile that gives us overhead cover. Now get down here," she said.

He stepped over the chain and followed. Nonsensica had very little trouble navigating the narrow path, but Non Sequitur found it just a little too thin and a little too close to the underbelly of the bridge as they passed under.

"Okay… Apparently this is for accessing… those bolts up there," he said, pointing out an array of fasteners with nuts the size of coffee cans and caked with red flaky rust.

"You mean the ones that are rusted beyond all recognition?" she said.

"Yeah."

"Seems like someone hasn't been using the maintenance walkway for maintenance."

"There aren't any doors though. No hatches. Nothing," he said.

"See, Non Sequitur, that's the thing about secret hatches, they're not going to be on the official schematic," she said.

"I was talking about in the actual reality," he said. "Unless you're seeing something I missed."

The dim, damp maintenance path didn't lead anywhere besides the opposite side of the bridge. It was far too narrow to hide a hatch underfoot, and no amount of knocking and scrutinizing turned up anything along the stone wall either. Nonsensica paused long enough to sneak a finger up under her goggles to scratch her cheek, then peered along the belly of the bridge.

"How do they inspect all that?" she said.

"It says they use special barges that are docked on the north end of ChiNoKo. There's this whole parade-type thing when they do it."

"Barges…" she mused.

She pulled a small pair of binoculars from her belt and scanned the belly of the bridge. It wasn't terribly easy to use binoculars without removing her goggles, but true to her sense of superhero professionalism, she managed.

"… What do you make of that?" she said, pointing and handing him the binoculars.

He held them up and followed her gesture. At first, he completely missed anything out of the ordinary. But after a few seconds of scrutiny, he saw what seemed to be a bundle of wires leading down from the belly of the bridge and vanishing into the cement pylon. Beside it, if he really focused, he could just make out a section of diamond plate with scrape marks above it.

"Looks like someone's been in and out that hatch recently." He checked the communicator. "And there's no sign of anything about hatches leading into the base of the bridge in the official materials."

"Bingo," she said. "And if that's a hatch, they have to get over there somehow. There's probably a switch over there that… I don't know, raises a walkway up or something. Any chance you could make the walkway appear, then use it to run over and flip the switch?"

"Only if I would be able to reach and activate the switch in thirty seconds. Also only if the switch exists," he said.

"Details, details," she muttered. "Fine. We'll do it the slow way. Give me a boost."

He laced his fingers and steadied himself. She planted her boot and vaulted up to grab on to one of the struts that ran along the bottom of the road surface. Hauling her slight, nimble frame up to dangle from the strut was relatively easy. Hooking her chunky boots over the strut was considerably less easy. It made for a slow, cumbersome process. After three minutes of pulling herself hand over hand along the strut, both of their communicators buzzed.

"Nonsensica! The Icon is on the move!" he hissed.

"Well what do you want me to do about it?" she called back. "I'm in the middle of something."

He looked at the alert on the communicator, then pressed himself to the wall and looked to the west. A silver point drifted through the sky. With Nonsensica as she was, if The Icon decided the bridge required an inspection, there was no way she'd reach safety in time. Best case, she let go of the bridge and let herself fall into the water, which would leave her considerably less exposed and slightly less helpless, but still a sitting duck for a meta-human with a bone to pick. She kept her mind on the task, pulling herself steadily toward the mysterious hatch they'd spotted.

Non Sequitur glanced back and forth between her and the distant silver spot.

"A little more," she huffed.

"He's headed this way," he said.

"High or low?" she said.

"High. And he's not moving fast. Not fast for him anyway." He huddled down. "I don't think he's got an angle on you. But he might have one on me."

He squinted as the form drew nearer. The full power set for The Icon wasn't known. His eyes wouldn't need to be much sharper than normal to spot the bright white-and-red uniform of The Other Eight. True, being dressed as a hero in theory meant he was safe from lethal force from The Icon. But time was short and they hadn't finished their mission. He couldn't afford to find out just how much force The Icon thought was not lethal. He needed to get closer to the belly of the bridge.

With no other options, he took a steadying breath, planted his boot against the wall, and tried to heave himself up to grab the same strut Nonsensica was climbing. His boot slipped against the stone of the river wall, robbing him of a few precious inches of height. His fingers just barely reached the strut, and for a heart-stopping moment, he was dangling over the edge of the maintenance walk by one hand. A mix of adrenaline and good luck got the other hand in place to grab hold before his grip failed.

He grunted and struggled, boots squeaking against the wall. With supreme effort he hooked one heel over a cable and the other onto one of the rusted bolts. Seconds later, the fluttery whistle of a decidedly nonaerodynamic human form pushing through the air in precisely the way it wasn't designed to do passed over the bridge. He held on until he saw the silver dot recede into the distance and loop along what he assumed was the opposite border.

"He gone?" she asked.

"He's out of range. I think. I hope," he said. He shakily lowered himself back to the maintenance walk and shook his arms. They felt like rubber. "I don't know how you are able to hang off that for so long," he said as she scrambled the last few feet and pulled herself onto an even narrower ledge that wasn't even visible from his advantage.

"Maybe if you did a few more pull-ups and a few less bench presses you'd be doing this too. Or maybe I've got a body made for heroism. Probably both." She huffed a few breaths. "Okay, this is definitely an access hatch, and it's definitely used fairly frequently. It's the only part of the bridge that actually looks like it's been maintained. And there's a manual chain winch here... and... ha ha! Stand clear."

He took a step back. She started slowly working at a crank on the side of the pylon. With the sort of smooth, silent operation that could only come from expert design and superb upkeep, a series of slats that had seemed to be nothing more than part of the superstructure of the roadway gradually inched down. It was a catwalk, suspended by cables and hidden among the stout supports of the roadway. The end of the catwalk notched neatly into two gaps in the maintenance walk. He gave the footbridge an experimental step, found it sturdy enough, and trotted over.

Nonsensica was already taking pictures with her communicator and passing them to the tech crew at the base.

She pointed. "The crew says this slot here is a card-key reader. There's no other latch or anything else. Your move, I guess."

"Any idea if there's anyone inside?"

She pointed. A small glass bead was positioned above the door, clearly a camera.

He nodded. "So either there's no one inside, they're confident we can't get in, or they expect us to get in but don't want to raise an alarm. What does any of that mean?"

"It means I bet we're going to have to kick some butt and get some answers in a minute. Now do the thing already. I'm getting antsy."

Non Sequitur put his hand on the hatch and closed his eyes. It would be some sort of a knob, or switch, or latch. The door clicked open. A latch, then. He swung the door open and found the mechanical release. A good hard yank clicked it into the position it should have had to be in to allow the door to swing open. Beyond the door was a long, claustrophobic corridor lit by a pulsing red light.

"I'll take the lead. You stick close," she said, a manic grin spreading over her face. She shook him by the shoulders. "Real hero stuff, buddy! Real hero stuff!"

Chapter 7

Bomb Sniffer, Gracias, and Chloroplast slinked through the hallway of the building they'd perceived to be The Icon's lair. Gracias's theory that they'd take extra good care of the hero and his home was well supported by what they found inside. Everything about the building was in vastly better condition than anything they'd encountered elsewhere in the city. Ever since the clash that damaged the power lines, anything in the city that needed power, from vending machines to streetlights, had become flickery and glitchy. The power in this building was rock solid. It had either redundancy or some sort of priority. Everything inside was clean. The air-conditioning was working. It was the way the building was intended to be.

It was also empty, and unlike much of the city, it didn't look like a recent development.

"I don't understand it," Bomb Sniffer said. "Why is it so... unused?"

Chloroplast inspected a doorway to one of the apartments. "The door is painted to the doorjamb. Like, as in the door was closed, then they painted, and it was never opened again," Chloroplast said. "Not only does no one live here, no one has ever lived here. Or not since the last paint job at least."

"Creepy..." Bomb Sniffer said.

They reached the doorway to the stairs and stepped inside.

"This whole thing is starting to get a serious conspiracy feel. This isn't a house. This is a set. Or, like, a laboratory," Gracias said.

Bomb Sniffer held out a hand, stopping the others. She shut her eyes and took a whiff.

"Ammunition," she said quietly. "Next floor. And something else. It's an explosive, but I don't recognize it. Might be one of those binary explosives that isn't mixed yet."

Chloroplast squinted at the doorway to the next landing. "That door's been opened and closed a ton. Look. You can see greasy fingerprints. Like a maintenance crew came through."

"What do you think?" Gracias said. "Do we skip that floor, or is that the floor we're after?"

"We can't just skip it, then we'll be above a floor with guns on it. If there's people there who want to kill us, we'll be trapped," Bomb Sniffer said.

"So we go in and clear it out," Gracias said.

"How do you suggest we do that?" Chloroplast said.

"We've been through boot camp. I'm gonna kung fu some fools," Gracias said.

Chloroplast looked at the door again. "Someone should stick around on this floor, get the elevator there, and hold it. It'll keep anyone from using it to get to us, and it'll give us a fast way down. That means if something goes wrong, the rest of us just have to get down one floor."

"I already said I'm going to kung fu some fools," Gracias said.

"I… uh… I think you're probably going to need me to sniff out the guns and bombs," Bomb Sniffer said.

"Fantastic. I'll hold the elevator, then. Stay in touch on the comms," Chloroplast said, dashing back through the door to the previous floor.

Gracias took the lead, creeping up the steps. He glanced back every few moments to see if Bomb Sniffer had any insight, but for the first few doors, she was simply anxious and alert. The floor seemed identical to the others. At least on the surface. But subtle bits of evidence scattered about revealed it to be different in some very important ways. Elsewhere, the place was utterly pristine. This looked a bit more lived in. The carpet was threadbare in some places and stained in others. The faint scent of cigarette smoke hung in the air, not from a recent smoker but from years of secondhand smoke leaving its residue.

Bomb Sniffer stopped him again. She pointed two doors down.

Bullets, she mouthed silently.

Gracias nodded. He dropped to the floor and crawled forward, eye level with the ground. Beneath the door, he could just make out the shadow of a pair of boots. He looked over his shoulder.

They know we're here. One guard, he mouthed. He climbed to his feet again and stood aside. Trust me, he mouthed, motioning for Bomb Sniffer to back against the wall behind him.

She pressed herself against the wall. He took a deep breath.

"Hey! Don't kill me, would you?" Gracias shouted at the top of his lungs.

A burst of words Gracias didn't understand, followed by a cluster of bullets, burst through the door. Gracias had been wise enough to stand clear of the doorway and was safe from the assault.

"Grassy ass!" he shouted.

The sound of startled dismay that followed transcended language. It didn't matter how much discipline or fortitude you thought you had. When two pounds of grass and soil appear in the seat of your pants, it demands your immediate attention. Gracias kicked the door open and dove inside. He collided with the stricken soldier and knocked him to the ground. In a flailing mix of panic and martial arts, Gracias knocked the rifle out of his hands and thumped him in the face until he started shouting what Gracias imagined were pleas for mercy thanks to his superior combat skills. He pulled a pair of flex-cuffs from his belt and cinched them tight around the man's hands.

Bomb Sniffer rushed in and zipped a second set of cuffs onto the man's ankles. The soldier shouted until they shoved an improvised gag in his mouth.

"Ha! Ha!" Gracias proclaimed. He spotted Bomb Sniffer's body cam and pointed to it. "You see that? You see how The Other Eight rolls? Put that in the highlight reel!"

"They don't do highlight reels for covert missions, Gracias," Chloroplast said over the communicator.

"Maybe not for you."

Bomb Sniffer huffed a breath and wiped her face. "That was intense. How did you know there was only one soldier?"

Gracias paused. "Right… yeah, there could have been two, huh?"

"Proof it's better to be lucky than good," Chloroplast said.

"Listen, armchair soldier, get up here and help us continue the investigation, would you?" Gracias said. "There's some weird stuff up here."

Now that they didn't have a guard to contend with, they could assess the room he'd been guarding. The room around them extended considerably farther than the spacing of the doors in the hallway would indicate. They must have knocked down a few walls and occupied nearly half the floor with this place. A control center of some kind occupied most of the west wall, blocking where the windows should have been. The bulk of the command center was an array of fifteen monitors, five long and three tall. They each showed stationary views of either fixed points in the city or the individual rooms in an apartment.

The room around them had signs of having been well used, even overused, in the past few weeks. The air stunk of burnt coffee. Assorted disposable food containers overflowed from a trashcan beside the door. A change of clothes hung from a tacked-up clothesline beside a sink on the southern wall.

"This isn't The Icon's house." Bomb Sniffer pointed at the monitors. "But I bet that is."

"Yeah, this has a real 'keeping an eye on the science experiment' sort of vibe," Gracias said.

He snapped pictures while Bomb Sniffer paced around the room. She kept sniffing, face scrunched up.

"Something wrong?" Chloroplast asked when he appeared in the doorway.

"I keep smelling that other explosive. The weak-smelling one," she said.

"Where?" Gracias asked.

"I don't know. Over here by the filing cabinet. Over there by those computers. Sort of all over," she said.

Chloroplast crouched and inspected the man they'd tied up. "Hey," he said. "Not to diminish your stunning combat prowess, but this guy doesn't look like a soldier. He looks like a technician."

"Oh, you can tell that just by looking, can you?" Gracias said.

Chloroplast pointed to the ID card clipped to the man's chest. Then pointed to the message on his communicator. "No. I can tell because the translator at the command center says this badge says he's a technician."

"This room looks like it should have way more than one person running things. But it also looks like it hasn't had anyone else in here for weeks," Bomb Sniffer said.

"Stands to reason," Chloroplast said. "If your science experiment went nuts and attacked a hostile foreign power, would you stick around?"

Gracias glanced at their prisoner. "How much you want to bet this guy was the FNG of the group? Stuck with the crappy assignments." He crouched to address him directly. "Bet you never expected you'd end up tied up with a pantload of sod, huh? That's what you get when you cross Team Green-plus-one."

"Look," Bomb Sniffer said.

The group gathered around the control center. In addition to the video feeds, there was a pair of laptops. One had been locked. The other was still logged in. The screen lacked any English words, but a vector representation of the city and its surrounding areas occupied the center of the screen. A blinking red dot was moving steadily along the border of ChiNoKo.

"They're tracking him," Gracias said. "That means we can track him, right?"

"Screw tracking him," Chloroplast said. "The guy isn't subtle. We don't need any help tracking him. We're here to get information." He grabbed the ID card and keys from the downed tech. "Let's start looking."

* * *

Non Sequitur and Nonsensica wove their way through the dim facility. The whole place had the feel of a submarine. Heavy metal doors broke the spiraling corridors within the bridge support into sections. Once they were a few levels down, the subdued sound of rushing water filtered constantly through the walls. It would have been nearly impossible to penetrate their defenses, if not for Non Sequitur. It turned out, the designers of secret scientific laboratories hadn't anticipated the possibility of someone who could open a door and then unlock it. The heavy, impact-resistant doors may as well have been curtains. So far, their infiltration had been without mishap and had consisted of working their way cautiously around a ring of corridors, descending a ladder, and repeating the process. Ironically, the most effective bit of security design was the decision to alternate the position of their ladders. That, at least, slowed the heroes down.

They reached the fifth sublevel. Nonsensica flipped through three quick hand gestures and dropped into a low stalk. Not quite as dedicated a soldier as she was, it took Non Sequitur a moment to remember what they represented. Proceed with caution. Two hostiles. Be ready for engagement. Non Sequitur wanted to respond with some signs of his own, but since he very much suspected there was no hand signal for "How could you possibly know that?" he settled for a nod.

The red light continued to pulse. Gradually, the tapping of boots echoed around the corridor. On this floor, the doors were already open. And sure enough, the echoing tap of boots seemed to be coming from either side. After five floors of no resistance whatsoever, they were being flanked. Nonsensica turned to him and executed two more gestures. These hardly needed military training to be understood. I take this one, you take that one.

Again Non Sequitur nodded. He moved as silently as possible across the steel grating of the floor and trained his ears on the approaching footsteps. Nonsensica slipped her non-chucks from their holsters and gave them a few twirls. Each hero reached the corner and stopped. The approaching footsteps stopped as well. A few tense moments ticked by. When the time came, Nonsensica made the first move.

"Gaji gwibul!" Nonsensica cried, somehow producing a phonetically faithful approximation of the words "Eggplant Earlobe" in Korean.

A semiautomatic burst of gunfire swallowed all other sounds into a white hiss of tinnitus. A soldier stepped around the corner in front of Non Sequitur, raised his weapon, and attempted to fire. The magazine dropped out from the bottom of his weapon, followed by the twirl of a bullet ejecting from the chamber. His confusion at being disarmed provided Non Sequitur with the opening to kick him in the gut, then drive a boot heel into his knee, sending the soldier to the ground. The hero picked up the rifle and pressed the release for the already-absent clip, then worked the bolt to eject the bullet that was already on the floor. He threw the weapon aside and put a knee on the chest of his foe. The struggle ended quickly, with the soldier's hands and ankles secured with zip ties.

His job done, he turned and dashed for Nonsensica. Neither she nor her target was visible. He rounded the corner and had to pull back as a non-chuck whistled past his head.

"Hey!" he yelped.

"You can't sneak up on me, buddy," she shouted. "Reflexes of a ninja!" She was standing on the chest of a similarly restrained soldier. "Did you hear that? I think I just spoke Korean! I don't even know Korean! My powers are even better than I thought!" she shouted.

"Why are you yelling?" Non Sequitur said.

"What?"

"I said why are you yelling!?"

She pulled off one of her martial arts gloves and screwed her pinky into her ear. "Stupid guy shot his gun in an enclosed space. I can't hear a thing. I'm not yelling, am I?"

He nodded.

"Gosh darn it." She hopped off the restrained main's chest and gave him a kick in the ribs. "You better not have screwed up my hearing for good."

Non Sequitur signaled for her to follow him. They moved slowly around the next turn. Again, the doors were already open. A cautious peer around the corner revealed the final stretch of corridor was clear. The pair approached an extra large and extra secure door. He grabbed the handle and gave it a tug, fully expecting it to allow him to open it and find the release as he had nearly a dozen times already on this mission. It didn't budge. He envisioned flipping switches, turning valves, pulling latches. Nothing that would open a door seemed to be within his capabilities to execute.

"What are you waiting for!?" she yelled.

"It won't open."

"What?"

"It won't open!"

"What do you mean, it won't open?"

"I mean it won't open. I'm trying to open it and it won't open."

"Eighty-five percent of your power is the ability to open doors! You could have just called yourself Lock Picker and let me be Non Sequitur like I wanted to be in the first place. And now you're telling me you can't open a door!"

"That's exactly what I'm saying."

A voice crackled across an intercom. "I am rather disappointed as well."

"Is someone talking?" Nonsensica shouted, tipping her head and wriggling her finger in her ear again. "I think the hissing is going down. I can sort of hear someone talking."

"This was a test," the voice said. "And a fairly remedial one at that. Two quote-unquote soldiers, the best we could muster in ChiNoKo but rather short of even a policeman's training. You found the lair, you defeated the defenses, but when it got down to it, all it took to stop you was a latch that takes forty-five seconds to operate. If I'd had the time and budget to put it on the outer hatch, you wouldn't even have made it this far. You are failures."

The mysterious person spoke with an odd accent, something in the realm of Slavic or Russian.

"I can't quite make that out, but he sounds like he's making fun of us. Is he making fun of us?" Nonsensica said.

"Yes," Non Sequitur said.

"Say that to my face!" she said, hammering the door with her fist.

"Why were you testing us?" Non Sequitur said.

"He was testing us?" Nonsensica said.

He motioned for her to let him take the lead. "What value is there in risking the lives of your guards as a test?" Non Sequitur said.

"I wasn't risking their lives. Not through your actions, anyway. You're superhumans. Victims of your own psychological complexes. The hero complex. Driven to do good, and driven to avoid undue loss of life. Aiken, for all his shortcomings, did a fine job of filtering out the antiheroes and megalomaniacs. The greatest danger presented to my troops was their own weapons. But as I observe you over the security cameras, and your other associates as they investigate The Icon's observation team, I don't see anything that approaches what it will take to defeat him, neutralize him, or otherwise solve The Icon problem. This is an issue of containment now. There is no other effective defense against The Icon but providing him with the constant task of maintaining vigil over the border."

"Hey, where are you, whoever you are?" Nonsensica called.

"That is hardly any concern of yours. I suggest you—" the voice began.

"Is he answering?" Nonsensica said.

"He's doing the standard supervillain taunts," Non Sequitur explained. "And generally deflecting."

"I hate when they do that," she said.

"If you believe I can be measured by the same damaged mental ruler as a meta-human, you are—" the stranger again attempted to say.

"How are your ears?" Nonsensica asked. "I'm mostly getting whistling right now. It'll be a minute before I can hear properly."

"I can hear okay," Non Sequitur said.

"If you cannot keep your mind on a task as simple as speaking to your target, how do you expect to—" the stranger spat angrily.

"Listen close," she bellowed, pointing at the speaker grill for the intercom.

He leaned close to it. She spun her non-chucks, then caught them both in the same hand. She pulled them back and put all her weight into bashing the door with them. After a fraction of a second of digital delay, the soft thunk of the blow to the door could be heard.

"Yeah, he's on the other side of the door," Non Sequitur said.

"I'm gonna go bust the cameras," she said.

"This is a pointless waste of your time and mine," the stranger said.

As Non Sequitur spoke, the sound of Nonsensica finding and shattering the cameras viewing them punctuated every few words.

"If you've been keeping an eye on everything, you know The Icon has killed several soldiers. And you obviously know an awful lot about him, so I don't think it's much of an achievement to unravel the riddle that you're a part of Project Icon."

"I am, shamefully, the project lead. ChiNoKo and its favored son are my handiwork. The product of more than twenty-five years of planning and execution."

"And you're calling us failures?"

"I am all too aware of the consequences of my miscalculations."

"Then why are you sitting there behind a blast door instead of getting out here and helping us solve this problem? You must have had a failsafe. Tell us what it is so we can take him out."

"The misstep, the only misstep, was the choice of failsafe. If we'd planned differently, the world would not even know about The Icon until he was deployed in a formal military mission."

"What was it? Maybe we can fix it!"

"I am uniquely qualified to inform you, that will do no good. Giving you insight into the failsafe will only exacerbate a dire situation."

"There's not much that can make the situation worse. According to the Chinese, the power plant is in a failure state."

"And you believe them, do you?"

"Why would they lie?"

"For the same reason the United States pursued every means necessary to deal with the threat of nuclear missiles being placed in Cuba. If an unfriendly territory has a weapon capable of making your nation bleed, you take whatever steps you can to ensure they are disarmed."

"No offense, sir, but hiding in a bunker while your creation runs amok pretty much destroys any credibility you have."

"The safest thing I can do for the world is remain beyond The Icon's reach."

"Yeah, again. If what you want is to stay hidden, that more or less clinches it that we're going to have to bust you out and drag you back with us."

"That will be quite impossible."

Nonsensica tromped back over and tugged at his arm. He followed her to the corridor adjoining the ladder up. In the center of the ceiling was a very heavily fortified grate. An emergency fire cabinet beside the ladder contained an extinguisher and a crowbar. She smashed the glass and pulled the crowbar free.

"What are you doing out there?" the stranger said.

"Boost," she said.

Again he made his hands and knee a platform. She stepped up and wrestled the grid free in a decidedly unstealthy maneuver.

"What was that?" the stranger said again.

Nonsensica grabbed the edge of the vent and hauled herself up. She dropped down again and gave a thumbs-up. At least that was one nonsubmarine aspect to this facility. Proper, unsealed ventilation.

"The Achilles heel of every supervillain lair. Big vents. It'll be a tight fit, but I can make it. It goes straight over the wall," she said, actually achieving a whisper. She unclipped her belt of gear and tugged the laces of her boots.

"Are you sure?" he whispered back. "You won't have your gear, what if—"

"What?" she whispered back.

He shook his head as she pulled her feet out of her boots, choosing instead to give her the boost again and hope for the best. In a maneuver she probably didn't realize was incredibly noisy, she tossed the crowbar ahead of her in the vent, then slid herself inside.

"You idiots... You have no idea what you're doing, do you?" the stranger said.

Non Sequitur trotted back over to the intercom beside the door. "Sounds like we're thwarting your efforts," he said. He grabbed hold of the door, ready to tear it open the moment either Nonsensica or his powers made it possible.

"I will be a liability if I am found outside this bunker. My mere presence in ChiNoKo, if I am found, will make an already unstable situation even more unstable."

"Uh-huh," Non Sequitur said. "That's exactly what a cornered rat of a villain would say as the good guys were closing in."

"Snap out of this idiotic hero/villain mindset for one blasted second. This isn't a comic book. A mentally deranged meta-human is essentially holding the entire region hostage, and the slightest prod to his psychological state could remove even the most fundamental inhibitors we sought to install in his psyche."

"And you're saying this isn't a comic book? Because that's a comic book plot."

Non Sequitur heard the thump of Nonsensica's crowbar rattling in the cramped space of the vent.

"Fine," the stranger said, his voice showing the frenzied beginnings of panic. "If you can't see beyond the facade constructed by your own mind, you leave me no choice. The truth of this project must never leave this place, because the myth that exists in The Icon's mind is the leash that holds him here. At least this will suit your worldview. This is a rare instance where this particular comic trope is actually justified."

The pulsing red lights suddenly switched on and stayed on. A message in Korean rang out over the PA system, followed by an English translation.

"Self-destruct in five minutes."

"I suggest you leave this place while you can. I am prepared to die to keep these secrets. Your lives would be better squandered in combat against The Icon."

A rattling sound rang out across the intercom.

"Zhidkost vombat," squawked Nonsensica's voice over the intercom, now approximating Russian.

The sounds of a scuffle followed. He heard something strike the door, then a heavy thump. Finally, Nonsensica called out.

"Door, door, door, door!" she shouted.

He heaved at the door. It swung open. He pulled at the interior latch to officially unlock the door, then nearly twisted his ankle stepping on the broken remnants of a hefty combination lock that Nonsensica must have bashed off the latch to allow him to open it. The room was equal parts survival bunker, control room, and data center. It was terribly hot. Multiple banks of servers lining the walls belched their heat into the room. An elderly Russian man lay on the floor, dazed. Nonsensica was standing at the keyboard of a rather antiquated desktop computer with a lot of Cyrillic type and roughly four minutes left on a timer.

"Fix it!" she said, turning to shout at the fallen man. "Fix it now!"

"It can't be stopped. Just go. You cannot imagine the danger of these secrets leaving this place, including the ones in my head."

Nonsensica and Non Sequitur got the same idea at the same time, checking their communicators. Both had gone dead: too far from the surface to get a signal. Nonsensica yanked the stranger's lab coat off and piled as many disks, notebooks, and other junk as she could into it.

"You grab the old man, I'll carry the crap, and we're getting out of here," she said, gathering it up like a sack.

Moving with a speed and efficiency that only desperation could provide, Non Sequitur bound the scientist and threw him over his shoulder. Nonsensica dashed along ahead of him, grabbing her belt from the floor where she'd left it on the way out and freeing both soldiers they'd incapacitated.

"Get out of here, or you blow up with the place," she barked. "And if you do something stupid like try to stop us from leaving, I'm scrambling your brains and leaving you in here."

They didn't linger long enough to hear the entire warning. The two simply clambered up the ladder. The heroes followed. Five minutes would have been a generous amount of time to escape, but the time spent subduing the stranger and pillaging his things had made it tight. Having to haul an uncooperative man up ladders wasn't making it any easier.

"Forty-five seconds," the destruct system alerted them.

"Hustle, hustle, hustle," Nonsensica said as they reached the second-to-last floor.

Above them, they heard a hatch slam.

"Those jerks!" Nonsensica hissed as she reached the top of the ladder.

The hatch to the outside was shut tight. She reached it and threw herself against it, but they'd wedged it somehow from the outside. The alert reached fifteen seconds. She grabbed either side of the hatch and drove both her bare heels against it. It popped open. The walkway was dangling in pieces, sabotaged by the escaping guards. There wouldn't have been time to cross it anyway. Nonsensica leaped from the ledge and plummeted into the river. Non Sequitur followed a lot less gracefully. They struck the water and vanished below the surface just as the thump of explosives started to go off. When they emerged from the water, flames were billowing out of the hatch and up through the road-way via pipes and drains.

"Whooo," Nonsensica said, drifting with the flow of the river as she watched the bridge begin to shudder and smolder. "That's our first dive out of a self-destructing secret lab! We've reached peak superhero!"

"There's a culvert. We need to get to cover!" Non Sequitur said.

They swam for the culvert. Above, there was the whoosh and clap of The Icon appearing with incomprehensible speed. Non Sequitur shuddered to think what would have happened if he'd spotted them, but as it was, a burning bridge was quite an able distraction. By the time they'd pulled into the culvert, the city's defender had fetched a dump truck from the street and scooped it into the water. He hoisted it over the bridge and dumped it. The same drains and vents that were spewing flames let the water flow into the pylon. Scoop after scoop of water plunged down, slowly dousing the flames. By the time Non Sequitur had hauled the stranger into the lower level of an abandoned office building, the bridge was barely smoldering.

Finally, The Icon darted into the sky. The heroes glanced at their communicators. The data team fed them video from long-range cameras. He hung in the air with the dump truck over his head. When he was satisfied the fire was taken care of, he scanned the ground for any perpetrators. The view on the communicators switched to the primary border crossing, where the troops, moving in formation, took a few steps toward the border and revved the engine of a diesel troop carrier. A plume of black exhaust belched up from the vehicle. The move, as intended, caught The Icon's attention. He darted toward the border, and for the moment, the heroes were safe.

"So... to recap," Non Sequitur said. "The goal was to do a superheroic mission and find a way to defeat the supervillain. So far we've set a landmark bridge on fire and kidnapped an old man. Meanwhile, the bad guy put out the fire."

"Oh, don't be such a killjoy. We captured the mad scientist who created the monster, we destroyed his evil laboratory, and no one died. That's superheroism in a nutshell. Now, the only question is, do we start the interrogation now, or do we wait until we get back to the base?"

"You have already made the terrible mistake of removing me from my bunker. If you do not get me to safety, without revealing my whereabouts to The Icon, I cannot be certain of the consequences, but they could well have global impact," he said.

"Oh, we're getting you out of here," Nonsensica said. "But because we wanted to, not because you want us to." She tapped her communicator. "How's everyone doing?" she said. "We're about ready for extraction."

"We need to hear from Team 4 before we deploy the exit strategy for you guys," came Aiken's hushed voice over the communicator.

"Well tell them to hurry up," Nonsensica said. "We're toting a mad scientist with us, and I don't want him MacGuyvering up some nerve gas or something to escape."

"I'm not a mad scientist," the man snapped.

"Well you sure aren't a happy one," Non Sequitur said.

"We're going to work our way toward the extraction point," Nonsensica said. "We ducked into a culvert to get to this office building, but it seemed like it led pretty deep into the city."

"I remember reading there's an extensive underground drainage network to deal with the river," Non Sequitur said.

"Let's see if we can use the drainage tunnels to get all the way to the extraction point. Safer that way. Then we'll be watching for the go-ahead."

"With any luck, it'll be hard to miss," Aiken said. "That's sort of the idea, after all."

* * *

"Let's go, guys," Bomb Sniffer said, staring at the communicator on her arm. "Team 2 has already blown up a bridge and captured a scientist."

She and the others were still in the observation room. Chloroplast was sifting through the reams of paper in the filing cabinets. Gracias was being coached through the process of attempting to penetrate the system of the computer that was still logged in. Even with the Chinese military coaching him via the communicator, it was no small task for someone who didn't understand the language the UI was written in. Bomb Sniffer was on lookout, alternating between the surveillance screens in the observation room and the feeds piped across the communicator.

"It's not our fault they got the juicy gig," Gracias said, clicking an icon that may or may not be sending him to the network settings for the computer.

"I'm beginning to think it would have been a good idea to get a language expert on the team," Chloroplast said. "It's one thing to try to read kanji when you don't know what they mean. It's another to read handwritten kanji when you don't know what they mean. This guy's writing is absolute trash." He snapped a few more pictures of carefully laid out pages.

"Have you found anything good?" Gracias asked.

"It's all daily logs of The Icon's activity. If you want to know what he eats for breakfast and when, I can tell you. By the way, he hasn't been eating well, and his favorite food is scallion pancakes. He makes them himself."

"Wow. 'Defends' his city against people trying to keep it from blowing up in a nuclear meltdown and makes pancakes. Real renaissance man, this guy," Gracias said.

Chloroplast returned the pages to their folders and slipped them back into the cabinet. "This whole drawer is barely two weeks of records."

Bomb Sniffer paced up to the screens and leaned on the desk. Some aspect of the system must have been devoted to automatically producing highlights of the best footage, because one of the lower screens was running a loop of footage captured from a camera on the bridge. It was captured in the moments following the last dump truck load of water being delivered to the bridge. She squinted at the screen.

"He looks tired," she said. "He looks miserable, too. Dripping wet, exhausted. He kind of looks a little scared, even."

"The guy was heaving around construction equipment," Chloroplast said. "What are you expecting?"

He slammed the drawer and skipped down to the bottom one. He slid the first folder out and kicked the drawer shut.

"I don't know. I guess I was expecting either cackling, fiendish glee at causing chaos, or stoic resolve. He's obviously shooting for stoic resolve, but I'm not buying it."

"Maybe he's starting to realize he's in over his head," Gracias said.

Chloroplast spread the pages out on the desk and started snapping pictures. "Here's the question, though. When he does realize that, what happens? Does he just give up? Or does he stop playing the hero and go for the cackling, fiendish glee?"

"This guy is like us, more or less," Bomb Sniffer said. "I don't think he can give it up. I don't think you can just decide to go full villain. I don't think anyone decides that. I think he's going to keep doing what he thinks is properly heroic until it kills him."

"Yeah, but what's it going to take?" Gracias said. "We've got to find that weakness."

"So far, all we know is it's not scallion pancakes."

"Maybe that's the source of his power. Maybe he needs to eat a scallion pancake every morning or he loses his powers," Gracias said.

The screen of the computer he was working on flashed and popped up a progress bar.

"Bingo! I got it connected to the Chinese computer system. They're downloading the stuff now." He brushed his nails on his chest and blew on them. "Guess you better add 'hacker' to my list of skills."

"You followed the instructions of a team of hackers. It's not the same thing," Chloroplast said.

"Hey, it takes a certain knack to pull off espionage at this level."

The screen flickered, then went dark. One by one, so did the screens on the wall. Bomb Sniffer's nostrils flared.

"We're getting out of here, now!" she said.

The trio dashed out of the room, snagging the bound soldier to drag him out. By the time they cleared the doorway, smoke was pouring out of the filing cabinets and the computers were sparking.

"Smooth move, Crash Override," Chloroplast said.

"Don't look at me! I was just following their directions!" Gracias said. "I guess there was a safeguard or something."

Ventilation systems kicked on to pull the smoke out. Whatever methods they used to destroy the files in the cabinet and fuse the electronics of the computer systems were stunningly well designed, efficiently wiping out the data and fizzling out again without spreading into a more general fire. If it wasn't completely sabotaging their mission, it would have been fascinating.

"What do we do now?" Chloroplast said. "So far this whole trip has done squat besides tell us what brunch menu he'd want to have."

"I think it's obvious, don't you? We have to actually get into his apartment, take a look around," Gracias said.

"We just saw what happened when someone clicked the wrong button on a laptop. What do you think will happen if we bust into a supervillain's lair?" Chloroplast asked.

"Nothing explosive," Bomb Sniffer said, sniffing once or twice. "That little display got rid of the smell I was picking up. This guy's rifle is the only source of explosive left in the building, at least that I can detect. And we know exactly where the apartment is now. The number for the unit was right there on the door. We could get in and get out really quick."

Gracias clapped. "No time like the present."

He dashed out the door. The others followed. As soon as they emerged from the stairs on the next level, the fiction the people running Project Icon had built up became even more obvious. The whole floor was downright palatial. Judging by the spacing of the doors, each unit was somewhere between three and five times the size of those on the other floors. The only thing about the floor that matched most of the other floors was the service elevator with a prominent notice listing it as out of order. And right at the end of the hall, in the place of suitable prominence, was room 808.

"Okay, so I feel like I'm getting pretty good with the rattle unlocker thingy," Gracias said. "So I'll get it open, then we just storm the place and take every possible picture and get out. Be ready as soon as the door opens."

They tensed, like track runners preparing for a sprint. Gracias grabbed the knob and prepared the strange, vibrating gun that would do the heavy lifting in the lock picking. He paused. With gentle pressure, the door just swung open. Not only was the door not locked, it wasn't even shut tightly.

"Wow..." Gracias said. "This guy feels like he lives in a good neighborhood, huh?"

When the wonder of the lack of security passed, they dashed inside. The interior to the living unit was, in a word, normal. Not normal in comparison to the other units. Again, this was practically a penthouse by those standards. But this was the home of a superhero, and it just looked like an apartment. It was a little untidy—dishes still in the sink and laundry on the floor. Most notably, there were bloodied bandages in the trash of the bathroom and a shredded supersuit hanging on a hanger on the door to one of the two bedrooms. But it wasn't loaded with flashing computers and high-tech weaponry. It was a home. A home with photos on the walls, with lines drawn on a doorjamb to track height. This was a place where a child had grown into a man.

They started snapping photos.

"This feels weird... This feels like we're stalkers..." Bomb Sniffer said.

"Investigators," Gracias said.

Chloroplast stopped in front of a wall in the living room. An assortment of photos had been lovingly framed and hung. All of them featured the person they knew only as The Icon, mostly as a child. Only one photo was recent enough for him to look like the same man they'd seen mangling military equipment. But joining him in most of the photos were a man and a woman.

"These must be his parents," Chloroplast said. "That's weird..."

"It's not weird to have parents, Chloroplast," Gracias called. "I had two of them."

"No, I mean, half of these photos are taken right here in this apartment. And this one is very recent. They clearly live here. But in those two weeks of chronicles I just snapped, the translator didn't say anything about the parents. And what's this?"

A fist-sized hole in the wall occupied a spot that should have been a rather prominent frame. Some fragments of broken glass and a dusting of drywall were on the floor beneath it. Chloroplast crouched and peered behind a side table. A frame had fallen behind and shattered. He fished it out. It was a fairly innocuous picture, not unlike the others, except rather than his parents, it featured him sitting on the knee of an aging Russian man. He snapped a picture and slid it back in place.

"Guys, get in here!" Gracias called.

He'd slipped into the bedroom with the ruined suit on the door. They joined him. It still very much had the look of a child's room. The walls were covered with superhero merchandise. There were Marvel, DC, Image, and every other sort of comic represented. There were also news articles, some clipped from newspapers and more printed from websites, showing off the formation of The Other Eight. But what outnumbered everything else, by a factor of three to one, were depictions of The Icon. Invariably, the hero was someone in a suit precisely like the one they'd seen, but depicted otherwise faceless. He was like a silver silhouette committing acts of heroism. Here he was holding off a tank with a fairly prominent Chinese flag on it. There he was punching a missile with the American flag on it. Most had words written in three different languages, like some sort of Rosetta stone. And all the words had variations of the same message. "ChiNoKo needs The Icon," or "Only The Icon can protect our sacred home," or "ChiNoKo awaits its savior, The Icon."

"Okay..." Chloroplast said. "This is shooting straight past propaganda into religious indoctrination."

"This kid never had a chance," Gracias said. "He fell asleep every night surrounded by dozens of images telling him a fictional hero was the only thing that could protect his home."

Chloroplast stepped forward and opened the door to the closet. Like everything else in this place, it was unrealistically large, the sort of walk-in closet you'd expect in the master bedroom of a mansion. Most of the clothes were quite mundane. But a silver case sat on the floor of the closet. It was the size of a steamer trunk and had a hand-lettered label on a bit of tape on the top, written in Korean. He snapped a picture, then gently lifted the lid. A stack of Icon outfits lay inside. He pulled one out and held it up. At that precise moment, all three of their communicators beeped.

"What'd you do?" Gracias yelped.

Bomb Sniffer glanced at the screen on her arm. "He's heading this way. Let's move!" she said.

They dashed from the living unit and shut the door. Bomb Sniffer did her best to keep her eyes on the communicator. A distant camera view showed The Icon vanishing into the tunnel system. They reached the stairwell moments before the doors to the service elevator slid open. The Icon drifted down the hall. If his gaze weren't so distant and dead-eyed, he almost certainly would have seen the door to the stairwell swinging shut.

The group continued down the stairs as swiftly as they could while remaining silent. When they reached the fourth floor, they abandoned stealth for speed and didn't stop again until they were on the ground floor.

"We're secure at ground level," Bomb Sniffer said. "Does anyone have eyes on The Icon? Is he still in the building?"

"Unconfirmed location," came Luo's voice. "You are advised to remain in cover until he leaves the building and we are able to continue our observation. The extraction operation can't begin until we are certain he will observe it."

"Great… okay. Keep hiding. I think we can manage that," Gracias said.

Chapter 8

Nonsensica and Non Sequitur were holed up in the alley behind a grocery store, snacking on some goods they'd liberated from the back room. Their captive hadn't said a word in hours. Neither had the folks in the command center.

"He's sleeping," Nonsensica said. "You know he's sleeping. He may be a supervillain, but he's still got to sleep. The guy is super strong, he's super durable, and he can fly. He's not going to somehow end up with the power to forego sleep forever."

"There was that one guy in the tryouts. What was his name?"

"The Remarkable Redeye," Non Sequitur said, digging at a tepid cup of ramen with a plastic spoon. "Gotta respect the guy for throwing in the alliterative adjective."

"Right, but the point is, The Icon isn't going to get the full Flying Brick and the Redeye. I bet we could just walk across the border."

"I would not take that bet," their captive said.

"Oh ho!" she said. "He speaks!"

"The entire border of ChiNoKo is dotted with well-hidden motion sensors. When someone approaches from either side, static electric generators in The Icon's residence begin to produce an elevated electrical field. The resulting tingle has been internalized in his mind as a sixth sense for interlopers. He will awaken and patrol the border if we attempt to cross."

"And why exactly did you decide to tell us this now?" Non Sequitur said.

"Because, as I have said, the greatest threat now is that The Icon sees me. I can't risk you trying to bring me across the border without some form of reliable distraction."

"Since you're suddenly feeling chatty, maybe you'd like to tell us who you are and what you did?" Nonsensica said.

"I imagine more skilled interrogators than you will be working with me shortly," he said.

"Don't you want us to put in a good word for you?" Non Sequitur asked.

"I attempted to commit suicide, you'll recall. I'm not concerned what the Chinese army does with me."

"Look, if you're hoping to come off as heroic, you should know that rings kind of hollow if you're just going to sit there and be obstinate rather than giving some useful advice to the people who are trying to clean up your mess. But that's fine. Sit there and stew while I eat my ramen with shrimp and…" She tipped up the cup. "Something else."

"I think it's just shrimp," Non Sequitur said.

"There's definitely some foreign matter in here. Unless they invented some kind of green shrimp."

"You won't be able to 'clean up my mess,'" the captive said.

"Make up your mind. You can either shut your trap or answer some questions. You keep sniping at us and we're going to gag you," she said, tapping on the camera on her communicator and pointing it at him. "So the next words out of your mouth better be your name or nothing."

He turned his head haughtily to the side. "My name is Ivan Borisov."

Non Sequitur raised his eyebrows. "Really?"

"You have heard of me?" he said.

"No, it's just that your name is, like, comically Russian," Non Sequitur said.

"Yeah. It's like if you said your name was Russia McRussiaface," Nonsensica said. "But what were you doing when it all went horribly off the rails?"

"The details are not important," he said.

"You have zip ties binding your hands and legs. What is or isn't important isn't really for you to decide. So what was it? A breeding program? A brainwashing program?"

"It was a holistic approach to crafting a meta-human. Parents were selected for their genetic makeup as well as the size and activity of their Liefeld lobes. Both parents had the meta-human gene but had never manifested powers. We then cultivated an environment built specifically around crafting a human who would believe, in the very fiber of their being, that the only way their home and their loved ones could ever truly be safe would be if a properly powerful superhuman were to arise. And it worked."

"Yeah, worked like gangbusters," Nonsensica said. "The whole city is under threat of nuclear meltdown, and the two most powerful countries in the world are hemming and hawing about how best to annihilate him."

"You joke, but that a single individual could draw the undivided attention of the US, China, and North Korea is evidence of his potency."

"And was it your plan to have it wig out and attack some soldiers? It seems to me that a good plan wouldn't involve you huddling in a bunker, absolutely convinced that if your creation ever saw you, it would cause some ill-defined disaster. How were you supposed to control him, and if you failed to, how were you supposed to stop him?"

"What is his weakness? You must have given him a weakness," Non Sequitur said.

"Even as someone with powers, you don't understand them. And you don't understand the thinking behind a project of this scope and import. We could not and would not give him a weakness. Honestly. A project running for decades, costing an incalculable amount of money and human effort... what good would he be to us if there were some simple way to defeat him? One does not build a fighter jet with a single point of failure, just in case it falls into the wrong hands. You make a weapon of war as invincible as you can manage, and then you ensure it doesn't fall into the wrong hands. The answer to the question of control and weakness were intended to be the same. Loyalty. His loyalty to us was intended to be completely foundational to his psyche. The idea of disobeying us was supposed to be unthinkable. But there was... a miscalculation. We came so close to flawlessly crafting a psyche to suit our precise requirements, but the human mind still refuses to behave as we require."

The communicator beeped. Non Sequitur checked it.

"As much as I'd love to hear what miscalculation that was, The Icon is on the move, and Team 4 is about to start the distraction to cover our escape."

"Time's up, then," Nonsensica said. "You're going to be finishing that story in a Chinese military base, and you'll be telling it to the guy whose soldiers your creation killed, so don't expect them to be offering you ramen."

***

Across town, distressingly near to the nuclear power plant, the members of Team 4 of the operation prepared themselves in an alleyway. Phosphor brushed off the flap of his messenger bag and peered out to the street beyond. He crouched to tighten his boots.

"I would have figured this place would be communist," he mused, tugging the laces tight. "And I wouldn't have figured a communist country would have banks. I guess back when I was in school, we didn't put too much effort into teaching kids about how communism worked. Only to watch out for it, since it wasn't capitalism."

The communicator on his arm chirped. Gen. Luo's voice rumbled from it.

"Earbuds in, and remember to position your communicator," he said.

"Will do." Phosphor tapped the screen to blank it.

He fetched his earbuds, powered them up, and slipped them in. The uncertain duration of the mission meant keeping the earpieces in place and powered for the entire time would have run the risk of them powering down at a crucial moment, unlike the bulky communicators with their multiday batteries and rapid recharge.

"Give it to me straight," he said, looking over his shoulder. "What are the odds this works?"

His partner stepped forward, dressed in a similar but slightly ill-fitting red-and-white-camouflage outfit.

"I don't work with odds," Dr. Aiken said, tugging uncomfortably at the costume. "But I wouldn't be here if I didn't think it was the best idea we had." He fiddled with his bright red gloves. "Forgive me, but I feel a little silly in this outfit," he said.

"It suits you, Doc. You look like part of the team."

"That's the important thing. If I'm right, my survival depends largely on how convinced The Icon is that I'm a proper foe."

"You look the part, Doc," Phosphor said. "One last question before we get rolling. Us getting out of here was supposed to involve getting The Number and Primadonna to put on another dance routine. We haven't heard back on whether they'll be able to pull that off anytime soon. Is there a plan B?"

"This is already plan F, Phosphor. From here on out, if The Number can't give us a way out, we're relying upon some combination of luck, military strategy, and improvisation."

"Oh. Well, we'll be fine, then. The Other Eight have only ever been so-so at planning, but we're aces at improv." Phosphor took a deep breath. "Time to break some rules."

Dr. Aiken hoisted a duffel bag to his shoulder.

"On three. One… two… three!"

The pair dashed out into the streets. It felt strange to be rushing in a mad panic through a completely deserted stretch of town, but when one's foe has superspeed, it is always best to act as though they are looming in the shadows. Their target was the largest bank in ChiNoKo. Like most other things in town, it was an indistinct concrete cube of a building. If not for the large plate-glass windows and conspicuous security cameras blinking on the walls, it would have been difficult to differentiate this from the half-dozen other buildings nearby.

The lights were off inside. Phosphor gave the door an experimental rattle, but it was locked.

"Looks like the entire staff evacuated, and they buttoned the place up before they did," he said.

"That's good. A supervillain taking advantage of a national emergency to pillage a bank is a classic scenario. It'll help cement our role in his mind," Dr. Aiken said, slipping a mini-sledge from the duffel and hefting it in his grip.

"I wish you wouldn't call us supervillains, Doc. This goes against everything I stand for," Phosphor said.

"We're playing by his rules right now, Phosphor. There's only room in his head for one superhero. Therefore, if we're going to position ourselves as equals, we have to fill the role of supervillain. Remember, low on violence, high on bluster."

Aiken reared back and bashed the glass. The tempered sheet exploded into a spiderweb of cracks, but still held in place thanks to the coating on the glass. An alarm bell rang out. It took two more blows to punch a hole through the safety glass, but it was enough for Phosphor and Dr. Aiken to hustle through.

"The alarm is going off," he said over his communicator. "Positioning comm. Move as soon as The Icon appears."

He pulled the device from his arm and strapped it to the vertical pipe of the fire-suppression system. Phosphor activated his own communicator and shoved it onto his messenger bag amid a cacophony of clinking and jangling of glass tubes. In moments, they heard the clap of a small sonic boom and the thud of something hitting the street out front. They turned to the broken window.

For an instant, the superhero looked through the broken window with uncertainty. Trepidation. When he saw the bright outfits Dr. Aiken and Phosphor were wearing, a brief flash of relief was swiftly replaced by a practiced look of stoic heroism.

"Evildoers," he rumbled, rising from the street and drifting toward the broken window. "You dare seek to pillage the fruits of the fine land of ChiNoKo?"

"He actually said 'pillage,'" Phosphor said under his breath.

"Focus, Phosphor." Aiken raised his voice. "The Icon! I should have known you'd show up."

"The Icon will always arrive when the forces of the evil beyond our borders stain our hallowed streets with their villainy."

Phosphor squinted and whispered, "We don't sound like that, do we?"

The Icon reached out and grabbed the ragged end of the sagging safety-glass window. He wrenched it aside like a curtain, scattering glittering fragments of glass to the street.

"What difference does it make?" Aiken said. "You clearly don't care about your city. You'd rather let it roast in the aftermath of a nuclear meltdown than do what it takes to keep it safe. We may as well clean out the bank before it's radioactive."

"ChiNoKo has the finest technicians in the world. The sabotage of the vile outsiders will be corrected, and ChiNoKo will shine again as the symbol of freedom and virtue it has always been."

Aiken nodded to Phosphor. He nodded back and slid a fluorescent tube from his bag, brandishing it like a sword.

"Let's just see about that," he said.

The Icon backhanded the bulb, shattering it into a cloud of sparkling dust. A second slap knocked the jagged stump from Phosphor's hand. The blow was calibrated to cause pain and disarm, but no injury. In a blurring motion, he darted forward and grabbed a handful of their thick canvas outfits, hoisting them from the ground.

"We have visual on Team 2. ETA for border crossing, sixty seconds. Team 3 still en route. ETA seven minutes," Luo informed them.

"I will send you back to the filthy land that sent you. Tell your masters that they will not profit from the sweat of the brows of the people of ChiNoKo."

In any other situation it would have been either an inspired bit of foresight or a profound bit of good fortune that the first notion The Icon had was to simply remove them from the city-state. But with seven minutes until both of the other teams were free, they couldn't risk The Icon returning to his patrols so soon. Aiken laughed. It sounded forced and insincere. He wasn't a very good actor, but dangling from the fist of a superhuman would test the skills of a Shakespearean.

"Perfect. Send us back. We'll return, again and again. You can't defeat us forever."

The Icon shuddered, pulling Aiken face to face. "Do you have a death wish, evildoer? Do you want me to end you?" he said.

"A-and you call yourself a hero," Aiken said. "What's the matter? Is there no justice to be found within ChiNoKo?"

"Justice…" The Icon said. "As with all things in my land, the justice within ChiNoKo is beyond reproach. Swift, fair, and thorough."

"You expect us to believe that?" Phosphor said. "The only one we see keeping the peace is you, and it hasn't been too peaceful."

"I am the shield that defends my people from the likes of you," The Icon said.

"Are they too weak to defend themselves?" Aiken asked.

"No mere human could defend this place against the evils of the world. That is why I had to arise. That is why I was necessary. That is why I was inevitable. Because when the light of righteousness exists in a single place, that light must never be extinguished. Nature seeks balance. And it took someone with my strength to balance the combined greed and hatred of the world beyond these walls."

"We don't seem to be much of a match for you. Is this what you call balance?" Aiken asked. "In all of these clashes, the only loss of life was at your hands. Is that what you call heroism? If you think I am a villain…" Aiken shut his eyes, as if mentally preparing himself for what he had to say next. "…We're not so different, you and I," he said, trying to deliver the tired line with as much force and conviction as he could.

"I'm nothing like you!" The Icon barked.

He dropped down to the ground. Both Phosphor and Aiken sagged in his grip until they were supporting their own weight again.

"I did what I had to do. I had no choice. They tried to kill me."

"The hostilities began with you," Phosphor said.

"They violated our borders. They poisoned the heart of ChiNoKo with their vile sabotage. It was right to do what I did. I was right…" He slowly drifted from the ground again, dragging them with him. "But you, too, are right about something. You should be left to the authorities. I have greater threats to see to."

He pivoted, Aiken and Phosphor dangling from his grip, and drifted out the window toward the police station.

This much had been part of the plan. The police station was farther into the center of the city, away from the borders. And unless The Icon had a complete disregard for their well-being, he would have to travel low and slow while carrying Aiken and Phosphor. Given his visible mental instability, such a regard for the health of his prisoners was not a foregone conclusion.

It took them three minutes to reach the police station. He entered not through the front door but through the garage, dragging them through its relatively spacious interior until he reached the officer overseeing the otherwise unstaffed space. The officer's presence indicated that at least some of the local law enforcement were among those who hadn't fled the city when The Icon's first violent acts occurred.

"Officer," he said. "I remand these two villains to your custody. I found them attempting to rob the bank. They are outsiders."

The man nodded shakily, treating The Icon less with the sort of respect one has for a revered hero and more with the sort of respect one has for a bull moose that has wandered into one's place of business. He stammered something in Korean.

"Of course," The Icon said magnanimously in return. "He has requested that I escort you to prisoner processing until they can be certain this jail can contain you. It was intended, of course, for those rare members of our saintly community who refuse to obey the law. It was not built with the intent to house supervillains, even ones as lowly as you."

He dropped them to their feet and landed behind them. A firm grip to the backs of their collars made sure they didn't run. The door ahead unlocked, and they were walked through a very modest police station. Phosphor very much doubted this place could accommodate more than a dozen police officers at a time. At present, there seemed to be only the garage attendant (walking nervously in front of them), a young woman working the front desk once they reached it, and one rather grizzled-looking officer lurking in an office behind her.

"Process these men. Bank robbery," The Icon instructed.

"Uh, yes," the woman said, displaying much the same level of wariness her coworker had. She stepped out from behind the desk and said, "Arms to your sides, please."

"Now that you've defeated us," Aiken said over his shoulder as he dropped a duffel bag to the floor, "what do you plan to do about the power plant? You've confirmed by now that it is approaching mechanical failure."

"I will not divulge state secrets regarding the heart of ChiNoKo."

"But what will you do if your people cannot fix it?" Aiken asked. "The lives of your people and the safety of the rest of the region hang in the balance. What is a superhero's purpose if not to do whatever it takes to protect his city?"

"The power plant is the heart of ChiNoKo. Its power is a balance of danger and bounty. If the power plant falls, we all fall."

"That's sort of the reason you should be getting help to take care of it," Phosphor said.

The officer finished removing the contents of the duffel bag. "Tools. No weapons," she said. "Remove the devices from your ears."

Both Aiken and Phosphor did as they were told. She logged the devices.

"And your bag, sir," the officer said.

Phosphor let her take his bag. One by one, she started removing fluorescent tubes.

"You must understand the scope of the danger," Aiken said. "If you do not allow it to be serviced, the loss of life will dwarf anything any so-called supervillain has ever done."

"Do not speak to me of the power plant. I know more than anyone its dangers. Though the ideals of The Icon and the righteousness he represents have existed in the hearts and minds of the good people of ChiNoKo for decades, the mantle did not fall to me until the awesome forces within the power plant granted them to me. And as with all great gifts, it required an equal sacrifice."

"Seems like if there was a price, it wasn't a gift," Phosphor said.

"Silence," The Icon said. "You will speak only to answer the questions of the police. My affairs are not your concern."

Aiken glanced nervously at the clock. Five minutes had passed. Two more minutes at least before the rest of the team was likely to be clear. Fortunately, Phosphor's powers were serving their purpose well. The officer had removed seventeen tubes, and the jangling mess within the bag hadn't reduced in the slightest. After three full minutes, she'd removed nearly two hundred bulbs. Mixed in among the rattles and clanks of her endless rummaging, a short sequence of vibrating buzzes alerted them that the final extraction had been completed. The others were safe.

"Just to let you know, ma'am," Phosphor said, "you're never going to hit the bottom of that bag. You could pull upwards of a thousand bulbs out and there'd be more where they came from."

"Enough." Icon grabbed the bag and tossed it aside. It struck the wall with a flash of broken glass and a puff of white dust. "Lock them up. They've taken up enough of my time. I have a city to defend."

The Icon thundered outside. The sonic clap of his departure sent a shudder through the building and the officer. Her carefully assembled pile of bulbs tumbled to the floor, shattering in a burst of broken glass that slowly faded to nothingness. The potent combination of the startling crash and the tension of the last few minutes caused the officer to practically collapse. She slumped against the desk. It would have been messy if Phosphor's power wasn't so obliging with its lack of cleanup.

At the risk of incurring some manner of wrath, Dr. Aiken stepped forward to comfort her.

"I get the feeling The Icon isn't as well liked around these parts as he thinks he is," Phosphor said.

* * *

Teams 2 and 3 were loaded into an armored personnel vehicle and sent thundering toward the base as soon as the last of them arrived. Any potential celebration at having not only survived but also acquiring the scientist in charge of the operation was instantly put on hold when it was revealed that Phosphor and Dr. Aiken were still in ChiNoKo.

"What the hell are we doing still heading back to the base?" Nonsensica said. "This was supposed to end with all of us free and clear. The two dancers were supposed to come back and—"

"The Number and Primadonna were still putting together a routine they can pull off injured, and if they don't dance, no one else does," Gracias said.

"So? There were other contingency plans. They were supposed to get kicked out, weren't they? They were supposed to commit a crime and get brought to the border."

"He needed more time. This was always on the list of contingencies," said their handler, the soldier beside the driver.

"That means we just left two men behind. We don't do that," Nonsensica snapped.

"To be fair, we've never really been in a position to leave anyone behind before," Gracias said. "Technically, this means we always leave two men behind."

"Gracias, if you start getting semantical with me, I'm going to scramble your brains so hard they'll be serving them on toast."

"Yeesh," Gracias said.

"I don't like this any more than the rest of you do..." Non Sequitur began.

"Apparently Gracias loves it," Nonsensica jabbed.

"Hey, that's not fair," Gracias said.

"The point is," Non Sequitur said, "we made most of this plan, but Dr. Aiken's part was his idea. And we have to trust him. He knows what he's doing."

"He doesn't know what he's doing any more than the rest of us do," Chloroplast said. "No one in the world could know what they're doing, because no one like The Icon has ever existed before. We're all just making wild guesses."

"Sure, but the doc was making scientific wild guesses," Gracias said. "I bet he's got plans within plans. An onion of plans. I bet right now he's cracking all sorts of mysteries back there."

"What good is that going to do us if we can't find out what he wants us to do afterward? They took away the communicators!" Nonsensica said.

Gracias tapped at his communicator. "Not really. One of them is still in the bank. Look, you can sort of see out the broken window. And… the other one is on audio only." He stuck his finger hard against the earbud and cranked up the volume. "There's conversation. Can't make it out though. Sounds like the doc talking to someone else."

"There, you see?" Non Sequitur said. "That's two points of contact available to him. And I bet the command room is doing all sorts of audio forensics on that one we can barely hear. The doc and Phosphor haven't been left behind. Their mission is on-going. The important thing is, we need to get everything we can out of Borisov."

Nonsensica glared at the still-secured scientist. "Oh, we're getting what we need out of him. Even if have to crack open that head of his to scoop it out myself."

The personnel carrier rattled into the base. Soldiers arrived to unload them. Medics attempted to check the team for injuries, but they marched after the pair of soldiers escorting Dr. Borisov to the briefing room. They were stopped by one of Luo's technicians at the door.

"This is as far as you go," the tech said, standing in their way as Borisov was brought inside.

"Like hell it is. That's our piñata. We get to break it open," Nonsensica said.

"We have experts for this sort of thing," he said.

"Yeah, so did we, and he's still in ChiNoKo," Chloroplast said.

"There's no official second in command when it comes to debriefing crazies, which means we're all second in command," Bomb Sniffer said.

"Yeah, that's how it works," Gracias said.

"This is a delicate process," the tech said.

"Not the way I plan on doing it," Nonsensica said, tugging on her gloves.

Luo appeared in the doorway behind his technician. "What is this about?"

"We want in on the interrogation," Nonsensica said.

"That isn't how this works," Luo said.

"How this is supposed to work is Dr. Aiken, an expert in psychology, would be here to plumb the depths of his mind," Nonsensica said. "But he was on the away team, and now he's locked up. So that leaves us as his protégés to pick up the slack."

"You have no expertise in this area," Luo said.

"We are this area," Chloroplast said.

"We went in there and faced a guy who could punch a hole through a tank and brought back his handler," Gracias said. "I say that earns us a chance to talk to him."

"Nonsensica and Non Sequitur already had him talking a little before they even got him clear," Bomb Sniffer said.

"We're the people who know things about ChiNoKo," Chloroplast said. "We can put pressure on him."

Gen. Luo looked about. "Where is Pvt. Summers? Get Summers over here."

"Here, sir!" she called, trotting over from across the way. "I was with the command team. They're working hard to filter the audio from the communicator that's still in range of Dr. Aiken and Phosphor to see what they can learn."

"In the absence of Dr. Aiken, you are the handler of his team. Tell me honestly. Can you keep control of them?" Luo asked.

"They don't typically require much control, sir," she said.

"If I permit them to enter the briefing room while we do our initial questioning of Dr. Borisov, can they be trusted to behave?"

"I stand by the discipline of this team," she said.

"Then listen closely." He turned to the others. "All of you, listen closely. You will be permitted to attend the briefing. You will keep your mouths shut and your opinions to yourself. If you feel as though you have something to contribute or a valuable question to ask, you will bring it to Pvt. Summers, who will bring it to my assistant, who will bring it to me, and only then will I determine if you should be allowed to speak. Is that understood?"

"The team will behave themselves," Pvt. Summers said, flashing a look over her shoulder to the team with a level of "stern mom" energy of which someone her age shouldn't have been capable.

"Then let us not delay any longer."

The group filed into the debriefing tent. Borisov was seated at the table, rubbing wrists still striped with the pressure of the recently cut zip ties. He managed to preserve some small amount of dignity despite his muddy, damp clothes. A pitcher of water had been set on the table before him, along with two glasses. Both were still empty. Lights and cameras had been set up to record what would follow. Luo took a seat across from him as the heroes arranged themselves against the back wall behind Luo.

The general filled the two glasses of water. He pushed one across to Borisov and took a sip of his own. Borisov declined to drink. Luo held out his hand. A thick folder was placed in it by his assistant. The general set the folder down and opened it.

"Dr. Borisov. Dr. Ivan Borisov. Former resident of Kazakhstan. Doctorate in psychology, specializing in mental conditioning and abnormal development. Two siblings, both deceased. Divorced in 1991. Never remarried. Is this accurate?"

"It is," Borisov said.

"As you can see, even with very little time to prepare, we have been able to pull together an intelligence file on you," Luo said. "Of course, most of this intelligence was fully prepared years in advance, but it was archived after this final entry. Date of death: 1994. Cause of death: pulmonary embolism. You are to be commended, or perhaps your superiors are to be commended. Very few individuals have faked their own death as successfully as you have."

"I imagine you are looking forward to correcting that oversight," Borisov said.

"Your crimes are not the matter at hand," Luo said. "There is no question of them, and this is not the venue to properly address them. The matters at hand are your mistakes, of which there have been many. The most significant of which—and perhaps the most significant one ever committed—is standing watch at the border of the Disincorporated Zone even now, staring down some of my soldiers. I understand you had a hand in the creation of The Icon."

"I oversaw the entire process."

"Then, as I have said, the matter at hand is The Icon. But please be aware that any leniency you may receive in exchange for your cooperation is contingent upon you being open, willing, and forthcoming. It is your obligation to your people, our people, and the world that you correct your errors. You understand the stakes."

"The stakes are that a small, independent state sharing a border with you has a potent weapon available that, under present circumstances, will not be deployed outside of its own borders. I can appreciate your distaste with losing the last element of control you had over the territory in the form of your sham nuclear inspections, but you'll have to become comfortable with the fact that ChiNoKo is now capable of enforcing its freedom regardless of your will."

"The blood of several soldiers is on the hands of your monster, Borisov, and we will not simply have to become comfortable with that. But your refusal to accept the reality of the power plant's state is easily addressed."

He nodded to his assistant. A device was set down on the table.

"A radiation meter," Borisov said.

"At the present distance, the radiation readings should be one-third of what they are now. Still within the safe range. But something is going on at the power plant."

Borisov looked dispassionately at the device. "You have tampered with the calibration."

"And did we tamper with the calibration over two weeks ago, when a similar spike in radioactive output inspired our initial inspection and attempt at maintenance?" Luo asked. "I want to know what happened. I want to know how The Icon was created, and I want to know how to destroy him."

"The operation took decades, but at its core it was very simple. Raise a child with the appropriate genetic makeup in an environment that produced a psychological imperative to fill a carefully constructed mantle. The Icon was the result."

"What is his weakness, Borisov?"

"He has no weakness, nor should he."

"What is the origin?" Dr. Liefeld said, approaching through the doorway.

"Why is this guy always showing up late?" Gracias grumbled.

Liefeld approached the table. "You've produced a meta-human with a lobe that exceeds all previously calculated theoretical limits," he said. "Some aspect of your experimentation must have enhanced the capacity of the lobe."

"Your calculations are trash, Liefeld," Borisov said. "They've been trash since the beginning. Terrible control groups, incorrect metrics. You are a poor scientist."

"I am the world's foremost expert on the mechanisms of meta-humanity."

"You are the third most skilled expert, behind me and Aiken. He and I understand the true mechanisms, those locked within the functioning of the human mind. Your so-called calculations regarding the strength of the lobe and its theoretical output are drivel. Dreck. You were lucky to have determined its role in meta-humanity to begin with."

"Enough!" Luo barked. "Dr. Liefeld, I am doing the questioning. Borisov, answer about the origin."

"The origin…" Borisov said. "It was supposed to be so simple. A lifetime spent building distrust in anyone but those of ChiNoKo, the origin was masterfully constructed to give The Icon a plausible source for his powers, a plausible reason for his powers to be used, and remove from him all but a single point of support. The boy's parents were both workers within the power plant. We engineered a simulated containment failure in the reactor. It was covered in the local news media as a temporary failure due to unreasonable oversight rules instituted by foreign regulation and flawed work by outside technicians. The radiation leak killed his parents and exposed him to a burst of radiation. His powers manifested within hours."

"The measured radiation spike would not have been sufficient to kill someone," Luo said.

"Of course not. It was scarcely the equal of a chest X-ray, even at close range. But it produced the desired effect. The Icon's mind now had its justification and motivation to manifest the powers that he'd been taught through his entire life were the only thing that could keep him safe."

"And the blame for the death of his parents fell upon 'outsiders.' Thus ensuring his heart and mind would forever be turned against us," Luo said.

"Precisely."

"And because the death is believed to be due specifically to outsiders performing maintenance on the power plant, he is assured to never allow anyone to repair it while he has the power to defend it."

"An unintentional but very real side effect of our tactics."

"What was the mechanism of control?" Luo said. "What was your intended means of enforcing control? You must have had one."

"The boy was raised with three members of his support system. His mother, his father, and a male mentor figure. The intention was for the death of his parents to leave him entirely dependent upon the mentor, and thus entirely under that mentor's control through his advice. Unfortunately, after the initial hostility, the mentor figure lost his nerve and was among the refugees to North Korea."

"What is his name?" Luo said.

"That is immaterial."

"That is not for you to decide."

"It is precisely for me to decide. I built that mind, General. I know its fragility. The moment his mentor fled ChiNoKo, all respect for him was dashed in the mind of The Icon. If he were to return now, he would be worthless, viewed as a traitor and quite likely to inspire a violent outburst."

Nonsensica tapped Summers on her shoulder and whispered something to her. Summers relayed it. When it reached Luo, he nodded. Nonsensica, Chloroplast, and Gracias stepped forward.

"You're full of crap," Nonsensica said.

"A bit more formality would be preferred," Luo rumbled.

"You're lying about at least some of that," Chloroplast amended for her.

"I resent the accusation," Borisov said.

"You made it abundantly clear that it would be disastrous if The Icon were to see you. You were willing to commit suicide to avoid it. What's that all about?" Nonsensica said.

"I was one of four people, including his parents, who were supposed to have died in the power plant mishap," Borisov said. "Seeing me alive could further destabilize his already-unstable mind by calling into question facts he considers to be incontrovertible."

"Bogus," Nonsensica said.

"Doubtful," Chloroplast corrected. "Gen. Luo, have your techs finished processing the photos and footage from our investigation into The Icon's apartment?"

"We are still processing and cross-referencing the data from the filing cabinet," replied one of the technicians on hand.

"Can you bring up the last photo I took on my communicator before we evacuated?"

He produced a tablet and flipped through the images until he found the relevant one. It was placed down on the table. A shattered picture frame featured an old man with The Icon in his youth sitting on his knee. The old man in the photo was Borisov. The scientist remained silent.

"Your explanation, Doctor?" Luo said.

"I don't imagine any statement I make at this point will further clarify the nature of the situation."

"Ha! I knew it!" Chloroplast said.

"It is within your power to end this and you were hiding that fact?" Luo raged.

"If it were within my power, this never would have started. Did you think I wanted an evacuated city and a meta-human going through the motions of comic book morality after assaulting a massive militarized nation? My official role with ChiNoKo, as he understood it, was as the leader of a covert security force within ChiNoKo. That way he would have had reason to believe that I had authorization to send him on missions beyond the borders and, ideally, to attract lesser meta-humans to form as a team beneath him. But as I was associated with security, he blamed me for failing to protect the power plant from intervention for years. He blames me as much for the death of his parents as any of you."

"Why would you lie to us about this?"

"Because even now, I am certain that some of you are considering having me presented to him to issue some order or another, which as I explained before would almost certainly result in a violent outburst."

"We'll have to discuss the matter with our psychologists, as Aiken is presently unavailable." Luo turned to Gracias. "Did you have something to add as well?"

"Yeah, General," Gracias said. He stepped forward, arms folded, and stared Borisov down with the air of a lawyer preparing for cross-examination. "You sculpted his mind from birth. He lived in a massive apartment compared to those around him. A luxurious upbringing. You taught him to have a great reverence and protection for his highly industrial city. His parents were in positions of importance within the community. Then, one day, through the actions of someone he was to view as the enemy, both of his parents were killed with the intent of him depending upon the guidance of an elderly mentor."

Gracias pointed accusingly. "You gave him Batman's origin!" he barked. "And even worse, you gave him Christopher Nolan's Batman's origin,"

"We had initiated the project several years before the release of the film in question," Borisov said calmly.

Gracias paused. "Irrelevant! The point is, you trained him up to have Superman's powers but Batman's origin. Of course he was going to be screwed up. Batman doesn't have a weakness either, because he's a Mary Sue."

"Technically he's a Gary Stu," Nonsensica said.

"No, Mary Sue is gender neutral," Gracias said.

"Mary and Sue are both lady's names. If they wanted it to be gender neutral, they'd have called it Pat Sam or something."

"Doesn't Johnny Cash have a song about a boy named Sue?" Chloroplast said.

"Even so, that'd be the last name," Nonsensica said.

"No, they're both first names. It's like Billy Bob or Barbara Anne," Gracias said.

"I fail to see the relevance of this tangent," Luo said impatiently.

"Oh, uh… the point is, he screwed up, and that's one of the reasons why. Or how. Or whatever," Gracias said.

"That will be all, thank you," Luo said.

"I have a point worth addressing," Liefeld said. "The parents, I presume, aren't truly dead?"

"They were evacuated to a secret location," Borisov said.

"And I presume the absence of their remains was explained away because they were still radioactive," Liefeld said.

"Correct."

"Clever." He turned to Luo. "We need to locate and present his parents to him."

"Absolutely not," Borisov said.

"If your entire premise is that his powers are conjured from his psychology, then revealing that his origin was false should undermine his powers. Simple as that," Liefeld said.

"His mind is a house of cards," Borisov insisted. "You have no concept of what you might bring about if you do this."

Liefeld waggled his fingers dismissively. "He doesn't want us to break his toy. That alone is reason enough to find, retrieve, and deliver his parents. You have your solution."

"I don't know," Gracias said. "I'm pretty sure Liefeld hasn't been right about anything since he got here. Or, like, for the last fifty years."

"We will take it into consideration. I have technicians doing their best to retrieve data from the waterlogged items taken from Borisov's lab, as well as processing all other audio, video, and evidence from the infiltration. We are beginning the planning phase for potential rescue missions for Aiken and Phosphor. All possible avenues of advancement will be pursued. Borisov, you have given me very little reason to believe you have any interest in aiding in the solution of this problem, so until such a time as we feel you have value to our cause, you will be held in custody. Everyone, dismissed."

Chapter 9

In ChiNoKo, Phosphor and Aiken were sitting in separate cells in the jail. There were only six cells total, and none of the others were occupied. Given the general state of mind of the police force, if they'd made an earnest attempt to escape, they probably could have done so. But there was little chance they'd have made it as far as the border, and zero chance they'd make it across. Better to be where The Icon wanted them to be, and thus safe from his ire, than to test the limits of Aiken's theory that he wouldn't kill people who a superhero wouldn't kill.

Phosphor leaned against the wall and gazed out between the bars. "What do you suppose'll happen next?" he asked.

"Mmm?" Aiken said vaguely.

"What happens next?" Phosphor said. "Do you think it'll be troops or the rest of the team that'll get us?"

"I suppose that depends on how useful Luo found this mission to be. But I very much doubt he'll be sending superheroes on another mission without me there to advocate for them."

"So soldiers, then." He shook his head. "Lord, I hope things don't get too bloody."

"Me too, Phosphor. Me too."

There was silence for a moment.

"Got a lot on your mind, Doc?" Phosphor asked. "You feel like you learned something? I know you wanted to get face to face with The Icon, and you did it."

"Not for as long or as openly as I would have liked. But... there is something that I can't get out of my mind."

"What's that?"

"The Icon can fly. He seems to prefer to remain aloft as often as possible. But he's dropped to the ground on multiple occasions when it wasn't strictly necessary. I wish I had the footage of it all in front of me so I could review it. We've spoken about it endlessly, that he must have a weakness. I think he does. I think something is weakening him. But it's… hazy. Vague. We structured our whole mission this way because he's more stable and predictable when he's fighting superheroes and supervillains. I'm a scientist. I like things to be stable and predictable. But at the same time, it's the volatility that shows us different outcomes, and showing us different outcomes is what teaches us new things, and learning new things is what makes things predictable."

"Can't really do much in the way of experiments when it'd endanger human lives, huh," Phosphor said.

The front desk officer approached with two trays. "Supper," she said.

"Oh, much obliged," Phosphor said.

He stepped up to the bars to take a tray containing a bowl of some sort of fishy stew. Aiken took his as well. The officer lingered.

"You're… you're really Phosphor," she said.

"Like I wrote on the form when you booked me," he said with a nod.

"From Power Picker."

He furrowed his brow. "Beg pardon?"

"The show! The show where they selected the hero team," she said.

"Oh. We just called it the Guardian Project," he said. "That got shown all the way out here?"

"Of course! It was about superheroes. Have you met The Number? Or Nonsensica? They're my favorite."

"The Number took some lumps dealing with The Icon, and Nonsensica's been in and out of town," Phosphor said. "I kind of figured you didn't much like us. Being outsiders and all."

"You're evil, deceitful, and contemptible. But I would like an autograph," she said, digging out a pad.

He set down the tray on the bed as she flipped open a pad and offered a felt-tipped pen.

"May I ask, ma'am," Aiken said, "what do you think of The Icon?"

She kept her eyes fixed on the pad Phosphor was jotting his name on. "The Icon is our shield," she said woodenly.

"Not to put too fine a point on it," Phosphor said. "But if you meant that, I don't think you'd be saying it like someone had a gun in your back."

The officer glanced over her shoulder. She took back the pad and pocketed it. "I didn't expect him to… I don't know if he can keep us safe. Life has become so difficult since he arose. My husband works at the power plant. Things are going poorly. They need help."

"And The Icon knows this?" Aiken said.

"He said The Icon came and explicitly asked. He was told that expertise and equipment from the outside will be needed to keep it running. Otherwise, they'll need to shut down, except they can't shut down, because the power lines to China have been severed. The plant needs power to shut down safely."

"You don't have generators? Things like that?"

"He doesn't trust them. They haven't started up for years. He doesn't even know if they will run. I'm frightened. The Icon can't protect us from a meltdown. I know he is a hero. The Icon can only be a hero. But…"

"That's it…" Aiken said.

"What is it?" Phosphor said.

"The Icon can only be a hero. He must be a hero. Why didn't I see it before? His very identity is built upon heroism as he understands it. A strict moral code. He is right, and he fights those who are wrong. He didn't bleed because of the glass. He bled because we were beginning to make him doubt his position as a paragon of virtue. And when The Number and Primadonna immobilized him, he ran off after that, he didn't fly. It was because they'd overpowered him. He realized that, if only for the length of a song, he wasn't invincible anymore, and it shook him. Weakness is his weakness. A legitimate threat to his power and to his righteousness." He ran his fingers through his hair. "My god, it's brilliant. It's a weakness that can't be exploited militarily. Fight him and it draws a line in the sand. Us and them. He is the defender, they are the aggressors. We have to hold up a mirror, make him see what he's been doing. That's what will sap his power."

"That's a little wishy-washy, Doc," Phosphor said.

"It's the mind, Phosphor. The human psyche is a bag of cats, squirming and clawing at itself. It's a miracle any of us are able to pull it together enough to function day to day."

"Is that, uh… your professional opinion as a psychologist?"

"It's the first thing they teach you when you declare your major. Now imagine having the weight of a city on your shoulders, no one to help you or even talk to you, and through your own actions, making the lifelong claim that the whole world is against you into a self-fulfilling prophecy."

He turned to the officer. "Ma'am, please. You have to let me contact the others. They need to know."

"I can't help you defeat The Icon. He's our hero."

"I assure you. I want to help him. The path he's on can only end in ruin. Not just his, but all of us."

She shut her eyes tightly. "I can't, sir…" She turned and hurried from the room.

"What now, Doc?" Phosphor asked.

"We have three options. We can get in touch with the others and tell them, we can find some way to come face to face with The Icon again and try to get him to see that he is the greatest danger, or we have to sit here and hope that someone out there comes up with a way to stop him without causing any more bloodshed."

"Seems like the only one of those we can do locked up in a jail cell is the last one."

"Maybe. But we can make plans for the first two regardless."

* * *

Gen. Luo stood with crossed arms in the command center. With no more active operations within ChiNoKo, he'd ordered his troops to withdraw. Tempting as it was to keep The Icon

149

exhausted by requiring him to be on constant patrol, for the moment it felt as though having the entirety of his force rested and ready for combat was preferable to simply taunting the superhuman. Data were still pouring in from The Other Eight's mission. It was with no small amount of irritation that he had to admit, for all their absurdities, they were well-suited to this specific task.

"Sir, Gen. Siegel is available," his assistant said.

"Get me on a call with him," Luo said.

"Shall I set it up in your quarters, sir?"

"No. Do it here. I want all of my data available."

"Yes, sir."

A complex communication sequence passed through a handful of military firewalls. Before long, the stern face of his US counterpart appeared.

"General," Siegel said.

"General," Luo said.

"Things have been awfully quiet," Siegel said.

"We pride ourselves on information security."

"The story that we've withdrawn the field members of The Other Eight for training exercises hasn't drawn any scrutiny."

"That's good."

"I'm still waiting on the formal briefing and materials from the penetration mission."

"The volume of data returned by Nonsensica and Non Sequitur in particular have been such that a full report will take some time."

"Any update on Dr. Aiken and Phosphor?" Siegel said.

"Due to either stunning ineptitude or complicity by the police force within the Disincorporated Territory, the communication device is still active and at the far end of the audio range. We can confirm that they are alive and in custody, seemingly without any form of duress."

"I have three units on standby for deployment for a rescue mission."

"Given the volatility of the situation, additional troops are inadvisable."

"Any change in condition of The Number and Primadonna?"

"Their capacities are diminished. The Number is certain he can concoct a routine in his present state. Primadonna is less optimistic and is being, frankly, a bit of a primadonna. I wouldn't consider them viable options for extraction plans right now."

"What is the plan going forward?"

"On the advice of Dr. Liefeld, and with provisional sign-off from analysts, we are attempting to locate and acquire The Icon's parents. We are operating on the theory that doing so will undermine the details of the perceived origin of his powers and potentially neutralize them."

"Have they given you odds?"

"We are far from certainty. We're still working through alternatives."

"How long will it take to decommission the power plant and render it inert?"

"The procedure necessary to restore it to functionality is a six-hour, high-complexity operation. It will require six skilled technicians in addition to the full remaining crew of the power plant. It also requires a stable power supply, which means the link to our power grid will need to be repaired. I'm comfortable calling that plan unfeasible in present conditions. An emergency plan to fully shut down the reactor can be done with the personnel on hand, provided there's at least one additional skilled technician on-site to deal with unplanned eventualities. But it, too, will require at least seven minutes of continuous external power. If the local generators are operational, they will serve the purpose, provided they are started and brought to speed before the procedure begins, and the power is not interrupted."

"Have the locals been informed?"

"We have no direct access to the locals. Most communication lines have been severed or interrupted. We have set up broadcasting beacons and are attempting to fill all television and radio channels with information, but we've yet to receive a response from within the Disincorporated Zone. And even if we did, the procedure can't begin until a technician is delivered to the power plant."

"What's the end game here, General?"

"We've analyzed footage of prior clashes with The Icon. Given the visible injuries achieved with conventional weaponry, I am assured that lethal force can be achieved with standard antitank weapons. The issue is the small size and high speed of the target. A broad bombardment is our best chance, but the collateral damage will be massive, and if it is done without precision, the power plant could be endangered."

"Far from ideal."

"I am open to suggestions."

"Short of sending troops, I have been informed I have one more key operative associated with the Guardian Project who has become available."

"Why was this individual not included in the initial or secondary deployments?"

Siegel plucked a pink Post-it note from beside the camera on his computer. "It's a little difficult to explain."

"Sir," said one of Luo's staff. "I'm sorry to interrupt, but we have located the mother. She has been apprehended and is en route to the base. ETA three hours."

"Excellent. Siegel, get your operative here, if they can be spared. We may be deploying a team soon, and in the event of failure, any and all available resources may be needed."

* * *

In the barracks, The Other Eight should have been sleeping. Between jet lag, the demands of the mission, and the likelihood of a future mission, it would have been wise to get as much rest and recovery as they could. As it so happened, sleep was the last thing on their minds. Far more important tasks took precedent.

"… Because he's a Mary Sue, that's why," Gracias said.

"Gary Stu!" Nonsensica said.

"No one is named Gary Stu!" Gracias said. "I've met people named Mary Sue. There is not and will never be a person named Gary Stu."

"That's absurd. There must be," Nonsensica said.

"Guys, can we please stop with this?" Non Sequitur said. "It's not doing anyone any good."

"What should we do instead?" Bomb Sniffer said. "Our mentor and our leader are locked up."

"All respect to Phosphor, but he's not our leader," Nonsensica said.

"Patriarch, then," Bomb Sniffer said. "And since when did being a superhero boil down to nitpicking words?"

"It's more of a nerd thing than a superhero thing," Chloroplast said.

"Are you calling me a nerd?" Nonsensica said.

"I'm calling you and Gracias both nerds," he said.

"We're all nerds," Non Sequitur said, jumping to his feet. "It is a prerequisite for this whole absurd life we've sought for ourselves. And one of the things nerds do best is argue passionately about things that don't matter. But believe it or not, I don't think that's going to help us much. So let's flex our nerdery in a different way, shall we?"

"I'm all ears," Chloroplast said.

"We've been spending all this time trying to learn stuff about who The Icon really is. Who his family was, what his life was like, right? But that's not who he is anymore, is it? We haven't even been calling him by his real name. We've been calling him by his superhero name."

"Yeah, so? We call each other by our superhero names," Bomb Sniffer said. "Frankly, if I'd realized that was going to be happening, I probably would have picked a better name."

"We could call you BS," Gracias suggested.

"Please don't."

"The point is," Non Sequitur continued, "we came to our superhero identities honestly. They are as much a part of our identity as our birth names. Unlike The Icon, we're proper superheroes."

"The man can fly and punch a hole through a building. He's a proper super-something," Chloroplast said.

"He's a super, that's for sure. But he's just playing a role. A role that was made for him and that he grew into, rather than an identity that grew out of him. I saw the pictures you three took in his room. The Icon was already a thing."

"What difference does that make?" Gracias said.

"The difference is, The Icon isn't a mystery, is he? The Icon was practically published like a guidebook for him to follow, but everyone in ChiNoKo knows all about him. And that's who he is trying to be. If we want to know what he can do, and what he will do, we can just read from the same instruction book."

"Right… Right, that makes sense," Gracias said. "But where are we going to get comic books?"

"The Chinese government has got to have access to that stuff," Chloroplast said.

"Are we sure? It's not like they knew they would be facing off against the star of a comic book one day," Gracias said.

"It's as good a guess as any," Non Sequitur said. "You should go see what they know."

"It could just be on the internet somewhere," Bomb Sniffer said. "Everything is on the internet somewhere."

"Great. You should go look into that too," Non Sequitur said.

"I'll bet if we head back to that refugee camp, some of the kids will have comics," Nonsensica said.

"Agreed. So we have three ideas to attack the same problem. Let's split up and see what Luo says. He can't turn all of them down."

***

"Permission denied."

They hadn't even been able to reach Luo. The assessment had come from the first Chinese military representative they could find, and it came after zero consideration.

"Since when are you the one who gets to deny permission for things?" Gracias said.

"The general is busy coordinating with his advisers. A new operation is likely to be launched sometime in the next seven hours. We cannot afford to divide our resources and split our attention," he said.

"You could at least ask," Nonsensica said.

"That would be splitting our attention, which I've already said we cannot afford."

"We've all met the general. The guy can multitask with the best of them. Getting a yes or no should take, what, five seconds?"

"Arranging for a visit to the refugee camp would require authorization, an escort, and oversight. The answer is assuredly no."

"But you guys must have a file or something of the goings-on in ChiNoKo," Non Sequitur said. "Let us go through it, try to find some information."

"The data available have been thoroughly processed, and anything of value has been included in the general briefing materials. You are welcome to review them again."

"We did and the only mention of The Icon that wasn't dealing with the wacko flying patrols out there was that 'the name and costume appear to reference a local fictional hero,'" Nonsensica said. "And then there's a picture and like four lines about how he has no secret identity or known weaknesses in the comics."

"Then there you have it," the assistant said.

"He's been steeped in these comics his whole life! Take it from someone in the same boat. You absorb a lot more than an outfit and a name from what you read as a kid," Gracias said.

"Look, can you at least give us internet access?" Bomb Sniffer said.

"You have access to the network," the assistant said.

"Unfettered internet access," she said. "I don't know if I've ever seen a network more fettered than this one. My school library let me access more stuff than this."

"It would be a security risk to allow you to access the internet directly from our system."

"Then give me a phone. I'm an American Zoomer. You'd be amazed what I can get done with two thumbs and a free afternoon."

"You'll find our cellular data networks are similarly 'fettered,'" he said.

"Did something happen in the last three hours to make you suddenly more dedicated to keeping us from helping than actually letting us solve the problem?" Nonsensica said.

"I am not certain you are cleared to know about the developments, and I will not be interrupting the general to make that determination."

"Cleared to know about developments? We're the whole reason there are turnip aggregate developments!" Nonsensica said.

The assistant flinched. "I'll thank you not to use your powers on me."

"Yeah, well I'll grassy ass you to actually do your job." After a moment passed without a poof of sod, Gracias shrugged. "Eh, it was a worth a shot."

"You will be summoned when you are needed and when things occur that concern you. Please remember that supersoldiers are still soldiers and must follow orders and respect protocol."

"Let me get this straight. Your army had two disastrous, tragic missions. Then we come in and get you the man responsible and a heap of intelligence, and then it's just 'thanks for the help, but go sit in the corner and wait to be called on'?" Nonsensica said.

"I don't recall thanking you for the help," he said simply. "Again, you are soldiers. You performed adequately. It doesn't excuse the clear discipline problems you are displaying now."

"Oof," Gracias said. "Sick burn on us."

Nonsensica looked to Non Sequitur. They both looked to the rest of the team. An unspoken understanding clicked into place in each of their heads.

"Fine. If that's how it is, that's how it is." Nonsensica turned. "Come on, everybody. The general's underling has put his foot down and doesn't want any useful research done. That's that."

As they marched away, the group huddled toward Nonsensica.

"I want to say that I know what you're thinking and I don't like it," Non Sequitur said.

"That's because you're a killjoy. That's your role in the team."

"Hey, I'm the official killjoy," Chloroplast said. "Non Sequitur's the official voice of reason."

"Just so we're clear," Gracias said. "We're talking about busting out of here and doing this ourselves, right?"

"That's the vibe I got," Bomb Sniffer said.

"It can't be all of us," Nonsensica said. "It needs to be an elite strike team. Like, for instance, someone with a stealth suit and someone with the ability to unlock doors."

Non Sequitur rubbed his eyes and sighed. "Why did I get stuck with the powers that are indispensable for all of the most inadvisable plans?"

"Some of us are cursed with insight, some of us are cursed with ability. And some of us, like me, have both. Plus, like I said, a stealth suit."

* * *

That evening, in what one could only hope wasn't a bad omen, a terrible storm rolled through the area. Non Sequitur and Nonsensica were already soaked as they crept through the darkened pathways of the base. The plan was a simple one. Rather, it wasn't a complex one. The execution would be a nightmare, certainly, but facing off against a supervillain and living to tell the tale had a way of putting challenges like this one in perspective.

"The motor pool is just ahead," Non Sequitur said. "Are you sure you remember the way to the refugee camp?"

"Of course I remember the way to the refugee camp. Don't you?"

"We were in the back of a personnel carrier."

"Pfft. It's a good thing you've got Class C powers, because if you had to get by on guile, you'd be a sidekick for sure. Next time, watch out the back and memorize the turns."

They flattened against the wall of one of the semipermanent structures and sidled along until they reached the corner.

"How are we going to cover the sound of the engine starting?" he said.

"We just have to wait for thunder, duh. Then we drive with the lights off and—"

"Stop right there," whispered a familiar voice behind them.

It wasn't the sort of command that was typically delivered in a whisper, but they froze in place and turned. Pvt. Summers was standing there, umbrella in one hand and thermal mug in the other.

"You know that without Dr. Aiken here, you two are my responsibility, right?" she said. "You go AWOL, the punishment hits me, too."

"We were just going to borrow some keys, borrow a car, and bring it back before anyone noticed," Nonsensica said. "They'd be none the wiser."

"I figured it out, and I'm a private. I'd like to think I'm not that special. And military vehicles don't use keys."

Nonsensica blinked. "They don't?"

"Nope. Push-button ignition. Really now, you should have noticed that."

"You never let me drive any of the vehicles during training," Nonsensica hissed.

"So what happens now?" Non Sequitur asked.

"Let me see if I can guess what you were planning. A visit to the refugee camp?" she said.

"Yeah…" Non Sequitur said.

"We were also planning to find a way to hack our way into the internet," Nonsensica said.

"Hack your way into the internet," Summers said slowly.

"You know what I mean," she said. "I have family in China. They taught me all about VPNs and stuff. Gotta master that if you want to watch streaming video."

"And how were you going to…" She shook her head. "No. No. Follow me."

"You're not going to rat us out, are you?" Nonsensica said.

"Rat you out? You should know me better than that," Pvt. Summers said. "Follow me."

She marched around the side of the building and knocked on the door. Nonsensica and Non Sequitur stood like scolded children while they waited for someone to answer the door. A dour-faced man of middle age answered.

"Lt. Bao," she said without checking the name printed on his uniform. She held up her credentials. "Pvt. Summers, acting under the authority Dr. Aiken and Gen. Siegel. I have to take Nonsensica and Non Sequitur out on some supervised drills under section eight, paragraph six of the meta-human policy document Gen. Luo signed off on."

Lt. Bao leaned aside and picked up a phone. After a short exchange in Chinese, he looked to Summers. "Duration?"

"Three to five hours, unless weather requires us to abort. We'll need to requisition a jeep."

He muttered a few more things into the phone. "You have a communicator?" he said.

"I do. Checked out from logistics under my name. I'll be the point of contact for the three of us."

"All right. Vehicle 0H6. The men at the gate will let you out."

"Thank you very much, soldier," she said.

She turned and marched toward the motor pool. When the door shut behind them, Nonsensica spoke up.

"What the heck was that?" she asked.

"Dr. Aiken drafted a document detailing special considerations that would need to be made when deploying meta-humans in a combat situation. Section eight, paragraph six: 'Meta-humans in a military setting are likely to become unmanageable if they do not receive assignments they consider to be commiserate with their powers and status with regularity. It may become necessary to deploy meta-humans on periodic low-impact training exercises to keep their mindset stable.' Basically, I'm authorized to take special measures, within reason, to keep the team sane."

"You just told them we need to go walkies," Non Sequitur said.

"Well, yeah. But in far more official language. Next time you want the rules bent, talk to me first. We're professionals at that sort of thing."

"They're not going to let us just go to the refugee camp though, will they?"

"No. But I'm the only one with a communicator, which means I'm the only one they'll be tracking the location of, plus the jeep. If you're good with hoofing it through a couple of miles of field, and can infiltrate the camp and get out again without being seen, then permission is of secondary importance. Just don't get caught. I'm not interested in a court martial."

Chapter 10

A jeep drove slowly toward the refugee camp. The rain had been hard and steady, leaving the dirt road a river of mud that threatened to mire its tires if it was not driven with care. When it passed a dense cluster of bushes, Nonsensica and Non Sequitur popped up. She held up a pair of binoculars and watched as the jeep approached the double gate of the refugee camp. Guards unlocked the gate and dragged it open, letting the driver inside. When the vehicle had vanished into the camp, she lowered the binoculars, and the pair tromped back into the open.

Pvt. Summers had dropped them off as close as she could while maintaining the ability to plausibly claim she wasn't headed directly to the refugee camp. That placed them about three miles due west of it, and the time since then had been spent making the pair progressively muddier. It was making Non Sequitur downright miserable. Nonsensica, on the other hand, was in her element.

"How crazy is it that 'hiking long distances in the mud' was the only part of boot camp that actually turned out to prepare us for a mission?" she said excitedly.

"I'd really appreciate it if you didn't sound like we were at a theme park," he said.

"Come on, man. This is what we live for. Covert missions that even our bosses don't know about?" she said.

"I'm not saying it isn't a job for the two of us. I'm saying maybe now isn't the time for manic enthusiasm," he said.

"I'll switch to serious mode when the time comes. And the time's coming pretty quick, the fence is straight ahead. You remember the plan, right?"

"Unless you've developed it more in your head, when we last left the plan it was 'Find some comic books about The Icon.'"

"Yep, you got it."

As they approached the refugee camp, some rather significant changes began to present themselves. For one, the number of lights in the camp were greatly diminished. They weren't just turned off, whole lighting platforms had been removed. The perimeter, formerly made from modular chain-link fences, had now been topped with barbed wire. The number of troops guarding the place had been increased as well. In short, it looked less like a refugee camp and more like a prison camp now.

"Guess this is why they weren't too keen on letting us come back here," Non Sequitur said.

Fortunately, during their first trip, Nonsensica had taken note of the location and direction of the surveillance cameras. In the dark and rain it was hard to be certain, but there didn't appear to be any additional camera coverage added since then. Also, though they were more frequent than during the first trip, the patrols were still far enough apart for them to reach a portion of fence in a camera blind spot and inspect it without much fear of discovery. A heap of displaced bushes and such that had to be bulldozed aside to make the refugee camp made for decent cover outside the fence.

"Okay, lockpicker. Get us in," she said.

There appeared to be only two ways into the camp, at least on this side of it. One was the double gate that allowed vehicles through. That one had a pair of troops lingering nearby, mostly because it had a permanent guard shack there and thus a place to stay out of the rain. The other was a single door with a camera fixed squarely on it. Both of them had one thing in common.

"Padlock…" he said. "And far enough on the inside that I'm not going to be able to reach through to grab it. And with a camera pointed at it. I can try that stunt the locksmith trained me to do, but not without—"

"Relax, I got you," she said.

She peered up at the wall. The razor wire would shred her if she tried to scale the wall. Latex suits were good for many things—at least, as far as she was concerned—but they didn't offer much in the way of protection. She nudged the mud with her combat boot. In their haste to build this place, the grassy field had been mostly churned to muck by the construction crews. The downpour had compounded the issue. Each step threatened to yank her boots clean off.

"Hold my stuff," she said. She unclipped her belt and slipped her pack from her back, then started working at her boot laces. "If I knew I'd be taking off my gear so many times on this trip, I'd have found some zipper-side boots," she grumbled.

Once she was stripped to nothing but her suit and goggles, she mashed at the mud beneath the fence. Only a few inches of ground were soft enough to shift, but that would do. She dropped to her belly. The slick suit combined with the rain and mud made her about as slippery as a greased pig. It was just enough to allow her to slither beneath the fence. It was wise to leave her gear behind, even if it meant running in her bare feet, because mere seconds after she'd popped up and dashed to the shadow of one of the dormitory tents, a stray soldier trudged sullenly through the area. If she'd so much as gotten her boot snagged on the fence, she wouldn't have made it to cover in time.

Non Sequitur took cover behind the debris. When the soldier was clear, both he and Nonsensica emerged from cover. Non Sequitur wouldn't be able to slip under in the same way without a shovel, and even if he did, it'd leave a much larger and more obvious divot. Nonsensica snapped her way through some hand signals, instructing him to head to cover near the gate.

He ventured as close as he dared, then reached into his bag and pulled out a small, cordless power screwdriver and a set of bits. Astoundingly, Nonsensica's stealth suit, now smeared with mud, was actually very difficult to see as she crept to the wire that fed the camera. Some struggling and cursing managed to pop the cable free of its connector. She jabbed it back in crooked, then sprinted to the single gate, now no longer under surveillance. Once there, she grabbed hold of the lock. He clicked a torx bit into the screw gun. Nothing. He swapped it for a flathead. Nothing.

Hurry up! she mouthed urgently.

He clicked in a Phillips head. The lock popped open in her hand.

"One chimpanzee, two chimpanzee..." he whispered under his breath.

She unhooked it and tossed it over the fence. He spun the shackle aside and jammed the screwdriver inside.

"Eight chimpanzee, nine chimpanzee..."

The screw backed out entirely, and the bottom of the padlock popped free. He tapped out the cylinder, then pushed it back in and spun the screw back in place.

"Twenty-four seconds," he muttered. "Not bad..."

He rushed to the door and slipped inside, clicking the lock back in place and scurrying to cover with Nonsensica.

Less than a minute later, a soldier marched irritably out into the rain and inspected the wire, but by then, the pair were far enough within the rows of dormitory tents to be in no threat of observation.

* * *

In ChiNoKo, neither Dr. Aiken nor Phosphor had slept a wink. The lights were off. The two officers who had booked them had cycled out to a single, much older officer, who promptly fell asleep.

"You know, all things considered, things could be worse," Phosphor said. "If you'd asked me to picture what it would be like to be locked up in a Chinese prison, let alone a North Korean one, I probably wouldn't have said 'three hots and a cot.' It seemed more like a 'one cold and the floor' situation. Maybe that's just me not knowing the world like I should."

"Maybe," Aiken said dully. "But I don't think ChiNoKo is representative of any real place. I strongly suspect this place has been subtly crafted to share features with the vague anytowns that comic books tend to take place in. The better to help The Icon settle into the role."

"Could be," Phosphor said.

"You're handling this incarceration remarkably well, Phosphor."

"They got my bag. Not much I can do but wait. But we got the best team in the world out there, teamed up with some really decent folks. We'll come through just fine." He stood and stretched. "You do have me thinking though, Doc. Care to answer some questions?"

"I welcome the distraction."

"Up until this whole thing started, there wasn't so much talk during training and such about how the powers worked. But since we got over here, there's been a lot of it. I never really thought about my powers. They're real. Can't deny it. But they're also all in my head? And the reason I think I got them isn't the reason I got them? It makes the ground I've been standing on all my life feel a little shaky."

"Your powers are in your head in the same way that your whole identity is in your head. Also, literally the lobe of your brain that facilitates them is physically in your head, but that's semantics. That they have a psychological basis in no way diminishes the reality of them. And your origin is your origin. It may not be the mechanism by which your powers are achieved, but it's the reason you have your powers and the reason they are what they are."

"But it's a hunk of my brain doing the powering. And somehow, some way, at some point it was me that made the decision of what those powers would be."

"Subconscious. You didn't make the decision. It was the natural result of a thousand factors working in conjunction. It was no more in your control than a phobia or a favorite color."

"Why not? What's to keep someone from just deciding to have better powers?" he asked. "Not that I'd do it. I'm happy with the ones I got. But now and then, a little more oomph would for sure solve some problems."

"That's the question that decades of research and endless observations and experiments have been seeking to answer. The Icon is the closest we've come to doing it, but it wasn't the hero's choice but that of his creator. Our best guess right now is that there literally don't exist the proper neuropathways to connect the full functionality of the Liefeld lobe to the conscious mind.

It's like… the engine of a car. You can press the accelerator and turn the wheel, but there are dozens of things separating you from the actual pumping of the pistons. You can only bring about the effects that the structure of the lobe has facilitated, but you can't choose the structure."

* * *

Stealth was a good deal easier during a late-night downpour. Nonsensica and Non Sequitur could have been stomping their feet as they walked and no one more than a few yards away could have heard them. The tightly packed dormitory tents and the knowledge of where the scattered cameras were also meant that staying hidden seldom required more than a quick sidle between two structures. But they weren't here simply for the thrill of a covert operation. They had information to find. And finding that information called for not only locating someone willing and able to provide it but talking to that person without alerting either the guards or other people who might not be so helpful.

Non Sequitur's powers turned out to be unnecessary, as the refugee tents were not only unlocked but lacked locks entirely. The "windows" were simply bits of transparent plastic that were stitched into the canvas walls with an extra flap of canvas to act as a shade. Most of them were covered, but they glanced into every open window in hopes of spotting a likely informant. Thus far, they'd only seen dim interiors and exhausted families.

"This isn't working," Non Sequitur said. "We need a new approach."

"I'm all ears," Nonsensica said.

"If there's any actual comics here, they'll be in the locked contraband shed on the far end, but it won't do any good to just go and search. We need an expert to at least point us in the right direction of where to look for good information. Just looking in windows and hoping for the best won't help us."

"Still waiting for a better idea, hot shot," she said.

"We need to go somewhere where we can be relatively sure we'll get access to someone on an individual basis. And really, there's only one place in this crowded camp where that might be true."

She wiped some rain from her goggles. "You're going to have us hide in the latrine, aren't you?"

"I was more thinking behind the latrine. This is a camp full of families. There's going to be at least one kid who can't hold it until morning. And the refugee latrines are opposite the troop ones."

"It beats creeping around looking in windows, I guess. And then what? Just whisper?"

"And be ready to make a run for it, I guess."

"You're the one making a plan that ends in a desperate escape from a swarm of guards if it fails," she said. "I love it. Let's do it."

Reaching the bathrooms without appearing on camera required a good deal more careful routing, because they were one of the portions of the interior of the camp that was undeniably under surveillance. Whether or not they fully succeeded would remain a mystery—they couldn't be sure of the field of view on the cameras—but no guards had come running. Like everything else in this camp, the restrooms were designed around efficiency: a long, narrow tent, a barely glorified outhouse. The walls were thinner than those of the dorm tents. Non Sequitur doubted they did much to keep the rain out, because they did nothing at all to keep the smell in. It made their wait a cold, wet, and unpleasant one. Mercifully, it was not a long one.

A boy in his early teens trudged unhappily toward the out-house, escorted by a soldier. He slipped into the latrine. Non Sequitur and Nonsensica maneuvered to behind where he was settling in. They crossed their fingers. Nonsensica spoke up.

"Hey!" she hissed through the thin wall, just loud enough to be heard over the rain.

The boy released a startled yelp.

"Relax! We're superheroes! Nonsensica and Non Sequitur," she said.

The guard in front said something in Chinese. The boy replied.

"I said a spider got on my leg," the boy said.

"Good thinking."

"Are you really Nonsensica?" he said.

"Who else?"

166

"Prove it."

"Ròu shīrén," Nonsensica said, her powers selecting Chinese this time.

"Whoa, again!" he whispered, presumably after the words made him twitch.

"We're in a hurry, kid. And we need your help."

"The real Nonsensica. And Non Sequitur is there too? Do something!"

"Not really much I can do through a wall. Sorry," Non Sequitur said.

"Aww... Well, how can I help?"

"We need to know more about The Icon," Nonsensica said.

"Are you gonna beat him up?"

"Only if we have to," Non Sequitur said.

"Good, he's the reason we had to leave town, and he's a Gary Stu."

"That's right, he is," Nonsensica said.

"What do you need to know?" the kid asked.

"Anything that might help us subdue him long enough to set things right again. We're thinking the comics might help. Does anything stand out?"

"Um... He has no weaknesses."

"We figured that much."

"He doesn't have another team yet. He's always talking about having a team, but he never gets one."

"Okay, good. What else?"

"Um... OH! There's the secret!"

"Shh," Non Sequitur said urgently. "Keep your voice down."

"There's a secret hidden in some of the comics. It's always the same. Something about dots and rings. And there's always the words 'The Icon will show, The Icon will know' on the page."

"What's the solution?"

"I don't know. Dad said they don't actually give you enough information."

"Anything else we should know?"

"He always wins, and he just goes on and on about how great ChiNoKo is when really it's kind of bad, and he never has any trouble fighting the evil outsiders. There's not even a main villain. He just fights everybody and beats them in a couple of punches."

The guard shouted something.

"He wants me to hurry up."

"Okay. You've been a real help, kid," Nonsensica said. "When we get this thing sorted and everyone can get back to their lives, you'll know you helped it happen."

They hurried away, weaving as direct a path as possible to the contraband shed. As with all other locked doors in the camp, it was secured with a padlock. But a quick application of Non Sequitur's powers opened, disassembled, unlocked, and reassembled the lock. They hurried inside and shut the door.

It was pitch-black, and there wasn't any lighting installed. Among Nonsensica's gear was a small LED light. They clicked it on to reveal endless rows of shelves, heaped with canvas sacks with little white tags attached.

"Look at this," Non Sequitur muttered. "These people's whole lives piled up here because one of us turned out to be too much to handle."

"It's not their whole lives," she said. "It's just what they could carry. It's our job to get them back home."

"I feel like this was inevitable. It's like if every human being had the potential to become a nuclear bomb or something."

"With great power comes great responsibility. That old chestnut. He just didn't have his head right when the powers showed up."

"Yeah, that's the problem. It's not like someone is out there handing out great powers to people with great responsibility. And this guy, they tried to create the responsibility and use them to create the powers."

"Hey, look. If things were going to go bad like this, better to get it out of the way fast."

"That's assuming this is the outlier. What if every hard-core power set ends up in the hands of someone without their head right? What if not having your head right is the only thing that can produce hard-core powers?"

"Then we'll have to make sure we're trained up and ready to take them out. Simple as that."

"That's assuming we make it out of this alive."

"Yeah, Non Sequitur. I tend to make plans that assume I'll be alive to carry them out. I'm silly like that."

"I just—"

"We don't have time for a crisis of confidence. Keep your eye on the prize."

They moved along, feeling the outside of the bags for the telltale flat rectangles of comic books. In any other community, the chances of finding any comics let alone the specific ones they were after would have been miniscule. Here, nearly every third bag contained some sort of comic or another, and nearly all of them were Icon comics. The printing was poor. More like a newspaper than a magazine. Most of them were ratty, not collector's items. They were creased. Dog-eared. Used. Non Sequitur focused on snapping pictures of any page that was dense with text. Nonsensica did a far more holistic analysis, fanning through whole issues and trying to absorb their contents.

"They worship this guy. This one actually has hearts drawn around his face." She held up the page. "Except he doesn't have a face. There's just a gray silhouette of a head."

"I guess because they couldn't print a mirror. They wanted people to imagine themselves in that role." He flicked a page in the book he was paging through. "Though a bunch of people drew faces in, like it was an activity page. This one gave him a mustache. ... And this one gave him cat ears and whiskers."

"They wanted one specific person to imagine himself in that role. Look at this view. Every issue ends with the same view of ChiNoKo, and it's a match for the view Bomb Sniffer shared from out the window of The Icon's house." She paused. "Wait a minute," she said. "How come they didn't find any comics in his house? How come they didn't find any equipment in his house? And the uniforms were just in a suitcase, right? Like they'd been brought from somewhere else? Why was that?"

"Those are good questions," Non Sequitur said.

She stuffed a comic back into one of the bags and replaced it on the shelf. The next bag had something that looked like an old-fashioned telephone book.

"Oh ho!" she said. "I bet we'll have our answer, soon enough." She held it up. "We have our winner. Omnibus. The Complete Icon." She snapped a picture of the bag containing the belongings. "Enough, we're done here."

* * *

Gen. Luo's eyes snapped open at the sound of a knock on the frame around the door of his quarters. He'd spent so much of his life staying in temporary housing, the sort of places where a door sturdy enough to knock on was the exception rather than the rule, that he'd developed the same instinctive reaction to the hollow tap of knuckles on extruded aluminum struts that most people reserved for their telephone or doorbell.

He hadn't been properly sleeping, simply dozing. Once again, the expectation of a full night's sleep was something he'd lost long ago. For him, "pajamas" were simply his uniform minus the jacket. He pulled on said jacket and smoothed any sleep-induced wrinkles, then opened his door. It was one of his endless legion of assistants and technicians.

"Sir, the mother is in the base. We've moved her to the briefing room. The members of The Other Eight who were responsible for the mission that penetrated The Icon's home are being gathered."

"Excellent." Luo stepped outside into the drizzle. "And Dr. Liefeld?"

"We're having a bit of trouble waking him. His advanced age, you see. But we're getting Borisov now."

"It's just as well. He's more valuable for his biological perspective, and this is well beyond that."

"There is, er, a bit of a problem, sir," the assistant said as they marched the short distance from his quarters to the briefing room.

"A problem? And why wouldn't you have made that clear before the rest of the information?"

"There is no immediate solution, so there is only one path forward without your insight. I wanted to set that path in motion before I disturbed you."

"What is the problem?"

"Our search for the parents of The Icon began even before Dr. Liefeld suggested it. We'd begun the search based upon the DNA in the blood sample. That was how we found this woman. She's inarguably the biological mother of The Icon, and her DNA was in a private medical database we were able to access."

They slipped into the briefing room, where an extremely rattled-looking Russian woman was sitting in a folding chair surrounded by soldiers, Gracias, and Bomb Sniffer.

"It ain't her, General," Gracias said, waggling some printed-out photos. "You got the wrong lady."

Luo took the photos. He recognized them as blown-up, isolated, enhanced portions of the photos The Other Eight had taken of the walls in The Icon's home. While there was a passing resemblance to The Icon himself, there was no resemblance at all to the woman who they'd identified as The Icon's mother, based upon her prominence in the photos.

"He's adopted, duh," Gracias said. "That, at least, is from Superman's origin. They got one part right."

"And we didn't suppose this was a possibility?" Luo said, radiating anger in the general direction of his subordinates.

"We had no leads to go on but the DNA. Our search of photo records for the woman in those photos came up empty. They were very careful in keeping her out of public records."

"Then we knew before this woman had even been found that she wasn't the one," Luo fumed. "Do we have a file?"

The assistant handed him a folder. He flipped it open.

"A resident of Sanhe Hui, naturalized Chinese citizen of Russian extraction. Inactive but highly developed Liefeld lobe. No children on official record. Egg donor."

"We have to assume that the woman in the photos is at least his adoptive mother, and possibly a surrogate," the assistant said.

"We don't have to assume anything. Assuming wastes time and gives us this, a woman with no value to us whatsoever, when time is running out."

Dr. Borisov was hauled into the room. Luo had to restrain himself from grabbing the man by the neck and wringing the answers he wanted out of him.

"What are the circumstances of The Icon's birth? What is his parentage!" he demanded.

"I see you've found one of his mothers," Borisov said simply.

"How many moms does he have?" Bomb Sniffer asked.

Luo raised a hand and motioned to his assistant. The woman was removed by the soldiers. The door shut behind them.

"Speak," he said.

"That woman is responsible for half of his genetic material. A surrogate mother was used for the actual birthing, and a trained operative was responsible for raising him. The Icon has three mothers and two fathers. We had anticipated this potential avenue of attack and muddied the question of parentage. One way to make the truth easy to disregard is to make it complex to understand. Bring him that woman and she will be a stranger to him. Somehow find photos of his actual birth mother and the woman in those photos will be a stranger to him. Find the woman who actually raised him and persuade her to tell the truth and blood tests will cast doubt on it. The Icon was engineered to lack any form of solid connection that would be in any way a potential liability to the program."

"So, what? We're back to square one?" Gracias said.

"You've never been anywhere beyond square one," Borisov said. "And you have very little chance of leaving square one."

"Borisov, that power plant is on borrowed time. You will aid us, or I will ensure that you are in the path of the fallout when it blows."

"Then so be it! Luo, we tried to create a sword and a shield, but in our fear that it might be used against us, we also created a bomb. Any attempt to defuse it will be just as likely to set it off. I cannot offer you information that can help you, because there is no information that can help you. I will not answer your questions, because if you get enough information to convince yourselves you can act, you'll only be risking setting off prematurely that which may at this point already be inevitable. That time that's running out is precious not because it gives you the opportunity to stop him but because it is the only time left before some sort of tragedy. We should be using this time for mass evacuation."

"We will not forfeit land and lives because you are certain your weapon cannot be safely destroyed." Luo turned to this assistant. "I want bombardment scenarios tested by engineers and geologists. I want to know at what range and at what intensity we can deliver ordinance to the Disincorporated Zone with minimal threat to the power plant. And I want a crew of technicians ready to deploy during the bombardment, both to react to failures and render the plant safe as quickly as possible. We're through treating this as anything but an extermination. Back to your quarters, all of you."

*　*　*

Gracias paced along beside Bomb Sniffer. The tail end of the rain wasn't enough for them to hustle to shelter or even try to shield their heads. Both of them had greater things to worry about than some wet clothes.

"Things are about to get bad," he said.

"They were already bad," she said. "They're about to get way, way worse. I can already smell all sorts of new explosives being moved into the base. Heavy-duty propellants. Mortars and stuff, I guess. And that's just what's here."

Gracias stopped and held out his hand to stop Bomb Sniffer. "Check it out," he said. "They're back."

Non Sequitur and Nonsensica were pacing along behind Pvt. Summers. They looked like they'd been through hell. Both of them were caked with mud. The rain had rinsed most of the muck from Nonsensica's slick black suit, but Non Sequitur's standard military camo was more brown than green. But rather than fatigue from a sleepless night, they both looked energized.

"That, Bomb Sniffer, is what hope looks like," he said.

They trotted toward their fellow members of The Other Eight.

"So, uh… what's—" Bomb Sniffer said, glancing back and forth between them and Pvt. Summers.

"I know about your little operation. I was the chaperone."

"Yo! You got Summers in on the scheme. That's next-level. How'd it go?"

"We got the stuff and we found the riddle," Nonsensica squealed, barely able to keep from proclaiming it at the top of her lungs.

"The what?" Gracias said.

"There's some sort of a riddle embedded in The Icon's comics," Non Sequitur said.

"Did you solve it?" Bomb Sniffer asked.

"Not yet, but how hard could it be once all of us put our heads together? Let's go!"

They slipped into their quarters. The Number was the only one inside who was still awake. Chloroplast was out like a light, and Primadonna was doing better than most at adapting to the local time zones, thanks in no small part to the earplugs and eye mask that turned her cot into something akin to a sensory deprivation chamber. Pvt. Summers and the rest of the crew gathered around a bunk, and the omnibus was laid out.

"A kid in the refugee camp told us there was a secret or riddle. We found an omnibus, and the thing shows up four or five times. Written on walls, stuff like that. It's always in English, and always says the same thing."

She found a page with the riddle in graffiti on a wall.

Three points to a ring.
Icon surrounds all.
Central is the thing
    that helps villains fall.

"That's it?" Gracias said.

"That's it. It shows up all over the place, but that's all there is," Non Sequitur said.

"So, we figure there must be a reason it's in English, that's one thing," Nonsensica said.

"Probably so it rhymes," Gracias said. "So we need to find out what 'three' is, and which way it's pointing. Because it's pointing to a ring, right? Maybe a power ring, like the Green Lantern's. These people ripped off enough other DC heroes, they could have thrown the Green Lantern in there."

"Icon surrounds it all? Are they talking about the border? Is this just where he learned he needs to patrol the border?" The Number said.

"I think that'd be pretty obvious," Nonsensica said. "I'm wondering if that 'central is the thing' line means there's a thing called Central?"

"Yeah, that could also be a power source," Bomb Sniffer said. "Central is the thing that helps villains fall."

"Central would be a good name for a supercomputer," Gracias said.

"What we're going to find isn't as important as where we're going to find it," Nonsensica said. "This is clearly giving a location."

"Forgive me," Pvt. Summers said. "But how important or valuable could the thing this riddle is pointing to really be? If it was in a published book that was practically assigned reading to the whole city."

"Well, the kid who pointed us to it said there wasn't enough information to solve the riddle," Non Sequitur said.

"Wait… they couldn't solve it, what are our chances?" Gracias said.

"This is meant for The Icon to solve. It's got to be," Nonsensica said. "The Icon comics are like a how-to book for what The Icon should be and what he should do. So it would require information that only The Icon has. And we know a heck of a lot more about the real Icon than most of the readers of this comic did, at least until The Icon showed up. So, come on. First line, 'Three points to a ring.' What is three, and what ring?"

The Number scratched his head. "Hold on. Hold on. This is only in English, right?" he said. "So maybe wordplay is involved. Though there's not a ton of amount of room for wordplay in this mess."

"What if 'points' isn't a verb, though? What if it's a noun?"

"It's been a while since I did Mad Libs last, buddy," Gracias said.

"Three points. Like a score," The Number said. "Oooh. Like someone has to score three points to win a ring? Three points in what?"

"No, no," Bomb Sniffer said. "Three points to a ring. You can define a circle with three points."

"You can?" Nonsensica said.

"Come on. They teach that in geometry class," Bomb Sniffer said.

"It's been a while since geometry class too," Gracias said.

"Well, three points on the edge of a circle define the circle," she said.

"On the edge," Nonsensica said. "So 'Icon surrounds all' could be referring to that. Icons on the edge of a circle."

"Don't tell me there are three Icons," The Number said. "We can't even handle one."

"No, no, no. Wait… Pvt. Summers, do we still have the un-classified briefing materials available to us?" Non Sequitur said.

"There's not much that falls under that heading. Basically population data, maps…"

"Maps, great. That's all we need," Non Sequitur said.

"Are you onto something?" Nonsensica said as Summers marched off to fetch them.

"I might be," he said.

He flipped through the pages of the comic. "There are issues where they dedicate statues. We breezed through them on the ride home. But there really is at least one statue of The Icon. Remember? We saw it."

"Right, yes. He was a lot more muscular than the real guy," Nonsensica said.

"Anyway, we found a statue dedication comics twice. …. Here's the first one. We figured it was just repetition. They repeat so much in this thing. But they don't give the address. There's the bridge in the background, though."

He flipped through until he found a second dedication comic. "And this one has the power plant in the background.

Those pages are way higher-quality than the rest of the art. Like they were working from photographic reference. And even in that short little jaunt into ChiNoKo, there's no place you could put one statue that would put those two landmarks in the background at those angles."

Pvt. Summers reappeared with laminated maps and dry-erase markers. Nonsensica unrolled one on the ground. They were aerial photos, and at the sort of resolution that was the hallmark of a disputed territory bordering a global superpower. That is to say, very high. She dropped to her hands and knees and looked closely.

"Okay, so, if the bridge is there, and it's at that angle, that first statue in the comic is the one we passed. Which was right… here. I can just barely tell that's a statue." She put a dot on it. "And for the power plant to be at that angle, the other one would need to be… somewhere… here. Bang. Am I looking for a third?"

"The third is the actual Icon, right? That's how you keep it a secret until The Icon shows up. It's going to be The Icon's apartment," Gracias said.

"Riiiight. Get down here and mark that," Nonsensica said.

He crouched and walked his fingers along the map. "It's this spot right here. Okay. Three dots. Bomb Sniffer, draw the circle."

"Why me?" she said.

"Because you know how."

"I remembered that you could do it. Now you expect me to remember how?" She grumbled under her breath. "Gosh darn it, you're going to have me doing integrals next. I know it was something to do with midpoints and perpendicular lines…"

Chapter 11

D r. Aiken shook from sleep at the clack of a heavy door.
At least once during every trip he'd ever taken, he'd
awoken in his hotel room and felt that moment of confusion and concern at waking up in an unfamiliar place. It turns
out, those moments were nothing compared to waking up in a
jail somewhere between North Korea and China. Rather than
realizing that the most worrisome part of this strange place was
potentially missing a questionable continental breakfast, in Chi-
NoKo, the looming threat of a mad meta-human and a nuclear
meltdown were on the menu.

Phosphor was snoring merrily away in the other cell as the
door to the rest of the station opened and the young officer who
had booked them walked in. She looked haunted as she paced
inside.

"Officer," Dr. Aiken acknowledged.

She looked over her shoulder and crept closer to the bars.
"Can they win?" she whispered.

"I'm sorry?"

"Your team. The Other Eight. Can they win? If I help you,
can they win?"

He sat up and tried to shake the lingering residue of sleep
from his head. "That is our hope. We certainly aim to."

"My husband came home last night and he..." She paused.
"Things are worse at the power plant than you think. A few
months ago, he said they had a crew of supervisors from the
city planning board. They had him and a small team disconnect
some monitoring devices. The sort of things that raise alarms if
certain safety measures aren't properly engaged. They were never

reconnected. And ever since The Icon showed up, systems have been acting up in the plant. All he has is a binder of procedures to go by. Half of the things in the binder aren't doing anything, either because of the thing he had to do months ago or because of the half-finished maintenance the inspectors did before The Icon chased them away. The other half were only buying time. But all the numbers are in the yellow now. A general fault warning has been lit for days, and they're out of pages. It's going to fail. It's going to fail soon. And we don't have the skills to fix it. The Icon knows this. He came and asked and we begged for help but he won't let anyone in. He just… recited some speech about how only the people of ChiNoKo know how to properly care for the heart of ChiNoKo. I don't want him to be killed. But, if something isn't done…"

"I understand. And I assure you, we are dedicated to doing whatever we can do. You can't let us out, I realize. The Icon will keep us from crossing the border, in all likelihood, and you'd be risking yourself by doing so. But if you could give us Phosphor's bag…"

"It doesn't contain a weapon, does it?"

"It contains an endless sequence of fluorescent bulbs and, with any luck, a still-functional communicator."

She hesitated, but only for a moment. She took a quick trip to the evidence room and returned with his bag.

"Phosphor," Aiken said.

He snorted awake. "Yeah, boss," he said automatically.

The officer shakily handed him his bag.

"The officer says the power plant is in bad shape. She's willing to help," Aiken said. "Get the communicator out."

"Oh, sure thing. And much obliged," he said.

He reached into the bag. There was a bit of clinking, but he was able to fish out the communicator, which the endless attempt to empty the bag when they'd first arrived failed to uncover, thanks to Phosphor's powers. The Icon's toss against the wall had done a bit of damage to it. The case was fractured in one corner, and the glass of the screen was feathered with fresh breaks. Nonetheless, it was still functional.

"Needs a charge badly," he said. "I think the doc's bag has a charger in it."

The officer nodded and scurried off. Phosphor depressed the push-to-talk.

"This is Phosphor. I've got the doc here. Anyone listening?" he said.

The reply was almost immediate: a communication officer in the Chinese Army. "Acknowledged, Phosphor. What is your status?"

"We're not hurt. We're still locked up. But it seems like the local law enforcement is ready to play ball," he said.

"We need to talk to command," Aiken said. "The power plant situation has deteriorated. We've been operating on a timeline that we can no longer trust."

"Acknowledged. We'll put you through to command now."

* * *

The Other Eight was as well rested as they were likely to get. It had taken twenty-five minutes, and a fair amount of scrounging, but they had been able to calculate the position of the mystery location indicated by the riddle. Using borrowed tape measures and a carpenter's square from the toolshed, two intersecting lines were scribed to pinpoint the center of the circle. The answer was quite convincing. It fell almost precisely in the middle of a small museum at the corner of a public park. Once they had that information, they'd resolved to rest up, because surely once they brought this to the command team, they'd be sent on an away mission to capture the source of The Icon's power—or whatever it was the museum held. They awoke to find the base to be buzzing. Lots of new military gear had been moved into place. Three new helicopters had landed in the wee hours of the morning, and six tanks had rolled in.

"You get the feeling there's not really a place for The Other Eight in a fight where tanks and helicopters are duking it out with a flying brick?" Chloroplast asked, peeking out the window at the latest piece of heavy gear maneuvering just beyond the walls of the base.

"They're getting the sledgehammer ready because they don't know we've got the surgical laser powered up and ready to fire," Gracias said.

Pvt. Summers opened the door and stood in the doorway. "We're bugging out," she said.

"We're what?" Bomb Sniffer said.

"They're withdrawing us. Breaking the base down. This area is no longer safe."

"What happened?" Gracias said.

"What's going to happen to Aiken and Phosphor?" Chloroplast asked.

"Gen. Siegel is in the loop. Everything possible is being done to—" she began.

"Bull!" Nonsensica snapped. "If they're not sending us in, then they're not doing everything possible. What's changed? Why is this suddenly so urgent?"

"Dr. Aiken and Phosphor were able to persuade local authorities to deliver the communicator they left in the bank to the power plant, and the situation is dire. A failure is imminent. It may already be in an irretrievable failure state. The only question is whether it will be catastrophic or not."

"Then they've got to get us in there," Non Sequitur said. "We've got to get Phosphor and the doc out."

"Unless Siegel convinces Luo that's the move, it is out of our hands."

Nonsensica gritted her teeth. "I'll show him what's out of our hands."

Pvt. Summers braced herself in the doorway. "Nonsensica, don't do something that will endanger the mission," she said.

"The mission is endangering us. They're going to carpet-bomb half a city, while the other half has a ticking nuclear bomb in it, and hope for the best. You tell me how anything we'd do would be worse than that."

"We've got to say our piece," Non Sequitur said. "The police station is awfully close to the bridge, which means Phosphor and the doc are going to be right on the fringe of the attack if they don't let them out of prison."

"I believe the police have agreed to release them in exchange for help taking care of the power plant," Pvt. Summers said.

"And how will they get out before the tanks start rolling and the bombs start dropping? And what happens if they fly a plane overhead to drop a bomb and The Icon just zooms up and punches a hole in it and the thing lands on the power plant?" Nonsensica said.

"We figured things out. We learned things they don't know," Bomb Sniffer said.

"It is a closed discussion," Pvt. Summers said. "It's between our superiors and Gen. Luo's team."

"You give me thirty seconds and I'll make it an open discussion," Non Sequitur said.

"Why are we here if not to handle this?" Gracias said. "Why are we here if not to be the last line of defense against the supervillain?"

Pvt. Summers shut her eyes and took a breath. "You're going to make me make a habit of bending the rules and stretching my orders, aren't you?"

"I believe you mean 'helping to save the day.' And yeah, like it or not, you're a part of the team. It goes with the territory," Nonsensica said.

She shook her head. "Follow me. We'll take one shot at it, but if they shut you down, you do as you are ordered. As much as you want to help, and as much as you worry they are taking the wrong approach, the surest way to loss of life is chaos and confusion, and that's exactly what we'll get if you try to go rogue."

She turned and marched toward the command tent. The whole team kept pace behind her. As they approached, the morning sun glaring down on the lingering puddles from the long night of rain, a soldier guarding the door straightened up and placed his hand on the grip of his gun in its holster.

"The team would like permission to join the mission discussion," Pvt. Summers said.

The soldier held his ground. He didn't even dignify them with eye contact.

"Hey!" Nonsensica snapped. "We're the superheroes, remember? You flew us in from the USA special to help you deal with this?"

"You know, you probably shouldn't be standing so close to the door," Gracias said. "Lots of really important people in there. If they have to leave in a hurry to do some military business, you might be in their way." He elbowed Non Sequitur and got a subtle nod in return.

"Part of our team is still behind enemy lines, and they're planning to make a massive mistake," Bomb Sniffer said.

The door popped open behind the soldier, bumping into him. He took a step forward, swiftly clearing the way for whoever was coming out.

"Oh, right, yeah," Gracias said, staring through empty doorway he'd stepped clear of. "The big boss is waving us in. See you when we're done."

Before they could be stopped, the team barged through, with Non Sequitur bringing up the rear with a conspicuous twist and shove of the door latch before yanking it shut behind him. The only familiar faces in the room were Luo, one of his assistants, and Gen. Siegel on the video link. The rest were presumably lower-level advisers and subcommanders.

"What are they doing in here?" Luo barked. "This is a confidential strategy session."

"Yeah, and we're a confidential strategy," Nonsensica said. "So we belong here."

"Get them out," Luo demanded.

Two guards on either side of the door stepped forward and gripped their weapons.

"Gen. Luo, this is your operation, but there are elements of this mission that would be better served by my team than yours," Siegel said.

"Your team is a parade of gimmicks and low-discipline wild cards, and there is too much on the line to rely upon them," Luo countered.

"We're the only people who have gone after The Icon and not gotten anyone killed or pummeled. We get things done," Nonsensica said.

Gen. Luo's expression remained steady and stoic, but the pressure smoldering under the surface was evident. "Put The Icon on screen," he said.

The second monitor populated with a grid of six views of The Icon. He was airborne, eyes flitting madly between troops on the ground and aircraft circling at high altitude. His expression was, in a word, volatile. He knew something massive was about to happen. The only question was whether the first blow would come from above or below.

"Does that look like a target you'll be able to subdue? He is currently one-hundred meters above the ground and on the verge of snapping," Luo said.

The Icon vanished from view. Cameras shifted and swept in search of him. A sonic boom rattled the walls. One by one spotters found and zoomed in on him. Non Sequitur looked at one of the lesser screens as one of the techs updated his location.

"He's almost directly over the power plant now. That took moments. You really think you have anything out there fast enough to hit him hard enough to take him out?" Non Sequitur said.

"You're sending someone in to fix the plant, right? And they actually have to make it there, right?" Gracias said.

"You need someone to keep him in position, to stall him," Nonsensica said.

"To distract him," Bomb Sniffer said. "That's what we do, remember?"

"There isn't time for an extraction mission," Luo said. "We can't have troops on the ground in ChiNoKo."

"We're not troops, we're superheroes. Or, I don't know, commandos. Whatever fits into your planning. We're special. And we're willing to take the risk," Chloroplast said.

"And we may have made a breakthrough in what it will take to depower him. There was a riddle in The Icon comics…" Gracias said.

"And we solved it," Bomb Sniffer said.

"There's a secret in the museum. We don't know what it is but—" Nonsensica began.

"You solved a riddle in a children's publication. It points to an unknown target of unknown value. And I don't recall providing you with the resources to acquire such information, but for the moment, that doesn't matter. We will be running two simultaneous missions to deliver nuclear technicians to the power plant. The combat operation will commence as soon as the power plant is rendered safe or at the moment it appears The Icon will interfere in its repair. Deployment of maximum force cannot be delayed. If you are in the area of the operation, you will be caught in the bombardment."

"You put us on the ground and there won't be a bombardment, because we'll have him handled, if not defeated, for as long as you need," Nonsensica said.

"You send us in and we'll go for the secret base or whatever. He'll try to stop us from crossing the border," Bomb Sniffer said. "If he tries that, you'll know where he is for as long as we can keep him there."

"If we get past him, he'll chase us. The bridge is the cutoff line for the bombardment, right?" Nonsensica said. "Good news, the secret place is south of the bridge. If we make it that far and it is an important secret base, he'll try to stop us and try to defend it and he'll still be right where you want him."

"And if what's hidden there is the source of his power, like we think it might be, then you won't even have to bombard him, because we'll depower him then and there," Gracias said.

"And if all that fails, then you drop the bombs and let us worry about how we'll survive," Non Sequitur said.

"I know your minds have been just as poisoned by the meta-human condition as The Icon's has, but regardless of your willingness to pursue a suicide mission, I have no interest in needlessly expending your lives in an ultimately doomed maneuver. If you attempt to defy my orders and enter the area of operation, my soldiers will detain you. Now leave before I have my troops remove you. This no longer concerns—"

A burst of alerts and radio chatter interrupted him. He turned to see The Icon streaking skyward, roaring toward one of the bombers circling the area.

"What is he doing?" Luo growled. "We're well clear of his airspace."

"I don't think he is able to make that determination accurately at that altitude, sir," his tech said.

The bomber veered aside. The Icon pursued. Spotter cameras strained to keep him in view as he drew closer to the aircraft. He reached the tail of the bomber and grabbed hold of it. He may have had a superhero's strength and speed, but aluminum was still aluminum. Regardless of what The Icon thought would happen, fingertips clutching a thin strip of metal did little more than punch through and tear a handful of metal away. It wasn't enough to significantly damage the bomber, but the lack of resistance when he pulled sent The Icon darting backward. By the time he recovered, he decided the bomber had drifted far enough from ChiNoKo and shifted closer to the center of the territory again.

"Maintain that perimeter," Luo said. "I can't believe we're letting this science experiment dictate our minimum safe distance."

"At that range, we'll add an additional forty-five seconds between the attack order and the first ordinance on target," one of the techs said.

"Noted." Luo steadied himself, as though he was expecting to take a blow. "How far beyond the borders of the Disincorporated Zone did The Icon travel?"

"Based upon the range finders from the spotters, at his maximum, approximately seventeen kilometers. We can get a more precise distance in a moment, based upon the moment of contact with the bomber," a tech said. He punched a few numbers into his console. "Maximum, eighteen thousand seven hundred and twenty meters," the tech clarified.

"Your FOB is only twenty kilometers away from ChiNoKo, correct? If he'd headed west instead of north, he would have been within visual range of it," Siegel said. "If he's beginning to challenge the borders, we need to plan for the possibility that he will venture as far as the staging area. That would be the wise tactical move on his part and would cripple the potential precision of the response."

"I don't think we need to worry about The Icon employing sound military tactics," Luo said. "More to the point, we have a larger issue. The border had at least made him predictable. If that benefit is eroding, then any hope of containment is eroding with it. I have very specific orders from high command regarding how to proceed if containment is lost. How soon can we have our tech in place in the plant?"

"Minimum time to insertion, thirty-seven minutes, assuming best-case scenario on both insertion missions," the assistant said. "And the most optimistic estimates of how long it will take to provide a reliable assessment as to whether the bombardment will be a threat to the operation of the plant is another twenty-five minutes."

"Never mind whether the bombardment will be a danger to the power plant. How long to render the power plant safe if we abandon all but the most critical safety measures?"

The assistant spoke softly into his communicator. "Absolute minimum of forty-eight minutes to stabilize the power plant, including at least seven minutes of uninterrupted power during the critical stage. Again, assuming our assessment of the plant is accurate."

"Define stabilize," Luo said.

"All reactors fully stalled and disabled."

"How long to remove all fissile material?"

"Weeks."

Luo rubbed his temples. "Eighty-five minutes from deployment to safe-state. He's already swiping at us at this range. If we pull back any farther, we may as well give Icon warning before we attack. He'll be able to be well clear before the first weapons can be fired." He stood in silence for a moment. "Gen. Siegel. You have been briefed on the high command's containment protocols," he said.

"I have," he replied flatly.

"Do you consent to elevating your team to the necessary security clearance to discuss containment?" Luo said.

"Section seven of the mission briefing," Gen. Siegel said.

"Is that the one where we're war criminals if we say anything to anyone about what we're about to hear?" Gracias whispered to Nonsensica.

"Yes," she said.

"I thought we were already facing that," he said.

"Would you shut up," she hissed.

Luo turned to his assistant. "We are moving this to the briefing room. Alert us to any significant changes."

* * *

Luo stood before the team.

"When it was made clear the scope of the abilities The Icon possessed, the high command determined that if The Icon could not be controlled or contained, then he would be considered the greatest threat to national and global security. Strategic weaponry is authorized."

"Strategic weaponry," Nonsensica said. "As in the next step up from tactical? As in you're going to take out the whole city!?"

"Whatever it takes to contain the threat."

"Greater than a nuclear meltdown? It'll kill hundreds of thousands of people. It'll irradiate millions of square miles."

"He is virtually immune to conventional weaponry. We've clocked his speed at bursts exceeding the speed of sound. He is capable of flight. Has been observed lifting twelve thousand kilograms. Someone like that could assassinate heads of state. Destroy infrastructure. The damage could easily surpass even the most dire estimates of the power plant's failure. I have my orders. The Icon is to be destroyed by any means necessary. But any attack can only succeed if he remains in place long enough to be overcome by ordinance. I don't want to wipe out the city if I do not have to. I don't want to trigger a nuclear catastrophe if I don't have to. But I can and will do both of those things if I do have to. The worst of all possible worlds is if the Disincorporated Zone is destroyed and The Icon survives."

He turned, arms crossed behind his back. "We have to run the missions concurrently. He must be kept within the borders. You want your mission? Keep The Icon occupied. Do what needs to be done to keep him in the city. If you neutralize him, the assault will be called off. If you don't, the bombs fall. But The Icon must be inside. Even if you are still inside. Are you willing to accept that?"

Non Sequitur crossed his arms. "General, just what did you think we were signing up for?"

Nonsensica nodded. "Yeah! Failure was never an option, right? If it comes down to him winning and lives being lost, do you really think we'd give up before we've given our all?"

"Once we step in there, we're leaving as heroes or staying as martyrs. That's just how it goes," Gracias said.

"We'll get the job done. Team Green doesn't lose," Chloroplast said.

"Then you have your mission. Go prepare. I have to handle my side of things."

The team left the room. Luo lingered with his staff.

"I want a strike team around the perimeter, rapid deployment, heavy weapons. The Other Eight have made The Icon bleed before. If he bleeds again, I want us to be ready to end it."

Chapter 12

The available members of The Other Eight gathered in the cover nearest to the badly battered north gate to Chi-NoKo. The remnants of The Number and Primadonna's gambit remained in the form of pavement shattered to gravel and gates slumping on their hinges. Once again, the team was outfitted with fresh communicators. Everyone, even Nonsensica, had foregone stealth costumes. They were in brilliant red and white. The crew looked every bit the part of a superhero team. Each wore a pack with the gear they'd requested, plus some assorted military supplies recommended by Luo and his advisers. Non Sequitur pressed his finger to the rugged earbud.

"Thirty seconds until the soldiers challenge the border to the south," he said. "Let's hope The Icon isn't in a border-crossing mood. We know the plan, everybody. On their signal, we make a break for our target. We want to get in and get hidden, but we don't want to be too stealthy. This only works if he knows we're there and starts looking for us."

"Imperfect stealth is kind of our specialty," Chloroplast said.

Non Sequitur nodded. "They're making their move."

"Should be obvious when it's time to make ours," Nonsensica said.

Sure enough. Within moments of the signaled motion of the soldiers, a thunderous clap burst from wherever The Icon had been lingering. It may as well have been a starting pistol. They took off at a sprint, navigating the broken pavement like their lives depended on it. Their earbuds kept them apprised of his actions as they desperately tried to close the gap between the border and the first reasonable bit of cover in the city. The story the communication team told was harrowing.

"The Icon is aloft, directly above the border," the tech described. "He is clutching a piece of rubble, a large fragment of concrete with exposed rebar. He appears to be more agitated than in prior noncombat border encounters. He is directing his gaze upon the commander for the unit. He is speaking."

The team threw broken gates wide on their way through, leaving them open both to save time and leave a trail of their arrival. The first forbidding concrete structures were a hundred yards ahead.

The tech continued. "He is speaking exclusively in Korean. The structure of the speech is less prepared and overtly heroic. He is demanding his people be left alone. He is warning that the aggression will be met with equal aggression."

"Before," Nonsensica huffed, vaulting over a traffic barrier, "he seemed like he was afraid of what he'd have to do. Now he's all threats."

"It's like Yoda says!" Gracias replied. "Fear leads to anger. Anger leads to hate."

They skidded into the shadow of a building to get their bearings. Non Sequitur brought up a map.

"Funny how when he's being insightful, he doesn't do the backwards sentence thing," Chloroplast said.

"Oh, yeah," Gracias said, leaning on his knees and trying to catch his breath. "Should have been. Anger, fear leads to. Hate, anger leads to."

"Guys, can we stay focused?" Non Sequitur said.

"Yeah," Nonsensica said. "What with the big guy sprinting toward the dark side at breakneck pace, maybe save your breath for running."

"Right, right," Gracias said. "… Maybe he was saying it backwards, backwards. Like, he had it queued up in his head backwards, and then he said that backwards so—"

"Focus!" Bomb Sniffer hissed. "If we're going to get caught and killed, let's at least make it to the first waypoint before we do."

"Two streets over, eight streets up," Non Sequitur said.

"We're in cover," Nonsensica said, keying her communicator. "You can pull back."

The crew hustled through the dank alleys behind tall semi-decrepit buildings. The tech narrated their withdrawal. The Icon rose higher as they pulled back. He hurled the debris he'd been holding. Either lack of accuracy or a purposeful miss left the rubble embedded in the road just shy of the rearmost soldier.

"He's throwing stuff," Bomb Sniffer said. "That's not good."

"At least he doesn't have laser vision," Gracias said.

Non Sequitur tried to split his attention between navigating the streets and keeping an eye on the face of the communicator. A manually updated location marker kept track of The Icon, while their own positions were GPS updated on the same map. Because someone had to punch in his estimated location periodically, The Icon's position jumped and shifted rather than moving smoothly.

"Looks like he's heading straight for where we came in," Non Sequitur said. "Taking his time though."

"He's getting cocky," Nonsensica said. "Good. That'll soften him up for when we make our move."

"We don't have a move to make, do we?" Bomb Sniffer said shakily, peering out from between two buildings to give the sky a wary look. "I don't remember us making a move against The Icon in the plan. We were a distraction."

"The only way we get out of this without a whole city becoming a smoking nuclear wreck with us buried in the center is if we find a way to take him down. So we're going to be making a move eventually," Nonsensica said. "And that starts now. Time to spit up. You guys have a straight shot to target A. Me and Non Sequitur are heading to target B. Don't get caught. And remember. If he shows up, we're the heroes, he's the villain. And the heroes always win in the end. He doesn't know it yet, but he's already lost."

"Hope he figures it out soon, before he wins by mistake," Chloroplast said.

* * *

Luo stepped through the door of his quarters and shut it behind him. It was early in the operation. He should have been in the command center, but this was a brief lull in activity. And what he needed to do right now was something that he didn't wish to have observed by technicians and underlings.

He took a seat at the meager desk set up in his quarters and logged in, slowly penetrating six separate layers of cyber security. Once he'd heaped the requisite amount of encryption onto the signal, he had the active call to Gen. Siegel transferred.

"General," Siegel said.

"General," Luo said. "I hope you don't mind that I am speaking with you privately."

"Private conferences are a part of every mission," Siegel said. "So far this operation is off to a promising start. All insertions successful, no active engagement."

"Indeed. But you and I both know that the numbers have been run, the simulations and speculations have been tabulated. As good a start as we've seen, there is no clear avenue to success."

"The fog of war makes success hazy in the best of times."

Luo opened a drawer and poured himself a drink. "If only this was a proper war. My training covers war. This is a threat we've never faced before."

"So we're writing the book on it, for the next poor grunt expected to deal with this."

"The next time…" Luo shook his head. "I don't want to imagine such a thing."

"We put our team together because we knew a day like this would come. And I don't know how you run things over there, but Uncle Sam doesn't like training up a team that he's only going to use once. Meta-human threats call for meta-human responses, and the kind of thing that can put the US and China on their heels isn't the sort of thing that a proper participant in an arms race is likely to give up on. The eyes of history are upon us, Luo. We're either writing the training manual of how to proceed, or we're writing the cautionary tale of how not to."

"I strive to set a good example."

193

"You should know, the news stations here are starting to pick up what's happening there. Specifically, the evacuations," Siegel said.

"I am aware. We've been monitoring them. So far, no specific mention of The Icon or his actions. As far as the world knows, this is a potential nuclear situation."

"Mostly people seem to be fixating on the fact that the North Koreans aren't evacuating."

"They'll do anything to get in international news. I assure you. The same drones keeping track of The Icon have been getting plenty of footage of the major population centers clearing out of the immediate fallout danger zone." He took a breath. "I've not been made aware of any major mishap in the mission thus far. You know your people better than I do. They are unquestionably dedicated, but they seem to have discipline problems. What is the likelihood of success?"

"All I can say is they'll surprise you. If they fail, I'm comfortable saying it is because success wasn't possible. If there is a way to succeed, they'll find it."

"Then for the next few hours, we shall hope that they find something my own people have missed, because as we speak, the evacuation vehicles are preparing for our own retreat. The expectation at this point is utter devastation."

"My crew makes a habit of defying expectation."

* * *

Chloroplast lingered in the shaft of sun coming down into the alley. Of the group, he and Bomb Sniffer were probably tied for "least foolhardy." That should have meant that he'd be even more motivated to stay in the shadows than the rest of the group. But he had the power of photosynthesis. Seeking out sunlight was a habit that was hard to set aside.

They'd made it as far as the alley between the two buildings directly north of the police station. The trip had been harrowing, particularly because it required a sprint across the fire-damaged bridge, but as luck would have it, The Icon had vanished into the underground tunnels after a half-hearted patrol of the border and hadn't shown his face again. The flashing white dot indicating his location was still firmly situated over the dormitory building they'd identified as his home. A neat little question mark beside it underscored that it was at best a guess.

The rest of the crew huffed and puffed after the desperate run across the city.

"How come you're not winded?" Gracias said. "You skipped out on the mandatory cardio during training at least as often as I did."

"Clean living and the power of the sun," he said. "One of the benefits of being carbon-neutral."

"Yeah, well, if you figure out how to shoot solar beams or something, let me know. That'd be another real good benefit."

"You'll be the first to know."

"It's tough to tell how many cops are in the station," Bomb Sniffer said, squinting at the building ahead. "There's a bunch of cop cars in the parking lot, but it's not like they commute in those things."

"We'll just be real sneaky. Then it won't matter," Gracias said. "You have that door-lock jiggler thingy for breaking in?"

"Of course I do, but I don't think it's really compatible with stealth. It sounds like a dentist's drill when it's running," Bomb Sniffer said.

"Okay, change of plans, then. We buzz the door, and when they unlock it and see who's trying to break in, we overwhelm them with superior force."

"They probably have guns, though." Bomb Sniffer took a whiff. "Correction, they definitely have guns."

"I'm open to ideas, then!" Gracias said. "Why do I always have to be the ideas guy?"

"We'll try the back door. I'll try to buzz in, and if we have problems, Gracias distracts them and Chloroplast disarms them."

"That's a good plan," Gracias said.

"It should sound familiar, that's what we came up with before we left," Bomb Sniffer said.

"Right…" Gracias said. "Still, good that we came up with it again in the field. Shows it's a solid plan. Um… remind me, what was the contingency plan if this ends up attracting The Icon?"

Bomb Sniffer glared at him. "You're joking right? Were you really not paying attention?"

"I sort of expected things to have fallen apart already," Gracias said.

She pointed to the storm drain. "The culverts under the city. They're huge, remember? Nonsensica and Non Sequitur found them. We get down there, hide, and wait for a diversion to give us cover to escape to someplace else."

Gracias nodded appreciatively. "We come up with some good plans. Let's get moving, then."

The crew checked the communicator. The Icon hadn't been spotted again. As far as they knew, he was still in his home.

"Maybe we're lucky and he's taking a nap," Chloroplast said.

Convinced the coast was as clear as it was going to get, they dashed across the driveway and through the garage entrance. Bomb Sniffer dropped to her knees in front of the door and slipped the lockpicker from the gear bag. Gracias pressed to the wall on one side, crouched below the presently unstaffed plexiglass window. Chloroplast took his position on the opposite side, crouching with his hand resting on Bomb Sniffer's back while she raised the lockpicker and inserted it in the deadbolt.

Operating the lockpicker was one of the stranger pieces of training she'd had to absorb for this mission, but certainly not one of the more difficult ones. It was little more than a metal prong that slipped into the lock. She depressed a trigger and turned the device, causing it to rattle against the pins of the lock and, ideally, jiggle them into the proper position. There was very little actual skill involved once you understood the knack of it. She slipped it into the deadbolt and pulled the trigger. Amid the sound of a jackhammer in miniature, the thing rattled at the pins and, within fifteen seconds, the deadbolt snapped open.

"Now the knob," she said shakily, ramming the tool inside and activating it.

This lock was considerably more temperamental. After thirty full seconds, she still hadn't opened it. But she did hear the rapid footsteps of someone coming to investigate. She yanked the tool clear, and Chloroplast pulled her out of the way.

The door opened, and a rather diminutive young woman appeared in the doorway, gun low but ready. Gracias stepped forward and grasped her wrist, wrenching it aside and knocking the weapon free. Bomb Sniffer kicked it out of range, and Chloroplast slipped behind her to wrench her arm up behind her back and cover her mouth. The whole sequence happened in moments and left the officer unarmed and at the mercy of Chloroplast.

Gracias blinked. "Wow... I kinda expected that to go a lot worse. I'm going to have to apologize to the general for saying his training classes didn't make sense for superheroes," he said.

The officer struggled. Bomb Sniffer placed a hand on her shoulder.

"Ma'am, I hope you can understand me. Can you?" she said.

She nodded as best she could while still being secured.

"We're not going to hurt you, but we need you to not scream. You have our friends here, and we need to get them out. Do you understand?" she said.

Another nod. The three of them moved inside and shut the door. Chloroplast slowly took his hand away.

"You're from The Other Eight," she said, her voice hushed.

"That's right," Gracias said.

"Are you going to do something about The Icon?" she said.

"... You want us to?" Chloroplast said.

"We need you to," she said. "Dr. Aiken and Phosphor are here. I can take you to them."

She hurried through the police station, the others keeping close enough to resecure her if need be. There was no need. She even went so far as to call ahead to her fellow officer and warn him to lower his weapon. They were taken directly to the cells, where Phosphor and Dr. Aiken were waiting.

"Chloroplast, Gracias, Bomb Sniffer! What's the plan? What's happening out there?" Dr. Aiken said quickly.

"Nothing good, Doc. If we can't figure a way to take The Icon out of commission..." Gracias paused. "Let's just say, the only win here is if he's 'neutralized.'"

"Where are the others?" Dr. Aiken asked.

"There was some riddle or something we solved from the comics. It leads to a lair or something. They're on their way now," Chloroplast said.

"I don't suppose you've figured out what we're going to have to do," Bomb Sniffer said.

"I have my theories, but like anything regarding the human mind, it's far from solid, and far from a sure thing. You see, I believe the seat of his power, or at least the foundation of the identity to which he attributes his power, is heroism itself..."

* * *

The Icon stepped from the tunnel and gazed at the clear sky. No sounds of combat. No groaning engines of bombers. He took to the sky and gave the border a cursory glance. The troops who had retreated had not returned. He drifted higher. The more distant troops were much less active. The larger weapons they'd attempted to kill him with were missing, and a great deal of the equipment had been removed. Perhaps the army had learned its lesson.

But the price for freedom was vigilance. His foes were devious, and appearances could be deceiving. A closer look was called for.

He took his time, drifting to the border at a speed that barely rustled his short-cropped hair. The main border was as secure as he'd left it. He traced along, moving north along the fence. It was secure, intact. The second border crossing drew nearer. He nearly dismissed it as untouched, as he had during his previous patrol. But his eyes came to rest on the heavy gates. Though they had been damaged during his prior clash, he knew he'd left them roughly shut. They were quite clearly open.

He dropped down and inspected. Fresh scrapes traced an arc along the ground. This gate had been shoved open. He clenched his teeth and stomped the ground, rattling the whole crossing. When had this happened? How had he missed it? He dashed along, seeking some sort of further evidence of infiltration. He found a footprint here and there, but otherwise, nothing. He was no tracker. He was a defender. And now there was an enemy within his city. Perhaps several.

The Icon narrowed his eyes and looked to the north.

They'd made no secret of what their target would be. He burst into the air and streaked toward the power plant. The city seemed even more dead as he swept over it. More refugees fleeing. They would return. He would make ChiNoKo safe again, and they would return. The city was nothing without its people.

He reached the main entrance of the power plant and pushed the door open. There was the telltale jingle of broken metal. A lock and chain fell to the floor. A worker in the short hallway beyond the door snorted awake. He was loosely gripping a crowbar. Dark circles around his eyes told the tale of sleepless nights.

"Is there a problem, citizen?"

"Icon!" he said. His tone was not one of relief. "There's... the reactor. Things are degrading."

The Icon marched past him into the adjoining hallway. The lights were dim and flickering. Red bulbs pulsed and flashed out of sequence. Every alert indicator save the warning sirens was active.

"How long until the plant is fully functional?" The Icon said.

"You're not listening. It's degrading. It's getting worse. We aren't on the way to recovery. We're on the way to complete failure. Quite possibly catastrophic failure."

"I believe in you. I believe in ChiNoKo. This plant is its beating heart. It will not let us down."

"Icon, we need help. You have to let us—"

The Icon raised his voice. "There are forces at work in this city. Invaders. I fear for the safety of the plant. Until I feel the plant is safe, I shall remain here in its defense."

"Please. We need expertise. We need additional labor. We need—"

"The power plant is the heart of ChiNoKo, and it will be maintained by its people," The Icon said with finality. "I am your defender. I will not allow danger to befall you. You were right to have locked and chained the door, and I see that you were guarding it. This was wise. But now you need not fear for who enters this place. Return to the task of resurrecting the power plant and making ChiNoKo shine once more."

The worker shakily backed away, then dashed down the hall. The Icon marched to the front door and drifted up to keep watch. No one would enter or leave this place without him knowing. The invaders would not reach the heart of ChiNoKo.

* * *

The worker rushed down the hallway and threw open the doorway to a long staircase. A combination of panic and weariness almost sent him tumbling down the steps six times, but finally he reached the secondary control room. Inside were two similarly frazzled-looking workers, a somewhat more collected older woman in a white coat and goggles, and a shlubby fellow in a white sweatshirt with the letter A emblazoned on it. The woman in white was reading the wall of dials and indicators, marking down her findings while the others shakily worked through piles of handwritten notes.

"It's no good," the worker said. "I told him we needed help. He said we have to handle it ourselves. And he says he knows there are people in the city. I don't know if he knows if it's you or not, but he won't leave."

The goggle-clad woman spoke crisply and simply. "I'll be brief, sir," she said. "We need bodies. The power plant, in its present state, cannot be brought safely to full power output or full stall without major maintenance. There are tasks that need to be done in tandem. They are low skill. Anyone with rudimentary mechanical knowledge and the ability to follow directions can do it. But for the final shutdown, we will need both of the diesel generators running."

"Generator two isn't working. Our diesel expert was one of the first people to flee," the worker said.

"It doesn't matter anyway," said one of the other workers. "The Icon will notice the generator is active. He'll know something is up."

"We need six additional workers, someone who can fix a diesel generator, and the opportunity to do a full shutdown, or this power plant will be irretrievable within eight hours and in full meltdown in less than ten. And these are rough estimates. The combination of the disabled security measures prior to maintenance and the prolonged maintenance mode has introduced a number of variables that I can't accurately allow for. I don't know how to solve this problem, but it needs to be solved."

The man with the sweatshirt raised his arm and pulled back the sleeve to reveal the communicator.

"We can tell the rest of the team," he said.

The workers and the expert all jumped as though a pistol had been fired. The worker from the entryway brandished his crowbar.

"Who are you?" the worker said.

"The Afterthought. I infiltrated with Inspector Wen during the last military action. We've spoken seventeen times since then," Afterthought said.

"I don't remember that."

He nodded. "No one remembers The Afterthought. I'll put you through to my team."

***

A few minutes later, Nonsensica and Non Sequitur were creeping through the darkened halls of the museum as the update was supplied through their earbuds.

"I'd be more worried about the eight-hour meltdown deadline if we weren't already working on a three-hour bombardment deadline," Non Sequitur said.

"Wouldn't be a superhero supermission if there wasn't a race to wipe us out," Nonsensica said.

"The cops have already rounded up some locals to help with the plant maintenance. They're escorting them to the plant now. I don't imagine The Icon will object to familiar faces showing up to do some repairs," Dr. Aiken said over the communicator. "But fixing the generator and starting it without him noticing is still up in the air."

"Can't they just convince him it's what they need to do to fix the plant?" Non Sequitur asked.

"Evidently they've tried. His parents worked at the plant. He knows a fair amount about its workings and knows the generators are emergency equipment. I suppose he sees it as a sign of failure. He will resist."

"It doesn't even matter if we can't find someone who can fix them," Nonsensica said.

"I can probably get the generator running. I've worked on diesel engines before," Phosphor said.

"We'll stick a pin in that. It would be a lot better if a local could be the one doing the work on the generators. They're outdoors, and you're rather obvious as a non-ChiNoKoan," Dr. Aiken said.

"We can purposely set off an alarm if we find one," Nonsensica said.

"Or, alternately, we could accidentally set one off," Non Sequitur said. "Since my training was mostly improving my ability to open locks and not so much how to locate and disable alarms."

"Either way, having his lair infiltrated is probably enough to get him interested enough to come try to deal with us. He can't notice Phosphor if he's too busy getting his butt kicked."

"How exactly are you going to avoid getting killed if that happens?" Chloroplast asked.

"With superior skills and cunning," Nonsensica said.

"We'll handle the situation at the power plant," Aiken said. "You two just focus on getting into the lair. With any luck, you'll find something inside to deal with The Icon."

"You got it, Doc," Nonsensica said.

They shifted the communicators to standby. In less trying circumstances, the museum would have been a genuinely entertaining place to explore. Not because it was well supplied with cultural or historical artifacts, but because it was practically a piece of performance art. It was propaganda sculpted into the shape of a building. So far they'd passed dioramas detailing terrible wars and atrocities committed against the people of ChiNoKo that were universally either misattributed war crimes that other nations had suffered or completely impossible imaginings. It was like the whole country had Munchausen Syndrome, claiming endless hardship for the sake of justifying attention and distrust.

Finally, they came to a section of the museum labeled The Hall of The Icon.

"Holy cow," Nonsensica said, looking about in wonder.

The only thing missing from the hall was a golden idol. There were busts, posters and countless video screens. The screens, at least, were dark. But the amount of worship on display was shameless. And subtlety was not their goal. A banner over a central platform read All questions of The Icon are answered here. The platform was about six feet tall, the sort of thing that would be perfect for another statue, but at the moment it was empty. The hall was located roughly in the center of the museum. A balcony surrounded it on all sides, giving a gallery view from both the second and third floors. Above, a circular skylight gleamed in the morning light.

"Okay. So. We're in the right place. Lowest level. Covered with Icon… iconography. And pretty much exactly at the point where the riddle said it would be. The question is, where's the door?" Nonsensica said.

"It's not going to be out in the open. I've got to believe they expected The Icon to be able to come and go even when the museum was open," Non Sequitur said.

"Mmm… But look at this place. It's all about spectacle. Maybe they'd want him to come here in secret, but they'd make a show of him leaving in costume. Give me a boost."

He put his back to the central platform and heaved her up. She laughed.

"You've got to see this."

She reached down and, with some difficulty, pulled him to the platform as well. It was topped with a brushed-metal circle. The I logo of The Icon was emblazoned in the center of what was obviously a complex iris-style hatch.

"Did he really need a riddle to find this thing?" she said. "Do your magic, buddy. We're going in the out door."

Non Sequitur crouched and felt over the door. He tapped at it and was rewarded with a hollow echo from beyond. "I'm trying to open it," he said. "Not getting anything. No latches. No knobs. No switches."

"Probably the controls are way down at the bottom. Either that or they fortified it against you. We know Borisov was onto us in his lair."

"Wait, I got it. Stand back," Non Sequitur said.

She leaned on a small plinth near the back of the platform. He got down on his knees and reached out, nudging at the emblem. He reached into his gear bag and removed a hefty pry bar. After a few experimental nudges, he suddenly reared back and clubbed the bottom of the emblem, torquing it aside. The petals of the iris mechanism rattled open a few inches. He hooked the edge of the opening with the pry bar and pulled it back, fully opening it.

"I could have done that," Nonsensica said.

"Yeah, well. Sometimes powers aren't necessary. And good news or bad news, depending on what our goal was, I don't hear any alarm," he said.

"Just as well. Much as I'd love a chance to put the 'chucks to the side of his head, I'd rather get a look at his hideout first."

The angle of the sun was such that they could only see a short distance down the concrete tube awaiting them beyond the door. She clicked on a flashlight and shined it down.

"Looks like, what, three stories?" she said. "That's why you always bring rope." She tossed the rope to him. "Anchor up and let's get down there. This better be good," she said.

Non Sequitur keyed his radio. "We've got the exit to The Icon's lair open. We're heading down. What's the word on everything else?"

"In a few minutes, you're going to hear some commotion. Keep focused on your task," Dr. Aiken said. "Team Green and Bomb Sniffer are getting ready to get The Icon's attention so Phosphor can slip inside and work on the generator."

Nonsensica gave him a punch on the shoulder. "You heard the doc. We have to get in and out quick, because they're about to have a bunch of fun without us."

One after the other, they rappelled down the shaft. This, at least, was a skill that had been drilled fairly effectively into them by the instructors back at the training grounds. They made their way swiftly down, stopping regularly to shine the flashlight to seek out anything that might be dangerous or that might alert The Icon of their presence. They were able to drop all the way to the bottom without a single sensor or boobytrap.

"I can't believe it. Completely undefended," Nonsensica said, hopping off the rope in the darkened room.

"It stands to reason," Non Sequitur said. "They led him here with a riddle. It wouldn't do him much good if he just set off the alarms or defenses once he got here. I think they were depending on the locals respecting the place too much to violate it."

They stepped off the steel platform at the bottom of the shaft. A mechanical click sounded off somewhere. They both reflexively dashed for the ropes. Fluorescent lights flickered on, but nothing else seemed to happen.

"Motion-controlled lights," Nonsensica said. "All the modern technology of a suburban driveway."

The pair of them crept out again. Calling this place a lair was a bit generous. It wasn't exactly the Batcave, though attempts had been made to dress it up like it was. The place was completely round, with the shaft at the center. Along the north curve of the wall, an array of Icon outfits hung in clusters of a dozen or so. There was the silver suit he was wearing now, along with a group of more heavily armored ones, some blue ones, and some black ones. On the wall opposite was a grid of screens. Of a dozen screens, only six of them were displaying anything besides the steady blue of a dead digital connection. They had a few views of the border and two shots of the power plant. A metal-topped desk spread below it, though there was nothing on top of it but a silver telephone receiver and a strange metal block attached to the table with a hinge. The only other significant feature was the doorway on the east wall.

"Looks like he's still standing guard at the front door of the plant," Non Sequitur said, staring up at the screens. "Or... floating guard."

"Gotta respect it. The man's got stealth suits," Nonsensica said, holding up one of the black outfits. "And those lumpy ones look like Kevlar. I guess they were worried he wouldn't be as sturdy as they wanted him to be."

Non Sequitur gingerly picked up the receiver of the phone, as though it would bite him if he wasn't careful. "Dead," he said.

"How much you want to bet it was a direct connection to the lab in the bridge?" Nonsensica said. She trotted over and thumped the metal box. "So this is it. If there's something in here that's going to turn the tide, it's in here." She tried to lever it up, but it wouldn't budge.

"I don't think it's locked," Non Sequitur said. "I think it's just heavy."

"Like Superman's door key." Nonsensica twirled her pry bar. "And just as dumb."

They worked their pry bars around the edge until they were able to flop it open. Beneath it was a leather-bound journal. Non Sequitur flipped it open.

"Aiken, you there?" Nonsensica said. "This might be good."

"You're spotty, but I'm listening," Dr. Aiken said over the connection.

"'If you are reading this, there can be no doubt. You are the one, true Icon. The defender ChiNoKo needs. The days ahead will be trying. But remember, to be The Icon is to serve The Icon's ideals. Without his ideals, The Icon is nothing. Your ideals are as follows. They are already a part of you, but know to put words and action to them are to give you power.'"

Non Sequitur turned the page. "'First tenet. The Icon exists to serve his masters. In times of need, and in times of confusion, the phone in this lair shall link you to the advisers who shall give you direction. These advisers are wise, and know things that you cannot. Trust them. If they deem it necessary, there is no other way.'"

"Oh, nice. They were hoping to make sure they could tell him to do whatever they wanted and he wouldn't even think about it. I guess they never expected the lab to get blown up."

"He was a danger for weeks before we did that. Either they were telling him to do that, they weren't stopping him from doing that, or he'd never even started listening to them." Non

Sequitur turned back to the page. "'Second tenet. Good exists only in ChiNoKo, but evil is everywhere. There is no such thing as a virtuous outsider. All who seek to cross the border seek to corrupt and control ChiNoKo. But there are those within the city, those native to your home, who would seek to collaborate with the outsiders. Do not trust them. Disloyalty to ChiNoKo is a sign of evil. A sign of villainy.'"

"These are some frickin' wordy tenets," Nonsensica said.

"'Third tenet. The Icon defends his people. ChiNoKo is its people. Those loyal to ChiNoKo must be protected, even from threats within ChiNoKo. Fourth tenet. The Icon is moral. The Icon is defined by these morals. Loyalty, obedience, righteousness, virtue.'" He flipped a few more pages. "That's it for tenets. The rest is… it looks like it's basically heroic phrases for all occasions. Recommended responses and explanations for challenges and provocations."

"That's it?" Nonsensica said. "No ring of power? No hunk of kryptonite?"

"It is not without its use. We now know how he defines his role. If we can properly challenge that definition, we have a chance of crippling him psychologically. I think it's time to find a way out of there. Things are about to start happening, and you might be needed," Aiken said.

"You got it, Doc," Nonsensica said, snatching the book from Non Sequitur and stuffing it in her bag. "Come on. Let's grab some souvenirs on the way out."

* * *

Bomb Sniffer checked the sky before ramming a pry bar into a cabinet on the back of a maintenance truck. She popped it open to reveal a package of cigar-sized metal tubes.

"Blasting caps," she said. "I'd know the smell anywhere. You'd be surprised how often they lock up the explosives someplace safe and leave these things just lying around." She grabbed them and threw them in a bag that was bulging with scavenged accelerants and explosives.

"Are you going to know how to set these off?" Chloroplast asked.

"Oh yeah. That's no problem. I almost got sent to juvie six times because of playing with stuff like this. I kind of thought becoming a superhero would have straightened me out."

"Being a superhero isn't about getting straightened out. It's about finding the job that needs someone twisted up in just the way you are," Gracias said.

"Any of you know how to hot-wire a car?" she said.

"Don't ask me, you're the delinquent here," Chloroplast said.

"Oh, hey!" Gracias said. "If you don't like the name Bomb Sniffer, you can go by the name The Delinquent."

"I feel like a name like that has an age limit on it, and I'm already on the upper edge of it."

"You never had a Sega Genesis or a Super Nintendo. You're still a delinquent for years," Gracias said.

"Whatever. Grab that brick, okay?" she said.

They fetched a dislodged bit of stone and followed her to one of the only cars on the street. She heaved the brick through the window and reached inside to unlock the door.

"We're on a hill, so maybe..." she muttered. She released the parking brake and put it in neutral. It started to roll toward the river. She slammed on the brake and parked it again. "Okay, this'll do. Let's load it up and find a good place to hide."

They wrenched the trunk open and upended the bag of ill-gotten explosives. It was a hodgepodge of everything they could find that would hold a flame. Emergency candles, rubbing alcohol, fireworks, gasoline, and now blasting caps. The last element was a long, old-fashioned fuse provided by the engineers back at the base.

"Okay," she said. "Time to grab a tiger by the tail."

"That's a dumb saying," Gracias said. "The tail's the best place to grab a tiger. It's shaped like a handle, and there's nothing pointy on it."

"I think that phrase means—" Chloroplast began.

He was interrupted when Bomb Sniffer thumped the steering wheel with a crowbar, blaring the horn. After two more bashes she was able to get it to break, producing a continuous wail of horn. Chloroplast lit the fuse dangling out of the trunk while she pulled the brake and put it in neutral. The trio took cover as their diversion picked up speed rolling down the hill. The Icon appeared almost instantly, snapping to a stop at the bottom of the hill with a thunderous clap.

"The Icon is clear, I'm heading in," Phosphor said.

As they peered out from the alleyway they'd hidden in, The Icon streaked up the street. The car was moving at a considerable speed by the time he made contact with it. The front end crumpled like it had hit a brick wall, but he slid back a few feet before he was able to bring it fully to a stop. He looked through the front windshield, expecting to find a foe, or perhaps a victim.

"So…" he rumbled. "More trickery." He stooped and levered the car up from the ground. When he had a proper grip, he drifted skyward.

"What's the plan here?" Gracias whispered.

"I don't know. I expected him to not stop it until it was already on fire," Bomb Sniffer said.

"Do you believe that such shallow ruses can fool ChiNoKo's one true protector, The Icon?" he called. "I am the vigilant eye that watches the weak. I am the unblinking gaze of virtue…"

As it happened, the heroes had two pieces of very good fortune. First, he was holding the still-blaring car over his head facing the front of it, leaving the still unnoticed fuse burning behind him. He'd also chosen to deliver his monologue to entirely the wrong hiding place. It gave them a clear and relatively safe view of the slow-burning fuse as it vanished into the trunk.

"This is about to get bad," Bomb Sniffer announced over the communicator.

The group donned heavy hearing protection. Smoke started to belch from the trunk. The Icon was far too deep into his speech to give it any attention. That changed once the fireworks started going off. The overpowered and underexperienced metahuman turned to see the source of the sound, pivoting his entire body far more quickly than the car's inertia would have preferred. The frame of the car buckled. The spin hurled burning fuel and flame out of the gas tank and trunk alike. Crackling fireworks and popping blasting caps filled the air. Flames doused the face of the streets on either side. The Icon gasped and dropped the car, causing what was left of its gasoline to billow up in an explosive plume.

"Crap, crap, crap, crap," Bomb Sniffer said, dashing down the alley and throwing her shoulder against a door. "We did too good."

The Icon darted to the river as the flames started to spread. Gracias helped her bust the door open.

"What's happening?" Aiken said, his voice clear as crystal through the earbuds tucked under their hearing protection.

"Good news, he's distracted," Chloroplast said. "Bad news, we sort of set the city on fire."

"Hey, it was him not us," Gracias said, barricading the door behind them before joining the others in a sprint down the hallway of the unfamiliar building. "Point is, he'll have his hands full for a minute."

Chapter 13

Phosphor fought with some fuel lines. A test ignition of the first generator had gone off without a hitch before he'd even fully entered the power plant. It would run just fine. It had taken one quick attempt to start the second generator to make it clear what the problem was. His policy with engines was always to start with the fuel tank and move out. After an anemic cough of foul-smelling fumes, it sputtered out.

"Fuel filter. It's the fuel filter," he said over his shoulder to one of the plant workers behind him. "If one of you can find the replacement fuel filters, I'll figure out where this one is and how to change it."

They dashed off to an equipment shed. He started following the lines.

"What's the word down there, everyone?" Phosphor said.

"The spread of the flames has been contained, but they have not been fully extinguished," said a tech.

"Hah! Here. Found the filter. Look at this thing. Have they ever changed it?" He fumbled through the toolbox and found the proper wrench to get started. "About how much time you figure we have?"

"The flames should be extinguished in less than two minutes, assuming he keeps the same intensity."

"I'd usually call this a fifteen-minute job," Phosphor said. "It doesn't have to be pretty, and it only has to run for seven minutes. I can maybe get that down to five. These folks are in position, ready to do their piece. So we're going to need at least twelve minutes."

"Phase 2 will earn us another six minutes and fifty-three seconds. Plus whatever time we can squeeze out getting The Icon in position."

He yanked the fuel filter off. "That still leaves us three minutes short."

"We'll get you the three minutes," Nonsensica said over the communicator. "With any luck, we'll get you all the time in the world."

"Start with three minutes," he said.

* * *

Gracias glanced at the video feed on his communicator. "He's just about to finish up and come looking," he said. "Here's where we split up."

Chloroplast slapped Bomb Sniffer on her back. "Don't drag your feet."

"I'll run like the wind," she said.

Bomb Sniffer dashed down a hallway. Chloroplast and Gracias hurried out the opposite side, sprinting toward the street on which they knew The Icon to be just finishing his firefighting. They paused just before the exit. Chloroplast took a breath and looked at Gracias.

"Don't get killed, okay? I don't want to inherit the role of 'dumbest powers on the team,'" he said.

"Can't inherit what you already have," Gracias said.

Chloroplast darted out first, running into the sunlight and hurrying up the street. Gracias lingered behind. The lean, green, carbon-neutral hero made it a fair distance up the street before The Icon was finally in a position to look for him. One micro-sonic boom later and The Icon was in front of him.

"You. You dare attack my city and dream of not facing justice?" The Icon seethed.

"Attack your city? We rolled a car down the hill, and you shook it around like a lunatic and lit a whole neighborhood on fire," Chloroplast taunted, attempting to juke to the side and get around The Icon.

The Icon snapped aside and blocked his way again. "I captured your fellow 'heroes' and locked them away. But they were simply trying and failing to rob a bank. This is inarguably a direct attack. The rules are different for soldiers in a time of war."

"Oh yeah? Ever heard of a little thing called the Geneva Conventions?" Chloroplast said.

The Icon grasped him by the neck and raised him from the ground. "Of course. We educate our people in ChiNoKo," he said, drifting upward and hauling Chloroplast with him. "One hundred ninety-six countries signed or ratified the Geneva Convention's protocols." He pulled Chloroplast closer. "ChiNoKo isn't among them."

"And you… call yourself… a hero…" Chloroplast croaked.

"I am a hero," he barked.

"Oh yeah, hero!" Gracias called from down the street. "If you're a hero, then you'll have the decency to face us as the team we are!"

He made ready to run, but he'd underestimated just how quickly The Icon would be able to close the gap even while dangling Chloroplast from his grip. He made it barely a dozen strides down the road before The Icon was in front of him, hand around his throat as well. He lifted them both from the ground, holding them a few inches above the street.

"You want to be beaten to submission like the villain you are while side by side with your partner in crime? I can respect that. Request granted."

Gracias grinned. "Grassy ass."

The snug costume bulged in the seat like he was suddenly wearing a diaper. Even The Icon proved incapable of ignoring the profound discomfort of having his rear end suddenly covered in landscaping. He dropped both Chloroplast and Gracias and tugged at his suit. The two heroes hit the ground running.

"Tell me again about the most useless powers on the team," Gracias said.

"One of these days you're going to find someone who likes having briefs full of sod and that'll be your archnemesis."

"Hah! All the best heroes have archnemeses."

Clearly the designer of The Icon's suit hadn't anticipated the need to quickly and efficiently clear away a mess within.

Jumpsuits are almost perfectly wrong for performing that task. After fighting with it for a few seconds, The Icon darted into the privacy of a building. They continued their sprint, finally reaching the riverfront before a window smashed in the building behind them and The Icon once again intercepted them.

"A temporary oversight," The Icon said. "I've studied your powers. You won't fool me again. Now will you come quietly, or will I need to render you unconscious before you join your friends in prison?"

"You studied our powers, huh," Chloroplast said. "If that's true, then you know all about Bomb Sniffer's abilities."

"She can detect the chemical signature of explosives with her nose," he said.

"And I bet you can't do that, tough guy," Gracias said.

"I have no need of such powers, and stop wasting time. You have one last chance to surrender before I give you the treatment invaders deserve."

"See, if you had bomb-sniffing skills, you'd know that we spent some quality time with that fancy bridge of yours," Gracias said.

"And being an expert in finding explosives goes hand in hand with being an expert in using explosives," Chloroplast said.

"But you don't have to take our word for it," Gracias said.

He pointed. The Icon looked. Bomb Sniffer was standing in the middle of the bridge. She had one hand raised and was clutching something in it. Massive canvas-covered boxes of some sort were on either side of her.

"You're fast!" she called. "But fast enough to get here before I can press a button?"

* * *

Nonsensica watched through binoculars as The Icon threw Gracias and Chloroplast aside. The binoculars quickly became unnecessary as he streaked toward the bridge, hand raised and ready to crush both the device and the interloper's hand if he needed to. He reached the edge of the bridge in moments. But just as he was closing the last bit of distance, the crates on either side of her thumped to life, billowing with sound and revealing themselves to be speakers. Two beats rumbled from a kettle drum.

They were just sound, but one could almost see them weave into The Icon's mind and take control of his muscles. He stopped near enough to Bomb Sniffer to hear her terrified gasp. More drumbeats rumbled, and the beginning of a spirited Irish folk melody lilted from the speakers. The Icon straightened. Two figures stepped out from behind pylons on the bridge. The Number and Primadonna. He had a brace on his arm and tap shoes on his feet. Impressively, Primadonna was wearing perhaps the world's first medical tap-boot.

They performed crisp, synchronized clacking steps on the bridge. He repeated them in a call and response. Soon the three of them fell into a perfectly matched Irish step-dancing rhythm. He couldn't help but play his part in the dance, helplessly in the thrall of their powers. The other heroes, their ears covered by hearing protection, scurried off the bridge. Nonsensica glanced at her communicator. A dancing waveform and a timer counted off the duration of the song. Minutes ticked by. In the earpieces of the team, chatter of this task or that underscored just how crowded this moment was. Members of two militaries, dozens of technicians, a whole team of superheroes, all unified in this single point in time. Finally a ragged rumble of ancient machinery thumped over the communication channel.

"Generators ready to go," Phosphor announced.

"All systems in standby, ready to begin stabilizing the reactor," said a technician.

"Do it!" Nonsensica barked.

The remaining time in the Riverdance ticked away. The generators were activated, and the final shutdown of the plant began. Workers and techs shouted out milestones. The song progressed. Primadonna and the Number had been steadily working her way to the north end of the bridge. The Icon had been working his way to the very center. As the heroes brought the routine toward its conclusion, they thumped their tap shoes all the more powerfully. The Icon matched their intensity, but scaled for his power. With thirty seconds left, both heroes were clear and their foe remained in the center, stomping thunderously on the bridge. It was trembling under the influence of his steps. They pushed it harder. He stomped harder. The music pulled toward its climax. With the final notes, the three dancers leaped and came down with a final blow. For The Number and Primadonna, it was little more than a triumphant clack of their shoes. For The Icon, it was a battering ram of a blow on a bridge that had been resonating toward its breaking point. That blow was the last straw. The fire-damaged roadway buckled, the towers failed, and the whole bridge came down in a cacophonous wreck with The Icon in its center.

Nonsensica stood alone in the street on the final stretch of city before the power plant. The rest of the team had taken cover. Her eyes darted between the bridge and the timer. Two minutes left before final shutdown.

The wreckage rattled. The Icon rose out of it.

A few fresh trickles of blood ran down the embattled meta-human's face, and his suit was terribly torn, but he was very much alive. And he was furious.

"Okay, team. Let's not screw this up," Nonsensica said quietly, blanking the screen on her communicator.

The Icon tore across the ground, moving so fast the light poles and traffic signs rattled in his wake. He was heading for the power plant. Directly for it, with no clear intention of stopping to grapple with Nonsensica. She reached into her bag and snagged the book of tenets, raising it in one hand and placing the fingers of her other hand in her mouth for a piercing whistle. The Icon turned. He came to a sudden stop as he realized what she was holding. He slammed down, stalking forward with angry stomps that left divots in the pavement.

"What are you doing with that book?" he fumed.

"Oh, this little thing? Your rulebook? We were in and out of your lair ages ago. Solved the riddle, broke down your front door. It was a cinch. That place? Heavy on the solitude, but light on the fortress."

"And now what do you suppose you will do? Attempt more trickery?" The Icon asked.

"Trickery?" she said. "Nah. Not my style. Oh, we brainstormed some stuff. We were going to do this big speech, complete with evidence, to tell you how you've been lied to your whole life. Video. Audio. Photographs. Try to teach you to see the truth. See you were being used. But after spending so much time with your people, both here and in the refugee camps that you chased your own people into, we realized there was no chance we'd set you straight. If there is one thing a ChiNoKoan is world-class at, it's self-delusion. That's the superpower your whole city shares. So we tossed that aside.

"We kicked around other ideas. Thought of putting one of your suits on someone else, trying to convince you they were the real Icon. Just about anyone we could find would fit the bill, and basically with equal claim to the mantle." She thumped the cover of the book. "First page flat-out says, 'If you're reading this, you're the one true Icon.' I've read it. Does that mean I'm The Icon?"

"I am The Icon," he barked.

"Yeah, like I said. The self-delusion is strong with this one. Anyway, not to talk your ear off, we all decided there was only one way to deal with someone like you." She tossed the book aside and punched her palm. "I'm just going to handle this the way heroes and villains have all throughout history. A good old-fashioned street fight. And I'm going to win."

"You," he said.

"That's right. I'll even let you throw the first punch."

"One punch is all it will take," he said. "You are like tissue paper to me."

She crossed her arms, raised her chin, and shut her eyes. "So? Get it over with. I don't have all day."

He hesitated.

"Do it. Hit me."

He clenched his fists and trembled with anger. "A hero doesn't hit a woman."

"Oh spare me the condescension. You put up a fight or you surrender. Now stop being a coward and hit me."

"I am not a coward."

"Then do what you were made to do. Defend your precious city from the interlopers. Hit me, coward. Hit me. Hit me!"

He pulled back and threw a punch with superhuman speed. The motion was a blur. In the time it would have taken to blink, he went from standing with his arms at his side to his fist whistling at full speed. It should have sent Nonsensica crumbling to the ground, broken. Except that it missed. In that same blink of an eye, Nonsensica dodged. With speed no normal human, and no meta-human but The Icon himself, should have, she shifted aside. It wasn't graceful. Indeed, it was a stumbling lurch that nearly threw her to the ground. But she was untouched.

He looked at her in awe and confusion. Both lasted only as long as it took for Non Sequitur to dash into the open and shove Nonsensica. She didn't budge when he did so. After all, she already had budged. She'd simply done it before he showed up.

"It is trickery," The Icon shouted.

"Trickery nothing. You missed. And now get ready for the pain," she said, twirling her non-chucks up to speed.

Again, he darted toward her. Again, she lurched out of the way. Non Sequitur circled around the other side to give her the shove that had pushed her out of harm's way while she delivered a punishing blow to the side of his head with the non-chucks. The weapon bounced harmlessly off him but left its mark on his pride. He turned viciously toward Non Sequitur. He reared back to end him first, but Nonsensica spat two random words and The Icon flinched, earning Non Sequitur just enough time to scramble clear.

What followed was something between a fight and a dance. It wasn't as tightly choreographed as the Riverdance, but it was no less effective. Little mental jabs in the form of Nonsensica's powers kept The Icon off balance whenever he went for Non Sequitur. When he went for Nonsensica, Non Sequitur's powers extended the window for a successful dodge from nanoseconds to thirty seconds. And each time she dodged, she followed up with a blow to his head. The first four successful hits were equally harmless. But slowly welts and bruises started to rise. More importantly, he was becoming winded, and his attacks were slowing.

"Let's face it," Nonsensica said, taking full advantage of the widening gap between attacks. "You're not the hero you think you are."

He swung and missed. She thumped him in the ribs.

"Tenet one. Follow orders. We both know that hotline is dead. You don't have any orders."

He lunged for Non Sequitur. She jabbed him with some words.

"Tenet two. Good exists only in ChiNoKo, but even some of those within ChiNoKo are evil." Another swing, dodge, and counter. "This town is empty. If you've been taught to consider those who abandoned the place to be evil, then there wasn't too much good here, was there? Unless you think you're the good one. And would someone good cause his fellow people to flee in fear?"

"Shut up. It's not true."

"Tenet three. The Icon defends his people. Again, what people? You chased most of them away. The ones that are still here are terrified of you. Every bit of damage and danger that's befallen this city since you put that suit on has been because of you."

"Stop it…" He tried to drift skyward, but his feet barely left the ground. His powers kept faltering.

"Tenet four. The Icon is moral. What about this is moral? What about holding your whole city hostage because you're too fearful of your own shadow to let someone help keep the power plant from blowing up is the right thing to do? And that's it. Every single thing that The Icon stands for has shattered in your grasp. If there is an Icon, it's not you."

He slumped forward and dropped to his knees.

"You could have been great. And you could still be great. But not like this," she said.

The Icon covered his face and crumpled to the ground, exhaustion and anxiety finally fully claiming him.

Nonsensica raised her wrist and tapped the screen. Phosphor was staring down into his own communicator. "The reactor is offline. The job is done."

Non Sequitur stood beside Nonsensica. The other's gathered around to look down at the broken Icon.

"Yeah," Non Sequitur said. "The job is done."

Nonsensica, breathless from the harrowing battle, crouched beside The Icon.

"It's not your fault, buddy," she said. "They screwed with your head. Tied you up in knots. You never had a fair shot at being a hero. But you killed some people. Probably broke some pretty major international laws, too. If you ever believed you knew what it was to be a hero, you know what you need to do now."

He hung his head and put his arms behind his back. Nonsensica applied flex-cuffs and helped him to his feet. The last of the lights and other electronics flickered and died. In the distance, the crackle of settling debris from the broken bridge could be heard.

But that wasn't the only sound.

The battle thus far had dislodged the earpieces of both Nonsensica and Non Sequitur. The others had mostly removed theirs as well. But there was hissing chatter going across the communication line. Nonsensica pressed her earpiece back in place.

"You guys getting any of this?" she whispered to the others behind The Icon's back as she led him toward the gathering soldiers ahead for the prisoner transfer.

They returned their earpieces as well. Most of the chatter, for the first time since they'd been brought on, was in Chinese.

"The Other Eight, please fall back to minimum safe distance," was the only order clearly intended for them.

They held their ground while the soldiers took over. Nonsensica listened close to the chatter. She knew very little Chinese. But she knew a few words. And what she was hearing made her uneasy. They were very sharp, very official words. With other things mixed in that seemed out of place. Codewords, she assumed. Mission shorthand. But something about the whole situation was off. As Non Sequitur, Gracias, Bomb Sniffer, Chloroplast, and Primadonna gathered beside her, all listening for further instruction, Nonsensica tipped her head.

"Dr. Aiken, where are we on the next steps?" she asked.

"Your jobs are through. Excellent work. I still have a fair amount to do. I'll need to interview The Icon. He should be considered unstable, and thus so should his powers. Given the degree of invincibility that was a necessary part of his identity, this defeat should be enough to keep him depowered for quite a while, possibly forever, but—"

The communication line crackled and shut off. Nonsensica and the others grabbed their communicators. Every screen said the same thing. "Secure credentials expired."

"I guess they're telling us not to let the door hit us on the grassy ass on the way out," Gracias said.

"Halfway through a piece of instruction from our mentor?" Nonsensica said.

She glanced up. The Icon had continued walking, but the soldiers had remained behind, fanning out a bit. Ahead, another contingent of soldiers cleared out the path. All in all, it looked less like they were escorting a prisoner, and more like…

"A firing squad…" Nonsensica said.

"They're not going to shoot him. They know they can't shoot him, right?" Non Sequitur said with a hush.

"He's beaten. He's lost. His story is over as long as they lock him up. If they try to kill him now, but don't succeed—" Gracias said.

"They're gonna give him vengeance as a motivation. Gonna make him—" Chloroplast said.

High-powered rifles split the air with their bark. These weren't simple antipersonnel weapons. These were monstrous, massive things. Antitank rifles. The kind of things meant to punch a hole through an engine block. One after the other, all six of the "escorts" blasted The Icon in the back. His suit shredded, fragments of cloth and speckles of blood flying everywhere. The attack should have cut him in half. He stumbled forward instead. More soldiers emerged from side streets and blasted with similar weapons at a right angle to the others. When they were through, those who fired the first salvo had reloaded and fired another.

The attacks were nearly relentless. In the brief silence between each cluster, a voice could be heard, ragged and pained.

"… forced away the people…"

A fresh burst.

"… squeezed your cold fingers around the beating heart of ChiNoKo…"

Another burst.

"… But we will rise again…"

Now The Icon was standing, bloodied and bare chested, but intact. He shrugged off another burst of weapon fire.

"We had him beat. We had him beat! All you had to do was trust us!" Nonsensica shouted.

"ChiNoKo will live again!" The Icon proclaimed.

He burst toward the power plant and smashed through the wall surrounding it. The Other Eights' radios snapped back to life.

"He was supposed to be depowered," Gen. Luo barked. "He was supposed to be vulnerable."

"And you weren't supposed to make him an antihero," Nonsensica shouted.

"This was a very delicate operation, General," Aiken said over the communication channel. "If you'd told me you were planning this, I would have advised against it."

"What's done is done. Get me visual on him."

They all stared down at their communicators. Everything from body cams to satellite views flicked across the video feed. It settled on a grainy body cam displaying the control room. It was angled oddly, as though the person wearing it was on the floor. But it showed that The Icon had arrived. The technicians inside were unconscious on the ground, and The Icon's hands were dancing across the controls.

"Tell me he doesn't know how to start that thing back up," Non Sequitur said.

"Better yet, tell me he does. The alternative is him just in there flipping switches, which strikes me as a good way to make it go boom."

"We've decommissioned the reactor. The control module has physically been removed and destroyed. The only reason the plant has any power at all is the generators. There is no piece of equipment left in the plant that can reactivate the reactor."

The image of The Icon blurred and he was gone. More video feeds flicked by until a sparkling black-and-white feed showed a barely visible form moving across what looked like a grid of metal slabs. The Icon slammed his fingers down, punching into the metal of one of the slabs. He slowly raised it up. A worrisome whistle and grind emanated from within the plant.

"He's physically raising the control rods!" shouted one of the technicians.

"Can he do that?" Gracias said.

"Not safely with the control modules offline. There's no coolant flowing. There's nothing to regulate temperature. We don't even have any temperature readings."

"What do we do?" Nonsensica said, tightening her gloves.

"Evacuate. Immediately," Gen. Luo said.

"No. To fix it," Non Sequitur said.

"Nothing you could would do any good so long as The Icon still stands," Luo said.

"We beat him once, we'll beat him again," Nonsensica said.

There was silence for a few heady seconds. Then Luo spoke.

"Give them procedures," he said.

"We need real-time readings back online. That will be a simple sequence of commands, if you can get to the secondary control panel," said a tech.

"I'm on it," came a voice over the communicator.

"Who are you?" Luo said.

The video switched back to the body-cam footage. A dumpy middle-aged man in sweats was now visible.

"I'm The Afterthought. I was standing in the corner when he came through. He forgot to pummel me. It happens a lot."

"Very well. Standby, Other Eight. Afterthought, my technicians will instruct you."

***

After The Afterthought followed the sequence of commands to the letter, the readings had slowly begun to flow.

"The temperature is rising slowly, but it will accelerate if he raises many more rods," a technician warned. "If the coolant system is completely flooded, it can be kept within safety margins for a few hours, but the rods need to be reinserted."

The few minutes spent gathering the information had given the rest of The Other Eight time to gather and recover.

"What's he been up to in there?" Nonsensica asked.

"Destroying cameras," Luo said. "All we have left are body-cam shots from downed soldiers."

"He can't have raised too many more rods, or the temperature would already be out of control," the tech said. "But it won't take many more. We need him occupied."

Nonsensica spun her non-chucks. "Oh, we'll more than occupy him."

"Coolant procedures are coming through now. And we have a possible tactic for forcing the rods back in with some rerouted hydraulic pressure," the tech said.

"Dibs on the coolant!" Gracias said. "Team Green is on that."

"I know a little bit about hydraulics," Phosphor said.

"I'll help," Bomb Sniffer said.

"That leaves the rest of us on Icon detail," Nonsensica said.

"I'm fresh out of routines, and without music, I won't be able to improvise one," The Number said.

"Not to mention the folks in the plant don't have hearing protection. We start a routine and they all start dancing," Primadonna said.

"Consider it a last resort, if you can come up with something," Nonsensica said. "That leaves me and Non Sequitur to finish what we started."

"Let's get in there and get it done," Non Sequitur said.

They charged forward, fully expecting The Icon to burst into place in the doorway to stop them. He didn't.

"Hydraulics is this way. Let's go, Bomb Sniffer," Phosphor said.

The pair dashed down a service corridor.

"Coolant is in the west wing. Let's go," Chloroplast said, leading the way.

For a moment, Nonsensica and Non Sequitur lingered behind.

"How do you figure we'll find him?" Non Sequitur said.

"I think he'll find us. I only hope he finds us first, because the other crew has jobs to do besides the butt kicking. I'd hate for him to be a hassle. Now let's go."

* * *

Gracias and Chloroplast rushed down the halls.

"What do you think, Chloroplast? Superhero team, racing to the rescue. Competing against the clock as a nuclear power plant gets ready to explode. Real superhero stuff, right?" Gracias said gleefully.

"Yeah. I've read this story a few times," Chloroplast said.

"I bet you a nickel someone comes out of this with a new superpower. One of the locals, maybe."

"Even money it's a tragic death instead."

"Pff. More like heroic death."

The pair reached the coolant chamber. It was little more than a divert for the river water with some gratings and filters to catch the debris. Like most of the plant, the place had seen better days. The primary coolant system was running, but it was clearly far below its intended level. Evidently, the diesel generators weren't quite up to snuff. Chloroplast rushed to the control panel and tapped in the emergency commands he'd been given. A few groaning motors did their best to shift valves and shutters on the waning current supplied by the generators, but the flow barely increased.

"Gotta go manual," Gracias said.

They rushed to the emergency divert. Huge handwheels and long hoists, antique technologies that nevertheless were able to function even without electricity, were the last line of defense between ChiNoKo and a meltdown. Chloroplast and Gracias each grabbed a wheel and started turning. Opening in sequence, the valves started shunting water from the river through the filters. Relatively clean, clear water rushed in to fill the open channels in the center of the room. They moved to the next set of wheels to move the flow of water further through the system.

"Guys, temperature is rising. We need that coolant," said Afterthought over the communicator.

"Hey! When did you get here?" Gracias huffed. "We're working on it. One more wheel and the water'll be headed where it needs to go."

Chloroplast rushed to the last wheel and gave it a spin. It spun free. The linkage connecting it to the rest of the mechanism had sheared.

"Uh-oh," Chloroplast said.

"We don't have time for an uh-oh, guys. I'm surrounded by flashing red lights," Afterthought said.

Chloroplast turned to the emergency tool cabinet on the wall and threw it open. He grabbed two pry bars and fitted the mil-spec earpiece a little more tightly in his ear.

"Fresh water coming up," he said.

He hopped onto the service ladder leading into the flooded channel. With a deep breath, he plunged underwater. Through the clear, rippling surface, Gracias watched as he levered the shutter open and water started to flow.

"Good, good. Keep it coming. We need that, continuous," Afterthought said.

Chloroplast, earpiece still in his ear underwater, nodded.

"Uh... for how long?" Gracias said shakily.

"Until the control rods are back in place," said a tech.

"Then you better get those things in place fast," Gracias said.

* * *

"Working on it," Phosphor shouted over the communicator.

"Are you going to be able to do this?" Bomb Sniffer said nervously. "Exactly how good are you with hydraulics?"

"It's all pipes and hoses," he said. "How complicated could it be?"

They threw open the maintenance hatch. A rat's nest of greasy tubing awaited them. Somewhere, an oil pump sputtered and groaned. The hydraulic jacks stood in clusters, directly below the rods they controlled. The whole chamber had the smell of overheated machinery, and the temperature was stifling. Crawling inside was like stepping into an oven. If they hadn't been wearing gloves, their hands would have blistered as soon as they touched the metal surfaces around them.

"Oh, no…" Bomb Sniffer said.

"Relax, relax. It's fine," Phosphor said. "It looks worse than it is. The techs said these things push the rods up, and gravity pulls them down. You can see the ones that are out of position. Those are the ones that are up. He just yanked them up, and I guess mangled them a little so they'd stay up. And those little jacks there at the top are, uh…" He checked the notes he'd scribbled down. "The scram jacks. They're supposed to work in a hurry. We just need to sort of hot-wire those so they activate even without the control thing telling them to. They'll puah the control rods back down and we're golden."

"But you said he mangled them to keep them up. What happens when you try to push a mangled rod back into the reactor?"

"I don't know. I suppose we'll hope for the best."

"Hoping for the best seems like something you should never do when a nuclear reactor is involved."

"Desperate times call for desperate measures," he said.

They made their way to the first of the control rods, trying their best not to slip on the leaking hydraulic fluid from the damaged jacks. For all of the intimidation of the network of tubes, it boiled down to adjusting a few valves. The undersized scram jack slowly started to extend, pushing the damaged main jack down and dragging the control rod with it.

"It's working. It's working!" Bomb Sniffer said.

Something above shuddered, then a nearby jack failed as another rod was pulled out of place.

"Nonsensica, Non Sequitur, he's in the reactor chamber, pulling more rods," Phosphor shouted into his communicator.

* * *

"We're on it!" Non Sequitur said, rushing alongside Nonsensica toward the reactors.

The route from the outside of the plant to its reactors was anything but a direct one. They'd been trying to get to them since they entered the building. Along the way they'd encountered intentionally indirect hallways—built with plenty of right-angle turns to keep explosions from having a straight path—to heavy, fortified doors. Non Sequitur had become something of an expert at finding and slapping emergency releases to keep them moving forward. But now they had come to huge blast doors that took more than a simple button or latch to heave aside.

"Come on. We're almost there. You've got to get it open!" Nonsensica said.

"It's like a vault door," Non Sequitur groaned. "It'll take more than thirty seconds to open it. My powers won't do the trick."

Nonsensica leaned against the door and peered through the tiny glass window. "I see him," she said.

"If he's in there and this door is shut, there must be another way. We just need to find it."

"No. I have a faster way," Nonsensica said.

She pulled out her non-chucks and doubled them up in one hand, rearing back and bashing the door. After three blows, she managed to get his attention. She put that attention to good use, raising her middle finger and thrusting it at the window. Whether or not the gesture carried the same weight in ChiNoKo as it did in the US, it did the job. The Icon darted to the massive door. One titanic punch caused it to lurch forward. The heroes cleared out of the way as a second blow sent it thumping to the floor. The heat of the room belched into the hallway. The Icon stood in the doorway, bloodied, but with focus in his eyes. Before, he looked lost. Now, he was certain.

"You..." he rumbled.

Non Sequitur and Nonsensica walked slowly backward. There wasn't much room in the hallway for a battle. And given how tag-teaming him with dodges was the only way they could hope to counter him, they needed all the room they could get. Not to mention the danger of doing battle so close to the reactor.

"How's it going, hero?" Nonsensica jabbed. "Sabotaging a reactor. Some top-notch virtue right there."

"You sabotaged the reactor. I am restoring it to functionality." He stalked closer. "And the word 'virtue' has no place in your mouth. I had surrendered. I was a prisoner, and you shot me in the back."

"We didn't do that. The Chinese military did that," Nonsensica said.

"And you are their tools. Puppets to their schemes," The Icon said.

They turned the corner. He followed.

"You bested me in battle once. It won't happen again."

"Let's see about that. Best two out of three," Nonsensica said.

They reached the first window. Nonsensica glanced at Non Sequitur. He nodded.

"If we're going to do this, let's take it outside," Nonsensica said.

The window popped open as she dashed for it. She hopped out and dropped a short distance to the courtyard below, where several of the plant workers were taking cover. Non Sequitur followed, flicking the latch on his way out. The Icon burst through after them, smashing through the wall itself and sending bricks raining down upon them.

They dodged the worst of it. He slammed down. Nonsensica grinned.

"Time for round two," she sniped, dashing forward.

* * *

Gracias had spent the last two minutes trying to find some way to wedge the damaged flow-shutter open, but the only tools that would do the trick were in the hands of Chloroplast, who was still below the surface, still wedging the shutter. There wasn't enough room for two people to be down there without one of them risking getting caught in the flow. And they were pulling up on three minutes since Chloroplast had taken a breath. He was starting to falter, the shutter starting to sag. And just that little bit of lost coolant brought a fresh shout of warnings from the techs on the communicators. Even the handful of seconds it would take for them to swap out, or for Chloroplast to surface, might be a few seconds too long.

"I don't know how he's held his breath this long, but he's giving out, I can see it," he muttered to himself. "Come on, man. We don't want the world to lose its only carbon-neutral… hero."

Realization dawned. Gracias turned to the ventilation windows of the huge vaulted roof. The sun was still high. He scrambled to the nearest ladder and scaled it, dashing along the catwalk. He eyed the angle of the sun and shoved at the filthy window hatch to open it wider. A few extra rays of sun came through, but not enough. Gracias grabbed a wrench and heaved it, shattering the muck-encrusted glass. Light streamed in, bathing Chloroplast in its glow. Photosynthesis may not have been the most impressive power, but when all it took was light to start pumping oxygen into his bloodstream, right now it was quite literally a lifesaver. Chloroplast rallied and leaned hard on the pry bar, increasing the flow and buying them a few precious moments of leeway.

* * *

Sweat streamed down Phosphor's face as he found the proper valve and adjusted it. Another scram jack activated.

"We've been at this for a while and we're barely back to where we started," Bomb Sniffer said.

"We just have to keep at it. So long as Nonsensica and Non Sequitur keep him busy, and the jacks keep firing, we'll get it done."

They moved to the next. Their boots were sizzling with each step now. Another valve. Another jack hissed to life.

"Fifteen more to go, by my count," Bomb Sniffer said. "The next one is this way."

They maneuvered around a block of jacks, headed for the second one, when the sputtering pump and flickering lights both faded.

"No…" Phosphorus keyed the communicator. "The generator gave out. We're dead in the water down here!"

"Get out of there," came a technician's order over the communicator. "If it wasn't for the force of the river pushing coolant through the system, we'd be on our way toward meltdown already. It's time to evacuate."

They clicked on flashlights and headed for the door.

"But what'll happen?"

"Meltdown, steam explosion. Fallout," the tech listed. "There's nothing more that can be done."

* * *

In the courtyard, the push had come to shove. Nonsensica couldn't spare a syllable to taunt The Icon. She was too busy peppering him with verbal zaps and being thrown this way and that with retroactive dodges courtesy of Non Sequitur's powers. She hadn't landed a blow on him in two minutes. The Icon was faster, more vicious, and more dedicated than they'd ever seen him. Every drop of their powers combined could only barely keep them free of his wrath. And no time for attack meant no time for retreat. All they could do now was buy time for their team and the handful of remaining citizens and soldiers to escape, because the moment The Icon wasn't preoccupied with them, he would be assaulting anyone trying to leave this place.

Warbling warning sirens, running on half-spent emergency batteries, broadcast the danger for all to hear. Attacks cut closer and closer. Both Nonsensica and Non Sequitur were running on fumes.

Finally, the inevitable happened. A single mistake.

The Icon had snatched a fallen brick and heaved it at the heroes. They were just a little too close to one another. A verbal attack was too late, not enough to foul his throw. Non Sequitur didn't have room for a superpowered, time-displaced shove. He did it the old-fashioned way, heaving Nonsensica out of the way. It left him square in the path of the projectile. A brick thrown with the force of a pneumatic cannon struck his shoulder. The blow was glancing but nonetheless devastating.

He fell backward, shirt torn and shoulder bloodied.

"No!" Nonsensica shouted.

The Icon charged toward her.

"Disaster investment, culture dome, corner desire, moseoli yoggu," she shouted.

He flinched with each assault. It may have been enough for her to make a break for it, but she'd never be able to get

231

far enough away for him to be unable to catch her. And right now, she had no intention of escaping. She continued her assault, jumping from English to Korean to Chinese. She spoke faster than she ever had. The mental short circuits hit harder than they ever had. Soon the subtle flinches were more intense, like The Icon was being punched in the face. And still she didn't relent.

He took wild swings at her. She barely evaded and continued her assault. He became clumsier, less steady. He covered his ears. She shouted louder, longer, faster. His mind didn't have time to recover between jolts. A trickle of blood oozed from his nose. He covered his head with his arms and slumped down.

"How... stop! You... aren't... how can you... my mind!" he wailed.

She spun her non-chucks up to speed and started interspersing blows with verbal jolts.

"You attack my friends! Steamboat dumpling! You attack your own people! Shovel eggshells! You threaten the world! Magnetic nostril! And you call yourself a hero!"

A fresh volley of verbal attacks left him curled up on the ground, barely able to breathe. She stood over him and leaned down, pulling him close to her face.

"I don't understand..." he wheezed. "You shouldn't have the power..."

"I'm a superhero. When I need the power, I find it. Now are you ready to listen? Or do I work my way randomly through three different dictionaries until your brain leaks out your ears?"

He blinked tears from his eyes.

"Listen. Do you hear the alarms? Do you see the smoke rising out of the roof? You damaged the reactor. People are going to die. Your people first, and then anyone unlucky enough to be near this place. You, with your bare hands, have condemned hundreds of thousands of people to slow death by radiation poisoning and cancer."

"No... I was... It was the heart of ChiNoKo. I had to."

"Lots of people ended up with a lot of blood on their hands and used that excuse. I had to. I had to do it. Well listen to this, hero. You want absolution? Then clean up your mess. Prove to yourself and the world that there is at least a speck of hero inside you right now."

The Icon looked toward the smoldering roof of the plant. If the anger and vengeance had brought focus, the sight of the ailing power plant brought clarity. For the first time, he truly understood what he had done. And what he had to do.

He rose to his feet and shakily into the air. Nonsensica watched as he drifted toward the roof of the power plant, then dropped down inside. When he was out of sight and the threat he posed vanished, so too did whatever well of power she'd been drawing on. Fatigue, far deeper than she'd ever felt, overtook her mind and body. She dropped to her knees, then to the ground.

* * *

No one will ever know what precisely happened in the minutes that followed. The only record was a grainy video feed from a heat-damaged security camera running on reserve battery. It is known that The Icon entered the reactor chamber. At the time, the temperature in the chamber was nine hundred degrees Celsius. The reactor's internal temperature sensors had long ago ceased to function. Seventy-three seconds after his entry was recorded, the camera feed failed. Ninety-two seconds after that, the internal temperature started to drop. Four minutes later, the generators and the cooling system were gradually restored to prevent thermal shock. Forty-three minutes later, the reactor temperature was estimated to be nominal.

The weeks that followed were far better documented. Moderately elevated radiation levels necessitated the full evacuation of ChiNoKo. All representatives of the United States military were withdrawn. According to the incident report following the event, nuclear technicians entered the reactor chamber to seal the fault in the containment and render ChiNoKo no longer a radiological hazard.

No remains of The Icon or any other individual were recorded as recovered.

Epilogue

Recovery had been slow for The Other Eight. Their intriguing variety of powers, alas, did not include an accelerated healing factor. Fortunately, Uncle Sam took the health of his only superhero team very seriously. Gracias was discharged immediately, though he stayed behind for a few days to make sure Chloroplast got a clean bill of health as well. It took two weeks for The Number to be sent on his way, his injured arm well on its way to recovery. Another week and Primadonna was sent on her way with a similar prognosis. Bomb Sniffer and Phosphor were released shortly after, once their burns had been treated.

The Afterthought remained behind in China for five weeks before anyone remembered he needed to be retrieved.

Now six weeks had passed, and only two members of the crew remained under medical observation.

"I don't believe it," Nonsensica said, scrolling through her social media feeds. "Still nothing. Not even conspiracy theories."

She was still laid up, confined to bed. Physically she was fine, but even now she had electrodes attached to her temples, with a machine beside the bed ticking off what was presently slightly elevated synaptic activity. In a testament to her powers of compromise, she was wearing a cloth mask in place of her goggles, lest her secret identity be revealed.

"You better take it easy, or they're going to come in here and do a full EEG," Non Sequitur said.

"Oh what else is new. They do it three times a day, what's four?"

"If you didn't want to have your brain scrutinized, you shouldn't have practically blown a cerebral gasket nuking a supervillain's brain," he said.

"Don't you have physical therapy to go to or something?" she snapped.

"Not for another forty-five minutes. So you'll have to deal with my company until then."

"Then I hope you don't mind listening to me gripe about not being a household name across the globe for saving a big slice of it."

"If I did, I'd have asked for my own room four weeks ago. You know, if I didn't know any better, I'd think you were in this for the fame. Not very superheroic."

"I'm not in it for the fame. I'm in it for the duty. But the fame is supposed to be a bonus."

"What can I say? Both the US Army and the Chinese military are really good at keeping secrets," Non Sequitur said.

She set her phone down and crossed her arms. "Tell that to FM. I wish they'd put him on the team. With the power to broadcast his thoughts over radio, he'd have leaked all the juicy stuff by now." She huffed. "Is the PT working, by the way?"

"Probably another surgery between me and being able to scratch my head and rub my tummy at the same time," he said. "But if the current rate of improvement is any sign, I'll be in tip-top shape again, eventually."

"That's good. We're the core of The Other Eight. I'd hate to have to train up another sidekick."

"Uh-huh," he said.

There was a knock at the door.

"Unless you're coming with a big front-page spread on the untold story of The Other Eight, we don't want any," Nonsensica shouted.

There was another knock. Non Sequitur turned the knob. Pvt. Summers pushed the door open with her foot, because, in typical fashion, she was carrying a quantity of coffees. Today there were three of them, one in each hand and another in the crook of her arm, while a sealed interoffice envelope was pinned under the other arm.

"Is carrying awkward amounts of stuff one of the things they teach you when you become a private?" Non Sequitur asked, taking two of the coffees.

"I wish," Summers said. "You pick it up on your own. Though, I'm happy to say, things they teach you as a private are no longer of any concern to me."

"Why's that?" Nonsensica asked.

She tapped the pair of stripes on her upper arm, now that she had a free hand.

"... I don't know what that means," Non Sequitur said.

"Didn't your parents ever watch M*A*S*H with you? She's a corporal now!" Nonsensica said.

"That's right! Successful field operation. I've got some medals and such, too. So, by the way, do you. Purple heart, naturally. And a couple more."

"I'm not in it for the glory," Nonsensica said.

"You were just shouting about wanting a front-page story!" Non Sequitur countered.

"Recognition and glory are two different things, thank you very much. One's about being honored, and the other's about letting the public know there are people out there fighting to keep them safe."

"Classified missions aren't really the kind of thing that gets you public recognition, but you'll be pleased to know that they get you a fair amount of private recognition. And on that topic, I present to you..." Cpl. Summers held out the envelope.

"Better give it to the person with two working arms," Non Sequitur said, passing it to Nonsensica.

She unsealed the envelope and slid out a pair of ribbons and a handwritten note.

"These things are usually handed out in ceremonies, but I think you know why that's not happening right now."

Nonsensica handed Non Sequitur his medal and held out the note to read it.

"It's from the general." She cleared her throat. "'To the distinguished members of Project Guardian. The events of your recent operation have illustrated in no uncertain terms that you serve a crucial and at times pivotal role in the defense of our nation and our world. Your performance was less than ideal, but you nonetheless rose to a level of service that I feel confident in stating no other soldier in this army or any other could have achieved. Through your actions and sacrifices, countless lives have been saved. Your nation and your world owe you a debt of gratitude that can never truly be paid. But for now, may these medals serve to remind you of your great deeds and the value your nation places upon you. Presented, for the first time, the Army Meta-human Medal of Achievement.'"

"Wow..." Non Sequitur said. "They made a medal just for us."

Nonsensica held the medal. It felt heavy in her hand. "I guess we get some recognition after all." She cleared her throat again and returned to a much snarkier tone of voice. "Kind of a mouthful, though. I'm gonna call it the Superhero Star."

"The general looks forward to getting the two of you back on your feet. It goes without saying that this little achievement of yours has ensured the Guardian Project will continue for the foreseeable future. Which means we need you veterans out there showing them how it's done. Because in the military, once something proves itself necessary, step one is making sure it's in tip-top shape."

"And what's step two?"

"Recruitment and expansion," Cpl. Summers said.

Nonsensica raised her eyebrows. "You mean I get to train a whole new crop of recruits!?"

"Provisionally, we are looking to expand to a second full unit."

Nonsensica rubbed her hands together. "I can't wait until the world gets to meet The Other Other Eight."

From The Author

Thank you for reading! If you liked this story, or perhaps if you found it lacking, I'd love to hear from you. You can find me online at my website, bookofdeacon.com. For free stories and important updates, join my newsletter.

Discover other titles by Joseph R. Lallo

The Book of Deacon – an Epic Fantasy Series:

Book 1: The Book of Deacon
Book 2: The Great Convergence
Book 3: The Battle of Verril
Book 4: The D'Karon Apprentice
Book 5: The Crescents
Book 6: The Coin of Kenvard
Book of Deacon Anthology: Volume 1
Book of Deacon Anthology: Volume 2

Other stories in the same setting:

The Rise of the Red Shadow
The Story of Sorrel Entwell
Origins: Anya
The Redemption of Desmeres
The Adventures of Rustle and Eddy
Jade
Halifax
The Stump and the Spire

The Big Sigma Series – a Sci-fi/ Space Opera Series:

The Free-Wrench – Steampunk Adventure Series:

The Shards of Shadow Series:

The Greater Lands Series:

Book 1: The Bygone Dagger
Book 2: The Bygone Archive
Book 3: The Bygone Mask
Book 4: The Bygone Caper
Book 5: The Bygone Plague
Book 6: The Bygone Way

Other Stories:

Between
Fallen Empire: Rogue Derelict
Top Level Player
The Other Eight
The Icon vs The Other Eight
Structophis
Paradoxes and Dragons: Volume 1
Paradoxes and Dragons: Volume 2
Paradoxes and Dragons: Volume 3